for you,

beautiful creature

we call 'reader,'

for daring to

journey where

only our minds

can take us

# THE LITTLE WOODS

BOOK 1 OF THE GOTHIC HORROR SERIES

# DISCIPLE

BOOK 2 OF THE GOTHIC HORROR SERIES

# • A Personal Note from A.G. Mock •

D O YOU FEEL you can always tell Good from Evil, Right from Wrong, Light from Dark? If so, you may be about to take a journey that will blur those lines and leave you wondering just how sure you really ever were.

The third and final installment of the New Apocrypha Trilogy, *Shadow Watchers* is the culmination of over twenty-eight years' unending passion and perseverance. That journey began with a young American newspaperman in an upstairs guest bedroom of his modest Lissett, East Yorkshire, home in England (a whole story in itself—hit me up on social media and I'll be happy to share it!) tapping away his first attempt at a novel that would one day, many, many, *many* years later become *The Little Woods.*

Little did that young newspaperman know that he'd be chatting with you over a quarter century later as you prepare to enter the final chapter of a story that began way back when, in a place far, far away.

I hope you enjoy this supernatural tale of Light and Dark and all things in between. And I hope it lives rent-free in your head long after its pages are closed…

So now it's time!

Come with me, and we'll head into the darkness together.

After all, you're not afraid of the Shadows, are you…?

*Spookily Yours,*

AG Mock

# SHADOW
## WATCHERS
Book Three of the New Apocrypha

*American Fiction Awards Winner*
# a.g. mock

**EPOCH**
EpochThrillers.com
AGMock.com

First paperback edition, Epoch Thrillers, October 2023.

Library of Congress PCN: on file with Publisher
ISBN: 978-1-7362919-6-2 | hardcover
ISBN: 978-1-7362919-5-5 | paperback

Published by Epoch Thrillers in Aiken, SC, United States
Epoch Thrillers and its raven imprint are trademarks of Epoch Thrillers

EPOCH THRILLERS
EpochThrillers.com
AGMock.com

*ET 10 9 8 7 6 5 4 3 2 1 First Edition*

# I

# ALPHA

# 01

## WAKING UP | ready to reveal it all

HIS HEARTBEAT THROBBED behind his eyes, each pulse fueling the unbearable pain as a stream of blood poured from his temple. He wailed through lips cracked and swollen, a haunting sound that reverberated in piercing echoes through the woods.

Now the thing coming at them loosed a cry of its own. Every minor chord at once, the shriek set fire to the man's nerve endings, a thousand blistering pinpricks.

*This can't be real*, he lied to himself as the angel wrapped around him and crushing fear took hold. "This isn't real!"

Folding into his shape as he lay in the frozen mud and stinging rain, the angel unfurled great wings like solidified light. They hammered the space above them, striking at a thing the man could not see and could not possibly understand.

*This is just another one of your night terrors,* his internal voice asserted. *A cruel mental torment, courtesy of your own sick mind.* The self-reassurance was bold and resolute.

But as powerless as it was untrue.

Savoring the rising acid taste of the man's terror, the thing screamed again—a warbling, ear-splitting yowl. And though he could not see it, a terrible deep vibration shuddered through the man, revealing to his mind's eye an ancient being so unhallowed it was beyond human comprehension.

The last thing the man would see was the dying light in the angel's eyes as it held him even tighter, refusing to yield as their bodies were pummeled beneath the trees in the stinging rain.

Again.

And again.

And again.

With each blow, the demon squealed in pleasure, growing stronger in equal proportion to the angel's dimming light. When that golden rod was extinguished altogether, the beast roared as all became nothingness.

Now the man's fear, his pain, the wet and cold and confusion, all slipped away to an empty space; a safe space.

All of it, that is, except one simple question: *How did it find her?*

To this, the man's expiring mind had no answer. For it was impossible to comprehend what 'it' even was, let alone a motive compelling its blistering, malignant hatred.

*Besides, none of this is real!* his mind persisted, clinging to a façade of hope, the last vestiges of which had been all but snuffed out with the angel's light.

Still, the question floated there.

Taunting.

Until the synapses in his brain slowly fizzled, then stopped firing altogether. And so, this one all-encompassing question became his last thought. Dissolving into the ether, it floated away as he, too, became one with the void…

That's how it happened. I don't mind admitting, I didn't understand any of it.

At first.

But I do now.

Now I know what that thing was. I know how it found the woman he was hiding. I know what it was after. And most importantly, I know the only option we have left.

Now, I'm finally ready to share it with you.

All of it.

But are you sure—*I mean really sure*—you're finally ready to hear it?

# II

# NEXUS

# 02

*hell's kitchen*

# 16 years before the end | June 1995

**W**AKING IN SHEETS sodden with his own sweat, Reicher Winslow had no idea it was the last morning of his life. Prematurely torn from an unfulfilling sleep, he kicked free of the twists and tangles binding him to the cold, damp mattress.

As superficial as Reicher's sleep had become after what happened last autumn, it still had managed to buoy him from at least some of the torments of his life. One in particular. But today it no longer afforded that benefit.

For here life was. Smacking him straight in the face.

His head was thick, the inside of his skull bristling with every move. Then came the serious pain, a marble that glowed like the tip of a blacksmith's iron inside his skull. Cradling his face with shaking hands, his brain chafed against what must surely be a lining woven from coarse wool.

"Yes, my love. The kind of lining that's so beautifully knit by cheap bourbon," his late wife had once chided and Reicher still chuckled at the joke to this very day. But laughing only made the emotional and physical pain worse, and he found himself focusing on nothing but the discomfort.

And, of course, the angel.

On the night it first appeared to him, Reicher had thought it the component of a dream, a hallucination, perhaps even one of his lingering night terrors from childhood. After all, the slightest of change in one's physiology had the ability to greatly impact one's psychology. And Lord knows, his physiology was more than slightly changing these days.

*What was that wonderful Dickens quote, again?*

Reicher dedicated himself to remembering the answer as he ran his bare feet back and forth across the hardwood floor, grounding himself and doing his best to ignore the sensation of a rusty nail through his skull. He racked his memory to not only recall the quote, but to do so as accurately as possible. Intense concentration on anything but the pain was one of the few ways he'd learned to take back just some of the power it had over him.

Slowly, the words surfaced and Reicher recited them in his mind. They were from Dickens' *A Christmas Carol*, dialog spoken by Scrooge himself to one of his ghostly visitors. A proud declaration of his disbelief.

*'You may be an undigested bit of beef, a blot of—' wait, what was it again... horseradish... Worcestershire...? No, no. I remember now, '—a blot of mustard, a crumb of cheese, a fragment of an underdone potato.'*

Permitting himself a thin smile, Reicher quietly spoke the rest: "There's more of gravy than of grave about you, whatever you are!"

He'd always considered this line one of the most underrated in English literature, but it resonated so much deeper now that his own restive nights had begun mirroring Ebeneezer's.

Following Liz's death, the notion of simply closing his eyes and falling peacefully asleep had become as foreign to him as the idea of starting his day refreshed and ready to face the world.

This had never been more true than today.

For sleep, which for the better part of a year had provided such scant refuge, now bestowed virtually none at all. At first, it had been the isolation and despair. Lying in bed, night after night, without his Lizzie lying next to him was the most soul-destroying pain Reicher thought he could ever endure. It scraped him from the inside out until he felt himself nothing but a hollow shell of what he had been and was meant to be.

But then came the spots of light. The memories too often flitting from his grasp…and the headaches. *Always the headaches.* And always the same penetrating pain at the base of his skull that could just as easily have been someone ramming a cross-head screwdriver through the back of his head.

Liz hadn't been gone even six months before the diagnosis, a one-two punch poised to destroy what little of his world remained. And in some ways, that was fine by Reicher, because he had thought many times of just snuffing it out himself.

Of course, he'd gotten on his knees and prayed first. Over and over. More times each day than he could count. Supplicating God for an act of benevolence he knew in his heart he did not deserve, Reicher concentrated so intensely that sometimes the pain did lessen…at least in those meditative moments. But as soon as his mind returned to the stark reality that was now his life, the marble in his brain would glow again. Grow again. Forcing him to suffer in excruciating abandonment.

Because his Lizzie was still gone.

*And she was never coming back.*

As the tumor satisfied its voracious hunger by devouring more and more of Reicher's cerebellum, so the pain increased by equal measure. Finally, with his every prayer falling upon deaf ears—if there were any out there to hear him at all—Reicher found himself trembling and pressed hard against the headboard of his Georgia home's bed, the barrel of the .38 in his mouth as the sound of the cicadas and the toads serenaded the night.

Now, he had awakened in a grungy Hell's Kitchen rental, the soundtrack of New York City his only bedfellow other than the incessant pain. He was here because something had stopped him from pulling that trigger, a thing so otherworldly and fantastical that the only word Reicher could summon to even begin to describe it was 'angel.'

It came to him the following night as well.

And ten more nights after that.

Each time it bestowed a little more of its unending wisdom. And each night it spoke of a chance at redemption, even hinting at the inconceivable possibility of Reicher's return to the life he'd once known and would give anything to have back.

So, Reicher made his sojourn to New York as was directed of him, whereupon the angel came a thirteenth and final time.

*'Your calling is here, my lamb,'* it promised its Chosen One without speaking aloud, deep vibrations filling Reicher's entire body until their warmth resonated from his toes to his nose. *'Your purpose will be fulfilled here. For here you will join the immortal, your name forever known as the nexus of the New Apocrypha.'*

God may not have ears for Reicher Winslow, but the angel did. And Reicher was only too ready to implore its graces.

Their nightly visits always started the same way...

# the dream

REICHER IS A child again, in the final days of the school year. It's that time when the boys' minds inevitably wander from dreary classrooms and final exams to a summer full of adventure. When that long-anticipated dismissal bell finally rings on the last day of school—its clanging peal officially announcing the start of summer—the children pour from the building in a human torrent. Sprinting through the hall-ways, they take the stairs two and three at a time while woeful teachers look impotently on. As they burst, and not a moment too soon, through the school's main entrance doors, many delight themselves by sliding headlong down the metal railings along the concrete steps. (Even though Nate Franklin Jr. had broken off a tooth last year in the most resplendent, blood-gushing fashion.)

They do this because...why not?

In what is then acknowledged as the most glorious moment of the year, each boy steps onto that first mud-encrusted stair riser of school bus #33...and into three months of glorious freedom.

One small step for boy. One giant leap for boyhood.

It's such a warm and carefree scene, Reicher wants so badly to welcome its arrival each night; to bathe in the joy of the dream.

*But how can he, when he knows what comes next?*

With no segue, the dream smash cuts to the boys' annual

March the next morning. The summer's first trek to the Little Woods, The March strides with purpose through the small figure-eight neighborhood, stopping at each boy's house along the way. This time, all but one is accounted for. Matt Chauncey does not answer, though they ring the bell and pound the door and rap on windows. Eventually, excited pleas for him to join them devolve into shouts of 'pussy,' 'chicken-shit' and 'wuss.'

At the bottom of the neighborhood a field sprawls as far as the eye can see. Its surface undulates upon the welcomed breeze of this blazing summer morning, stalks of immature corn dancing and swaying in unified, almost hypnotic rhythms. This is the beginning of The Wild Place, and through it two deep ruts from the passage of countless knobby tractor tires have formed a rough path. Reicher follows this, bounding over small mud puddles and stopping here and there to investigate things he finds along the way.

At the Twin Ponds, he drops to his knees and begins fishing through the murky waters. He turns over rocks with one hand while preparing to swoop in from behind with the other. Usually this reveals nothing. But occasionally there is a tiny beast like a wannabe lobster, and Reicher is adept at grabbing these 'round the head, just behind the pincers where the crayfish cannot reach. They squirm and curl up their tails as the pincers open and close in the most threatening display. He often brings them close to his face, staring into their little black pin eyes as they snatch and click at his nose.

Without warning it is now the previous year.

It's the moment Reicher thrust a crayfish in the face of Craig Dalton. Craig is strolling ahead of him with Ian Cockerton and Jimi. They're laughing at some joke the creepy Dalton kid just made about Farrah Fawcett and how he 'has a faucet she could drink from' when Reicher taps him on the shoulder.

Still chuckling through a smile as broad as a wide mouth frog,

Craig turns to find a writhing swamp monster staring him in the face. He screams. Reicher laughs and repeatedly jabs the crayfish closer as Craig winces and ducks. He prods the little beast too close, and the pincers find Dalton's cheek just beneath the eye. Craig screams as the tip of the crustacean's claw clamps down on the soft tissue and a blood blister instantly colors the skin purple. Swatting at his face and stumbling over the tractor ruts and clumps of dirt, Dalton falls on his ass. The crayfish releases its grip and goes airborne, just missing Ian. It sails into Jimi's hair and becomes entangled in the boy's thick curls.

"What the—you friggin' douche-nozzle!" Jimi is clawing at his scalp, frantic and digging harder than the poor crayfish which is dazed and merely trying to find purchase on something as eight spidery legs twist through his hair. "Jack, I'm gonna kill you!"

"Not if I kill you first," Reicher rebukes, tackling his younger brother as the crayfish is dislodged. It scuttles away through the weeds and puddles as Jack and Jimi wrestle in the mud.

Until the scene jumps like a bad 8mm film splice.

It is now the next summer once more.

Reicher is again on his knees at the pond's edge. Again, he snatches an unwitting crayfish from beneath a rock.

Ahead of him, Matt Chauncey, Ian Cockerton and Craig Dalton are jostling and pushing one another as Dalton starts gushing over ABC's Tuesday night primetime lineup. He guffaws as he grabs the air ahead of him, rotating both open hands back and forth as if he's miming the testing of a pair of cantaloupes' ripeness. He's mentioned Suzanne Somers—something about her tits, then sniggering that he'd 'keep those babies company'— when Reicher taps him on the shoulder.

Dalton turns, still laughing, but screams when the wet pincer *claaacks* at his face. This time he ducks and swats the creature from Reicher's grip.

"Get away from me!" Craig wipes a thin streak of pond water

from his cheek, eyes glaring. He unconsciously runs his fingertips over the small scar in the soft tissue beneath his left eye. "Not this year, Jack, you fuck-tard."

Smash cut. Same dream. New scene.

They're in a dark wood, standing beneath a colossal tree he knows is called the Father Oak. It dominates a cluster of lesser oaks, beech and other trees, all of which form a rough perimeter around it. A meticulous arrangement of rocks and stones have been placed between these outlying trees, linking them together like a dotted line. The attentive work of generations of kids long before them, it highlights the circumference. At the center of the clearing is an oval of brushed dirt where several logs lay parallel to one another, facing a carved tree stump close to the Father Oak.

They are church pews before an altar.

Bryan Cockerton and another boy—who is both him and not him at the same time—are standing together near the stump, each taking turns to jump upon it and tower over the boys who watch with intense focus as the teams for their game of War are picked. The process is already underway when Reicher joins it.

"…In that case," Bryan declares as he steps into the oval clearing, snagging Jack's younger brother by the collar and all but dragging him to the stump. "I'll take Jimi."

Reicher visibly winces. He knows he should have expected the retaliation but contests the selection anyway. "Shit, you can't do that, Cockerton!"

"Sorry big guy. No vetoes. You know the rules. All's fair in love and war…. And all that jazz."

Reicher needs to think. He pauses as he contemplates his next move. He carefully scans the faces. His younger brother Jimi had been a big part of his plans. Time to adjust his strategy.

"Fine. Then Dan's with me."

Dannie Mercer—a.k.a. Big Dan—is a mutual friend of them both. He's big. Very big. But slow as syrup…and twice as stupid.

What he lacks in brain cells he makes up for with muscle cells, and that strength is a bonus to whichever team he's on, well worth his cerebral challenges.

In short, no one messes with Big Dan.

"OK. Then I'll have Woody."

"Take him. See if I give a shit, Bry'. But while you're at it...." Reicher smirks. "You can take the *Three Douche-keteers* too. All for one, and one for all!"

He gestures toward Bryan Cockerton's brother, Ian, Creepy Craig, and Matt Chauncey.

*Weird little Matt Chauncey,* Reicher thinks as the scene wavers like heat on a highway, a twisted grin beneath his mask of mud and red. It is darker in the woods now, and he is holding the frightened boy's flute. As if on cue, Reicher screams acrid breath into it. The cheap bamboo pipe shrills to inharmonious life, and from a limb of the Father Oak as thick as an elephant's leg, Stu Klatz takes this cue from his best friend. While Jack continues to pump sour notes from the flute, Stu retracts a muscled arm far behind his ear. He fires it blindly at Matt Chauncey's face.

The fist is off target. But powerful as a piston, it makes little difference. It strikes with a popping sound and Matt's nose spreads wide. Thin strands of red sling in all directions, weaving a concentric pattern across the drying mud which masks Matt's face; spots Stu's shirtless torso like a bout of instantaneous measles.

Chauncey cries out in a delayed, muffled cry as he cups a bloodied hand over his face.

Stu revels in indifference as he artfully sweeps his leg around and perfectly executes a lightning fast roundhouse kick.

It happens so fast, it's impossible to dodge.

Matt's legs sail out to the side and up. For a moment, his feet are level with his head before he crashes back down on the great branch of the Father Oak and his ribs make a sickening cracking sound. The air bellows from his chest. His body goes slack and bends unnaturally around the curve of the branch.

Then, Matt simply slides from the limb.

Falling through the entanglement of offshoots and vines, he plummets towards the ground screaming. One hand futilely clutches at empty air; the other for the loop around his neck.

When the rope reaches its full extent, intense momentum jolts him violently back up. Matt's tongue darts from his mouth and his own teeth cleave it clean in two. Blood sprays as the severed tip drops into the raging bonfire below. It sizzles in the flames and the sound grows louder as the moisture within the tongue begins to boil, the tip instantly wizening.

Above the flames, the boy continues to bungee up and down. With each cycle, the noose tightens even more. It constricts Matt's throat until the tongue boiling in the fire and the boy's choked-off scream become a single, snake-like *hissssssssss*.

It is this sound that fills Reicher's ears until it is all he knows. Except now it has become the sound of his wife's name through his own screaming lips: *Lizzzzzzzzzz*…

# 04

# 17 years before the end | Oct 1994

L IZZZZZ!" HE SHRIEKS as he attempts to pry her mangled left hand from the food processor. Having sliced off every finger, blades like serrated razors continue to devour them. Traveling from nail all the way to the metacarpophalangeal knuckle, the blades only stop when they finally embed in the bones of Liz's hand. Wrapped in a tight coil, the meat of her shredded muscle, tendons like rubber bands, and long strips of skin constrict the spindle. Amongst these is Liz's wedding band, the platinum still shining from the mound of pulverized flesh. The food processor's motor has begun to smoke, untenable levels of torque making it scream.

It's the only thing that is.

Liz is soundless. Unmoving. Staring straight ahead as though she sees something a thousand yards beyond the subway tile backsplash just two feet in front of her.

"Hang on, baby, hang on!"

Liz shrugs. "I'm fine."

Reicher reaches over the machine and pulls the plug. The iron stench of the blood is as prevalent as the spatter that's painted a conical spiral across the stove, backsplash, cabinet uppers, ceiling…his wife's torso, neck and face.

"I'm going to call 9-1-1 babe, I won't be—don't move—I'll be—"

He's already out of the kitchen and running for the living room handset. Plucking it from the wall, he pulls the chrome antenna so hard that it comes free in his hand. He checks the dial tone as panic begins to roil in his gut, the acid taste of bile rising to his chest and mixing with the iron taste of Liz's blood. In the mirror over the buffet he can now see that it's oozing through his hair, thick lines dripping down his face. A famous logo depicting a pail of red paint drenching the world immediately enters his mind.

The phone has a dial tone, but it's filled with static, crackling brown noise. He punches the three digits, and a faraway voice addresses him like the adults in a Charlie Brown animated show.

Reicher slams down the cordless handset and runs upstairs to the bedroom. The old fashioned phone on Liz's side of the bed is a rotary style. Black. Long coil of cord. He dials the three numbers, the first one's journey around the dial taking longer than any two seconds of his life.

Reicher leaves the phone off the hook after shouting their address and the word 'ambulance' as quickly as he can, while still ensuring it will be understood by the operator the first and only time. The woman's voice continues to emanate from the receiver in tinlike tones as it spins in circles, coiling then uncoiling beside the nightstand as it dangles from its long, twisted cord.

He leaps down the stairs, descending the flight in two moves, to find Liz on the kitchen floor, the food processor attached to her hand as if it were a catcher's mitt. The other is clenching her chest. She's unconscious and unresponsive when he speaks to her; she does not react when he touches her cheek. She does not close her beautiful green eyes that are frozen wide-open in terror, their color all but swallowed by pupils big and dark as night.

A pool of vomit is revealed when Reicher pulls her to him, and now he sees the bluish tint to her skin, the strained neck muscles as she gulped for air that refused to come.

Reicher rolls her on her side and begins striking her between the shoulder blades with the heel of his hand. More vomit expels from Liz's mouth with a thick, fatty stench like vinegar and rotted meats. He rolls her almost completely over and it pours from her mouth as he continues to pound on her back.

Liz does not move.

"C'mon baby! C'mon babe. C'mon!" he urges over and again as the sound of his palm slapping her back changes from a solid noise like finding a stud in the wall, to a more hollow one like tapping your knuckles against drywall over the channels in between.

Reicher would not remember the ambulance arriving, or the paramedics who took over. He would not remember the chest compressions that cracked his wife's sternum or the suction plunger that syphoned away the rest of her bile.

He would only remember the blanching of her already pale skin and how the bluish-purple tone first settled on her neck, appearing so stark and lifeless against the warmth of her flowing, naturally ginger hair.

And the prank.

*He would always remember the prank...*


Finishing work on his book earlier than expected, Reicher turned off the monitor which went dark like a black hole sucking down a neighboring star; the computer and printer. He waited until the fans slowed before closing the studio door for the night.

"Done already, babe? That's *fabtastic*!"

"D-U-double-N, DUNN!" he joked, joining in on the wordplay fun. "Smells great down here, by the way."

Tucked in the corner of the kitchen, Liz was already busying herself with anniversary meal preparations. Making from scratch a three-course dinner that would be the envy of any Michelin star chef was her way of marking the occasion. This was her gift to him, to them both. A rare spectacle for the pomp of it. It wasn't every day you marked another year of marriage, after all. Especially nowadays. And Liz's famous anniversary meal was also her way of feeding not only his body but his heart. Acts of Service was one of Reicher's five love languages and an entire morning procuring every ingredient fresh from two local markets, followed by an entire afternoon in the kitchen, were just one way she communicated her affection on this day. Every other evening might be delivery pizza or chicken fingers, but not this one.

Of course, he always offered to help. And of course, Liz always politely declined. These days, anyway. To the point that it had become something of a running joke. Being more a cabin than a house, the kitchen was far from grand. But it was hardly the smallest she'd ever had, and there was plenty of space for two people to work just fine without tripping over one another. Which made Liz sometimes wonder if Reicher just slapped food out of her hands on purpose or spread stuff all over the counters, just to get out of ever helping her again.

"Uh, no thanks, Mr. Bull-in-a-China-Shop. I've got this," was her inevitable reply. He took no offense by this, because, quite frankly, she was right. He was about as dexterous in the kitchen as he was in bed. And that wasn't saying much.

At least he was honest about it.

"So, I see someone's having fun with some carrots. Mmmmm." He mimed going up and down a 'vegetable' shaft while giving Liz a deliberately awkward wink. Think cheap seventies' porno where the plumber asks for payment from a wife whose husband's out of town but can't pay for the repair, and you'll be getting close.

"You're an idiot, do you know that?"

"Yes. I do know, as a matter of fact. But I'm *your* idiot."

"That you are, babe," Liz confirmed and laughed, turning the food processor to dice. "Especially as these aren't carrots, Einstein. Since when've you seen a carrot the color of clotted cream? They're parsnips."

"Ahhh," Reicher recanted, stroking his chin like a villain as Liz fed the smaller of the two through the food processor's clear chute and the blades made easy work of turning the thick root vegetable into a dozen-plus medallions. "And what's a parsnip, when it's in town, exactly?"

"Reicher, are you being serious with me?" She began feeding the second through the chute but only a small portion of the root would fit. She twisted off the cap of the processor's clear bowl. "Are you trying to tell me you've never had a parsnip?"

"Uh, maybe?"

"Oh, babe, come on." She turned away from her husband and carefully fed the fat parsnip directly into the bowl. The serrated blades began tearing through it as though it were butter.

"Oh, I'll come alright!" He snuck up behind her and threw his hands around her body, cupping her breasts and squeezing them while humping her like a dog from behind.

The sound of the processor was suddenly different.

Its rhythmic sound, like the tearing of cardboard, changed to a cycle of four *thwumps* which repeated several times before one final sound, the loudest of all, stopped the blades and the motor began whirring.

Something thick and wet hit Reicher's hands.

"Ewwww, Liz, your parsnips are bleeding," he joked but with an element of genuine disgust as warm runnels began to flow through his fingers. "Are they supposed to be that color? And what is wrong with that food processor?"

Leaning over Liz's shoulder to see exactly what was going down with these stupid parsnips—and to give his bride a kiss while he was at it—Reicher first smelled his favorite of Liz's perfumes which she'd spritzed on the nape of her neck. Then he smelled her blood, the pungent ferrous odor, before he saw it.

*Everywhere...*

# 05

## 16 years before the end | June 1995

AS THE TREES dissolved with the dream into the dark and dingy walls of his rental, Reicher Winslow sat bolt upright in his bed. Three stories below, the occasional car and passerby on the street reminded him that he was no longer in his Blood Mountain, Georgia home.

He squinted and rubbed his eyes, adapting them to the dark. Atop the studio's writing-desk-cum-dining-table-cum-TV-stand, the LCD clock dimly blinked.

*3:33am.*

The surreal dream in the woods had come to him *(again)*. And just like the twelve other times, it segued into the unbearable memory of his Lizzie *(again)*, consumed by a pain so unthinkable that her heart had no other choice but to bring it to an end.

Reicher's breaths shallowed as thick tears welled *(again)*.

*You can't lose it, buddy. Just... no. Not today, Satan.*

Breaking down was a luxury Reicher Winslow knew he could not afford. Because something deep inside, a feeling more than a thought, forewarned that the next time would be his last.

Tangled in sheets that were cold with his own sweat and reeked of ten-dollar bourbon, Reicher decided he no longer cared.

And he no longer held back the tears...

# II

He felt the figure's presence before he saw it.

Beside his bed, motionless and draped in a flowing cloak, its indistinct edges blended and merged with the shadows and shapes of the room around it. A sock slung across a tattered armchair reeking of cat urine became one of the robe's deep cuffs; a T-shirt drying on a small plastic card table, the figure's torso. The head was formed by a dark corner where plumbing stack met the ceiling, the figure as tall as the room itself.

*I'm still in the dream.*

He waited for the figure to disappear, along with the Father Oak and the flames and the screaming.

They did. The figure didn't.

Which made the pulse in Reicher's neck throb hard, its every beat palpable.

*'What would you give?'* The voice was raspy. Low. Its source was not the faceless void deep inside the figure's cowl, but somehow a sensation taking place in Reicher's own being. More than a voice in his head, the words vibrated like a subwoofer throughout his body. A deep bass that agitated every cell.

With the angel having posed the question a dozen times before, Reicher did not have to clarify, for he knew of what it spoke.

This time, his response was different.

*'Anything,'* he answered only in thought, feeling the word flow from his soul to be absorbed by the angel. *'I would give ANYTHING if you'll only give her back to me and rid me of the torture that devours my heart, soul… and mind.'*

There, he'd said it. He would do anything.

And it was the truth.

The angel did not respond to his admission as Reicher's tears fell. It only stared upon him from the depths of a cowl that shielded no face as it silently absorbed every word.

This is no longer what Reicher saw, however.

What Reicher saw was his wife.

*'Shhhhh. I know you would, my love,'* she comforted, leaning over him to stroke his face with fingers once again whole. An aura surrounded her, a warmth that enticed him into her energy.

"God, I've missed you, Lizzie." The words did not match the tone with which they were delivered, something deep inside refusing to accept what his eyes were seeing.

Lizzie sensed this and held her left hand before him.

*'Look upon it, my love.'* The gesture was as delicate and provocative as it was intended to bluntly refute his doubt. Her fingers were long. Slender. Perfect. Her wedding band, wide platinum, sparkled as glimpses of moonlight caught it through the curtains to glimmer in hypnotic prisms. Her nails were deepest crimson, accentuating her ivory fingers all the more.

He did not have to ask for her to slide them under the sheet. Nor did Liz have to offer. Gliding her hand to the polyester hillock now jutting above the rest of the sheets, she wrapped each finger around his swollen cock. One…slender…finger…at…a…time. When her ring finger gripped, Liz rubbed the cool metal of her wedding band against him. In contrast to the soft heat of her hand, the cool firmness of it was erotic, akin to an ice cube rubbed across an erect nipple.

Reicher did not resist. Instead, he closed his eyes and leaned into it as his wife began stroking him gently up and down. First her nails ran down his length. Then around and around in teasing, repeated circles until it verged on the edge of cruelty. He was wet when Liz played them over his glans and again rubbed the cool metal of her ring over his tip before gripping and pumping in that intense slow-fast rhythm she'd perfected over the years.

It was mere moments before he came under the sheet, a patch soaking immediately into the fabric. A slick film coated his cock, Liz's hand, his groin, and she laughed in that way she always had when they both had come together: that perfect exclamation of relief and rapture in one glorious sound.

But then came the smell.

Not the salty, musky scent of sex…but the earthy, iron stench of blood. *Old* blood.

Reicher opened his eyes to a sheet soaked in a red so dark it was almost brown, and the breath caught in his throat. In a panic he tore the covers from his body…

…and found the remnant of Liz's mangled hand wrapped around him. Deformed fingers and fibrous ribbons of skin and muscle were coiled around his still-erect penis, just as they had coiled around the spindle of the food processor. His crotch was drenched in thick, clotted blood from Liz's mutilated hand as she continued to pump him up and down while strips of her flesh stuck here and there like raw chicken in decoupage gel.

Then Liz dipped her torn and twisted claw through the burgundy puddle dappled with Reicher's semen, raised it to her lips…and began licking. With each lap of her tongue her face grew thinner, more grey, deathly gaunt.

And she began to cackle.

A nerve-shredding din like a vinyl LP caught in the middle of a recurring skip, this deranged laughter persisted in cycles that abruptly hiccupped before resuming at the beginning again.

When her body broke out in cadaverous lesions and rawness that squirmed to life with maggots and creeping insects, Reicher released a scream so intense that it was little more than a silent rush of air from a mouth stretched ghoulishly wide.

'*Anything!*' he had committed to the angel just minutes earlier. '*I would give ANYTHING to have my wife back. My life back…*'

Having fulfilled half of that deal, the angel now accepted Reicher's invitation. It leaned down and spread atop him in Liz's lifeless shell, placing her fetid lips over his. Sucking in his lifeforce, it then absorbed everything within that made Reicher, Reicher…

# 06

*9:07am*

HIS HEAD FELT dull, thick, something he was suddenly aware of rather than merely being a part of him. The morning sun and abominable noise had penetrated the cheap unlined curtain, stripping him from a sleep that provided no rest and a night he would not remember. Twisting free of the sweat-soaked sheets, Reicher ran his soles across the hardwood floor, kicking aside the bottle that tumbled unevenly across the warped planks. Bourbon sloshed out, splashing a loaded revolver as it rolled to a stop against it, halfway across the room.

With every move he made, Reicher readied himself for the inside of his skull to bristle. *(Again.)*

It didn't.

A surprise, given the amount of bourbon he'd consumed.

*But we'll just thank God above for these small mercies, eh?*

The glowing marble always came next: that white-hot orb inside his skull.

This time, it did not.

Reicher lowered his head into hands that shook not from pain, but disbelief. For years he had described his hangovers to Lizzie as his 'brain chafing against what must surely be a skull lining woven from wool.' Since the cancer, those hangovers had become indiscernible from the invasive destruction of the tumor. And still,

Liz's one-time comment about that lining being best woven by cheap bourbon was always capable of making him smile.

Always.

At least it did, up until yesterday.

Today, there was no humor in Reicher Winslow. Because today he would submit fully to the shadows—just this once, mind you—then step right back into the Light with his Liz returned to him and the tumor dispelled. For the angel had come to him again, that much he remembered. And in this last visit it shared why Reicher had been summoned to this place…and exactly what it required of him in return.

*Yes, you're making deals with the undead,* Reicher joked. *Pardon me, Mr. Angel,* he added while raising his hands before him in mock prayer. *I meant, making deals with the immortal.*

The very thought of it was absurd.

Yet he knew it to be true.

Either way, he had nothing more to lose.

*What was that famous Dickens quote, again?*

"There's more of gravy than of grave about you!" He hadn't had to think about it this time around, the quote instantly retrievable as if his mind had become seven times sharper overnight.

Now he laughed, a caustic sound filled with venom—

*stupid fucking Dickens*

—and began burning the skin off his finger with a lighter.

II

It was excruciating. At first.

The flame of the lighter danced to life with a simple flick of the strike wheel. In seconds, the studio's stagnant summer air grew even hotter as he held the flame before him.

He passed it under his right index finger.

*Too quick. I feel nothing.*

Now he passed it again, this time more slowly, and the nerve endings shrieked to life. He could bear it but a moment before reflexively pulling his finger from the flame.

He thought of a life where this brief pain would prevail over the constant debilitating torture inside his brain...

*...He thought of Liz.*

Again, Reicher leveled his finger over the brilliant, almost transparent cone. It was so small, so innocuous in appearance. How could it possibly burn at a temperature that melts aluminum?

This time, Reicher did not pull his finger away.

*One-one-thousand...*

Still little more than the remnant of pain from a moment ago.

*...two-one-thousand...*

In an instant, the nerves were screaming.

*...three-one-thousand...*

And now, so was Reicher.

*...four-one-thousand...*

He refused to submit to instinct, and the tip began blistering and popping. The volume of his scream exceeded any sound he'd ever made. From a faraway place in his mind, he may have heard someone banging on the shared wall of the rental.

*...five-one-thousand...*

The temperature sensing cells in that finger now dead, Reicher's brain began to interpret the pain as the sensation of sudden cold, as if the lighter's blazing cone had become an ice cube. Now someone in the rental directly above began stomping on their floor.

*...six-one-thousand...*

Reicher's scream descended to a wail as the skin turned black, a rank, sulfurous odor like burning hair wafting in the smoke as his fingernail softened and all but melted.

*...seven-one-thousand.*

Now Reicher felt nothing at all.

The third degree burn had killed all sensory nerves in the epidermis, dermis, the subcutaneous fat, and even some of the muscle layer. Though he felt no more pain, the smell of his own flesh cooking lingered in the air and Reicher vomited. The odor of bile and regurgitated bourbon mingled with the sulfurous scent of the burn, and he threw up again.

He held the charred finger to eye level.

*Compared to the pain Lizzie would have felt,* his brain assured him as he vomited yet again, *this is nothing.*

He did nothing else until his breaths were governed and the appearance of the dead tip, which only minutes before had been a living part of his body, no longer pulled so hard at his stomach.

He then painted it with a heavy black marker.

Pressing its tip firmly against a piece of white card stock, the ink transferred beautifully. But instead of organized whorls, the pattern was chaotic and offered no visible friction ridges. He now compared this as objectively as possible to the card he made from the same finger last night.

No resemblance, whatsoever.

### III

After all five of the right hand were complete, Reicher's brain no longer acknowledged the pain. Those on his left hand therefore felt more like an uncomfortable pinch than the 1,112° heat of burning butane.

All-in-all, it took less than an hour (vomit breaks included) to turn every fingertip into ten blistered pieces of leather.

On the off chance that his parents had made a stamp of his baby feet at the hospital, Reicher decided to set about erasing the prints on all ten toes as well.

*Just in case...*

# 07

*11:47am*

THE LATE MORNING sun achieved what the tumor no longer could, and Reicher averted his eyes to avoid the piercing pain it dished out. Despite his nearly black sunglasses, he found himself staring at the tarmac and concrete, even shielding the sides with his hands. Every now and then, the stench of his fingertips filled his nostrils and Reicher's stomach would roil.

Striding upon legs that no longer felt his but as if they belonged to an automaton and he were simply along for the ride, Reicher headed southeast towards Times Square. Walking against traffic, he did not look up to see where his legs were taking him, not even when the sidewalk was full and they chose to stride down the street instead. Busy as it was with cars and taxis and MTA buses hurrying from one part of the city to another, none posed a threat. Without a sound—not a honk, not a shout, barely even a look—they all respectfully (and unknowingly) obeyed the invisible buffer that seemed to encase him like a force field the way two magnets of the same polarity simply press away from one another.

Times Square opened up before him and under normal circumstances, Reicher would have been enthralled by the high energy and vibrancy. As a writer himself, the idea of Broadway and what it stood for had always been a thrill he wanted to experience. While he was not one for musicals, he was a hundred percent behind any medium that told a story. And over the decades, Broadway had told a *lot* of stories. For Reicher, it played an integral role in helping keep theater of any kind alive and well in a television society which had become so addicted to stories told in just twenty-two minutes. Not including those mind-numbing commercial spots, of course, which ate up the remaining eight minutes of every half hour.

Today, however, the excitement and lights and all the hubbub of Times Square made for just another city block, in any other city. Reicher paid it no more attention than he had the previous blocks…or those that followed. Clad in a heavy camo jacket while all around sported shorts and tees, Reicher cut quite the figure with his thick dark beard and glasses resembling a purchase from the Ray Charles line of accessories. Making a beeline through the plaza where *New Day, USA!* was filming live, for a moment (and for reasons unknown) Camera Operator #1 followed his progress. From its position behind the great glass studio windows, the cameraman even cut away from the host introducing Alanis Morissette, who would be 'joining us to play her new single, "Jagged Little Pill" live after the break.' At this point, the Floor Producer barked to 'get that camera the fuck back on Lara befor—' when the power surged and the broadcast went black. When it came back on in less than three seconds, Reicher was nowhere to be seen.

Thirteen minutes later, he all but glided across Fifth Avenue, Manhattan's backbone and arguably America's most stylish address. He did so without opening his eyes which had become so sensitive to the light, realizing he could simply keep them closed with no impact to his progress whatsoever. Meanwhile, other pedestrians averted theirs with a gasp of expectant tragedy as barreling vehicles, certain to turn him into a blot of human pâté, simply veered around him at the last moment.

All without making a sound.

Minutes later, Reicher was at East Forty-Second and third, opening the door to a hole-in-the-wall sports bar he'd never been to, or even heard of before. He did not look up when he asked the bartender for a beer, raising his voice to be heard above the crackling din of two boxy Zenith TVs, one at each end of the bar.

"No problem," the bartender replied, only it came out more like *'noah problem.'* To Reicher's right, two men sitting at the bar debated the qualities of a buxom blonde on the TV as she inhaled her slim cigarette with a look of climactic joy. When she sensually wisped the smoke from plump, red lips, the first of the two men puckered his own and blew the dusty old TV a kiss in return.

"Man, you're into *that* chick?" the second man admonished. "She's way too false. And too…" He surveyed the bar, seemingly to ensure that none were within earshot. "And way too…*blonde.*"

"No such thing," the first man—the kiss-blower—replied.

"I agree with Felipe," the bartender chimed in, handing Reicher a glass that glistened from the condensation that speckled its surface. His comment had been directed at the two other men, and propping his elbows on the bar, Tony continued polishing a glass as he joined the debate. "She's too blonde, my friend. That's your trouble. You should find yourself a nice, dark Italian girl who knows how to cook her mama's pasta and…"

The increasing static in Reicher's head buried the rest of the man's advice, and he moved to a booth at the farthest corner. Cloaked in shadows, he took off his sunglasses and scanned the bar nervously, his unease about being here—about *why* he was here—building. As it did, the noise in his head grew by equal measure until it became a thunderous assault. Now the pain at the base of his skull threatened its insidious return, the nausea of extreme migraines starting to churn his gut as the marble, while not yet glowing, began to warm up inside his cerebellum. He knew this was the angel's way of reminding him that, while far less painful and debilitating, the tumor was still very much there.

For now, at least.

Meanwhile, as Reicher grappled with more suffering than was humane for any one person, it was clear to him that the two men at the bar took for granted every blessing they were so privileged to enjoy. Though he knew nothing about them, this was nonetheless a matter of fact in Reicher's mind.

The way they navigated their charmed lives with such disregard only fueled Reicher's unease. Except now it was no longer the product of anxiety or lingering doubt, but annoyance. Which immediately turned to anger; anger to hatred.

*Hatred to wrath.*

As this emotional progression descended from seed to certainty, so the pain in Reicher's head lessened...until the marble in his skull was all but gone; the bowling ball in his stomach dissolving.

Now Reicher guzzled his beer, patting his waistband with his free hand. Though his fingertips were no longer capable of feeling, he was fortified by the reassuring sensation of the revolver's cool metal in his palm. He rotated it gently, positioning it to where his leathery-tipped fingers would slide effortlessly around the textured handle, through the guard, and over the trigger in one seamless move.

As he did this, the noise in Reicher's head went silent, for all but the most inconsequential of conflict remained. And so the man who had once been Lizzie Winslow's doting, creative and thoughtful husband was all but an empty shell readying itself to become the catalyst of the New Apocrypha.

Surveilling the bar and everyone in it, Reicher steadied his grip on the .38 and welcomed his descent into darkness...

# 08

*12:59pm*

H OMER! SWEETNESS!" THE first man (the kiss-blower) exclaimed and beat his hands against the bar. He swiveled a full three-sixty, the shrill squeak of the barstool grating through the shell of what was barely Reicher Winslow lying wait in the corner booth.

The gaze of the kiss-blower's Latin friend was stone-like, eyes drilling into the guy as if he wanted to rip his tongue out.

Disconsolate, the bartender shook his head. "Scored? Already? I don't believe it. Just don't *believe* it…"

"I know," the tongue-ripper said and extended his hands to the bartender. They bowed their heads in mock mourning while the kiss-blower perused the various disappointed faces…and started to dance…and scream…and laugh.

"Homer, homer, homer, homer, HOMER!" he chanted, the grin on his face so wide he looked on the edge of sanity.

On the two Zeniths above the bar, the stadium—or at least a tenth of it—went wild.

Pirates 1. Yankees 0.

"Did you see that, Menendez? Did you see that?"

"Yeah, yeah, Cockerton. I saw it."

*Cockerton?*

The floor of Reicher's stomach gave way, the skin of his back, neck and arms prickling. Deep in a place that was getting farther from his grasp by the moment, Reicher was sure he had once known someone with that name.

*Hey COCK...erton!*

A boy's voice in his head; an echo of a past life.

*Wotcha doin', COCK...erton?*

A whisper of a dream.

*Ian...?*

A memory of a childhood stolen long ago.

Reicher wanted to call out his friend's name, to connect with a part of his humanity he'd long forgotten and which, in this very moment, was slipping between his dead and blistered fingers.

Instead, a grating voice—earthy and foreign to him—bellowed from his throat, resonating through the shadows where he sat at the back of the barroom. "HEY YOU. PIRATE BOY."

The intonation was flat, deep.

And unyieldingly malicious.

Unsuspecting, Ian turned to find a burly man stepping from the shadows of a booth in the corner. Sporting a camouflage jacket and dark, matted beard, it was the anonymous customer Tony had served earlier whom Ian had barely noticed. In fact, he wouldn't have noticed him at all if the man hadn't been so strangely withdrawn and silent.

For a moment, Reicher said nothing more. Then, as he found his legs carrying him across the barroom, the unfamiliar voice in his throat calmly but oh-so clearly instructed Ian to shut up. To "shut the fuck up right now, PIRATE BOY."

The bar fell silent. Except the two boxy televisions which, oblivious to the drama about to unfold in a small saloon on 42nd and 3rd, were crackling with a tinny organ melody as a cartoon Yankees pitcher threw a strike across the stadium's Jumbotron, then winked to the crowd as the rally text 'Let's Go Yankees!' spun across the giant screen.

It was a disturbingly surreal backdrop to Reicher pulling out a .38 caliber from his waistband and aiming it squarely at Ian.

Ian Cockerton's gut loosened as his chest tightened, pulling his body internally in two different directions at once. His lungs constricted, the ribs pressing down upon them. A thousand ants crawled down his back.

Reicher stepped forward and the barrel of the revolver was now so close that Ian felt he was staring down the mouth of a cannon.

"N-now look. Buddy," Ian stuttered, trying hard not to stumble over the words he forced through his lips on the barest wisps of air. He swallowed. A hard, dry effort. "Look. I meant no offense."

Reicher did not move—*Ian, it's me. Don't you remember? Don't you recognize me?*—except for the loose and leathery tip of his index finger which tightened on the trigger. While the movement may have been imperceptible to everyone else in the bar, to Ian it was terrifyingly tangible. The .38's cylinder softly clicked along its natural clockwise rotation and the hammer pulled back.

Ian did not answer the voice which only Reicher heard coming from the lingering remnants of his mind.

*See, Reich?* that voice pointed out. *He doesn't even know you anymore.*

"Fucking outsider bastard," Reicher proclaimed, and with the words being incongruous to any substantive emotion, they came out in an eerie, almost soothing monotone.

*Or worse,* the voice posed, *he recognizes you and doesn't want to know you. Because you mean nothing to him. So, you see? Even your friends have abandoned you. Your oldest—and allegedly dearest—pals. Buddies for life, isn't that what you promised one another in the woods?*

Reicher laughed out loud. It came not from a place of humor but as a scoffing indictment that what little still remained of him was fully aligning with the reality the voice was divulging.

*You mean nothing. To everybody. And this guy right here's no more part of your life now than Lizzie is. Speaking of which, fancy wanting to get away from you so badly that the bitch was willing to put her fucking hand in a blender. Now that's really saying something, isn't it, Reich?*

Burying the words, the static in Reicher's head returned with a vengeance. In an instant it escalated to become a pain that resonated through his skull with such ferocity that it felt like a vice grip crushing his head. A pain so unimaginable that death would have come as sweet mercy.

*Everyone abandons you, Reicher. Everyone hurts you. God hurts you. Because he doesn't care, you know. Not really. The darkness is all you have. The darkness is all you need. Let it swallow your pain and make you whole in the eyes of the one true Lord…*

Now Reicher shouted the words with every emotion that had been absent only a moment before: "Fucking bastard scum!"

Felipe Menendez, with his hands up and palms out in the universal gesture of non-confrontation, eased off his barstool. "Look, I think we can—"

The last ember of what had once been Reicher Winslow fizzled away and was extinguished, only the soulless shell of an anonymous predator remaining. He spun the revolver toward Felipe so swiftly the move was astonishing. "Fuck off, Tex-Mex. Now sit back down *right now* before I blow your spick ass all the way back to Tijuana, where it belongs."

Shaking, Menendez complied and climbed back upon his stool.

Though Reicher returned his attention to Ian, he did not alter the .38's aim, which remained steadfast upon Menendez.

"Now, Pirate Boy. Tell me one good reason why I shouldn't blow your friend's cock off." Without breaking eye contact with Ian, Reicher lowered the revolver's barrel just the right number of degrees for it to be squarely aimed at Felipe's groin. "TELL ME."

"Wait," Ian cried out. "You've got no argument with him. It's me that's pissed you off. Point that damned thing at me!"

Reicher shrugged, his mouth pulling into something like a twisted mimic of a smile. "How sweet. Sticking up for your faggot boyfriend. But you see, I do haVE AN ARGUMENT WITH HIM! AN ARGUMent with all of you…" Rising to a disturbing crescendo, his voice flattened just as abruptly as he swung the barrel back toward Ian.

*Silence.*

Except for the baseball game which played on.

Seated on his own at the end of the bar, an elderly man began to hyperventilate. He clutched at his chest as his breaths escaped in shallow, rapid bursts. Between these, a mix of shrill, hissing whimpers issued as he then sucked the air right back in again.

It was the excuse Reicher needed. He spun toward the sound and pulled his index finger.

Twice.

The first shot exploded the old man's chest, throwing him from the barstool as his insides came out. Despite the thunderous blast, it was the sound of the hollow-point round shattering the old man's ribs that none in the bar that day would ever forget.

The second round removed half of the elderly man's face as he had already begun sliding from the stool and fell into the shot. Lifeless, his body slumped to the greasy tile floor. In sharp contrast to the centrally cooled air, a small plume of steam rose from the man's skull where the friction of a hundred red hot fragments of the hollow-point spun through his brain at over five hundred miles per hour, boiling the moisture in the organ.

Soft moans and wails filled the bar where, only minutes before, all had been laughing and swearing, reveling in the venue's inherent machismo. Now, all of that had vanished to insignificance as the murmur of stifled cries lent an odious, unnatural quality to the new vulnerability of this microcosm.

"Jesus! He was only scared!" Frozen with his palms still held high, Ian saw from the corner of his eye that even Menendez was weeping in silence.

*Not Jesus,* Reicher sniggered to himself. *No. Wrong team.*

He pivoted and the revolver was leveled at Ian's forehead. This time, it was held a little less steadily, the smoking barrel swaying in the smallest, wavering ellipses. The gunmetal and sulfur scent wafted foreign amidst the odors of stale beer and sweat. Then came the stink of the old man's ruptured organs, reeking like liquid iron.

Ian doubled over and retched. No vomit came with the reflex, but the acid taste of bile rose into the back of his throat.

It was the aggressive move Reicher had been waiting for, and his blackened index finger pulled the .38's trigger a third time.

An explosion of noise filled Ian's ears, the echoing, unbearable percussion of a turntable's needle dropping onto a vinyl record at maximum volume and bouncing across the tracks.

*BOOM—boom—boom...*

The world faded to grey as Ian collapsed—while behind him, Tony Lamont was reeling from the recoil of the sawn-off 12-gauge he'd drawn from its mount hidden beneath the bar.

Reicher's face dissolved, features shredding as the shotgun's flash of light and concussive sound filled the room. His body buckled unnaturally as it pitched backward, arms windmilling as his index finger completed one final pull upon the .38's trigger.

The wild shot embedded into a far wall at the end of the bar as Reicher, or what was left of the husk that had once been the man, crashed through a table, the revolver spinning out of his hand and across the floor.

With his teeth and most of his jaw no longer existing, and all traces of identifying prints burnt from his hands and feet, the transformation of Reicher Winslow to anonymous harbinger of demonic prophecy was complete.

Still, the angel had fulfilled the three covenants to which both were bound. For Reicher would indeed, many years from now, become known as one of the agents of the New Apocrypha. Though the name by which devotees would come to know him would be only 'Anonymous.'

Reicher had also been reunited with his Lizzie, even enjoying the experience of his late wife pleasuring him one last time in this day's early hours. The fact that she was a decaying, animated corpse when she did so was neither here nor there.

Finally, as promised, Reicher's dehumanizing, debilitating and unimaginably painful cancer was no more. For the tumor had truly been obliterated…along with most of Reicher's brain stem and the cerebellum upon which it fed.

As his dead body lay sprawled on the floor in a gleaming crimson puddle, the energy that had been Reicher Winslow gave itself to the universal vibration. All the light Reicher had cast through his life—all the love and giving and selfless affection—was snuffed out like a candle in a breeze. What remained were the instances of loathing and hatred and self-absorbed pleasure Reicher had embraced over the years.

That, and the pain he'd caused.

*All the pain.*

These shadows cast throughout Reicher's life were what the angel now guided into the darkness over which it presided. Without the balance of their counterpart in light, every corruption, misdeed and transgression melded into a conduit of pulsing, untethered power. They now became the totality of Reicher's existence…an entire life having been unwittingly lived for the singular purpose of drawing Ian Cockerton back to a state of being he had managed to refute for eighteen years.

Sparking to life just a hint of abilities suppressed—and the memory of a horror long forgotten—the liquid of Ian's stomach released itself. Overwhelmed by confusion and fear, he closed his eyes to the nightmare scene before him. His consciousness followed suit, permitting the brown noise that enveloped him to carry him away.

II

Ian's eyes reopened to find a young boy staring at him, their faces so close to one another that the boy's was all but a blur. Ian winced, flinching back and blinking until the face came into focus.

It was a boy he knew—a friend.

A friend who would never age beyond his eleventh year.

*'Quite the reunion we have going on here. Isn't it, old pal!'* Matt Chauncey declared with an intense grin. *'You, me...Jack...Who could possibly be next, I wonder?'*

Ian scuttled backward with a gasp of disbelief. Instead of beer-sloshed linoleum floor tiles, his knuckles scraped warm, rough blacktop. He was no longer in Tony's Major League sports bar, but in the middle of a road. A road Ian recognized as the place called 'Hamburger Hill,' the fast food haven of his childhood.

Matt was jumping up and down, clapping his hands with excitement as a tractor trailer barreled towards them.

*'Did you really think you could run away? That you and your stupid brother had won?'* Matt Chauncey giggled. *'I've missed you! The gang's all here, and they've all missed you, too!'*

Ian's parents were traveling up the hill.

*'Watch, Ian! Just watch!'*

Carl Miller's truck was traveling down it.

Chauncey shrieked with delight as the semi veered across the double yellow, jack-knifing into the path of the blue sedan driven by Hare and Veronica Cockerton.

*'Time to come home and finish what you started, Ian. Just wait 'til you see what we have in store for you! Our game isn't over. Oh my, no. It's only just begun...'*

# 09

*slaughter creek*

# 16 years before the end | July 1995

THE DARKNESS WAS coming. Of this, Eddie was certain. He had felt it strengthening over the past month now, a physical sensation as tangible as the gleaming steel head of the axe in his grip, the surety of the hickory handle worn smooth by his calloused hands.

It had been absent from his life for almost two decades, more than enough time to expect that it had gone forever. Yet Eddie continued to honor one anniversary after another, waiting for the day the abomination they had awakened as boys would return.

*Today was that day.*

Splitting wood to dry for the long winter months ahead, he abruptly stopped when a sonic boom of dark energy rang through him. In an instant, every fiber of his being resounded with a deep, bass vibration.

"It is time," he exclaimed as he fell to his knees, lifting his eyes to the dusk sky to find that an impossible darkness had swallowed the sun. And in his mind, he was once again in the Little Woods...

# III
# MUTATIO

# 10

# 6 years before the end | July 31, 2005

SHE FELL IN and out of sleep as the hours passed. All around her, strangers who were becoming acquaintances chattered about their reasons for the trip, who they were going to see, what awaited them at home, or what adventures lie in wait. She remained on the bus as those same acquaintances, now becoming friends, departed two and three at a time to jostle into line at the Chantilly Café while hunger pangs pulled at their stomachs.

"Excuse me, uh..." a woman in her early forties half-whispered and gently touched Diane on the shoulder. Flinching, Diane sucked in her breath as the dimensions of her dream world crumbled, the awakening to stark reality as brutal as a spray of ice water. "Oh, my. I'm so sorry. I did *not* mean to startle you! I just wanted you to know that we're in Charlottesville, Virginia. End of the line. For today, at least."

The woman's gentle smile wavered, just perceptibly, when the sleeve of Diane's hoodie pulled taut to expose the scar in her wrist an inch in diameter.

Diane had no memory of how it had gotten there, nor could she begin to fathom what had happened. The last thing she remembered was Simon Peter's followers grabbing her in the cathedral, so it must've happened then. Whatever had caused it, it looked angry, boasting a blush rim around its periphery that smacked of infection.

When Diane caught her looking, the woman averted her eyes and pretended to peer out the window over Diane's shoulder, going so far as to give a little wave to someone outside the bus who did not exist.

Diane tugged her cuff halfway up her palm. Soft as the material was, the cotton was steel wool as it passed over the puncture. "It's…nothing," she dismissed.

The words were strained and painful, the muscle tension of her throat overcompensating for vocal cords damaged from the prolonged and repeated screams she did not remember.

A smile returned to the woman's face, though more forced this time. It still conveyed a warmth that made Diane feel less alone.

"Well," she extended a hand to help Diane up from her seat. "Whaddya say we grab dinner? After all, two refined ladies such as we, and traveling all by our lonesomes, ought to, by rights, stick together. Don'tcha think?"

II

Shrimp and grits never tasted so good.

"So, it's a favorite of yours, hun?"

Diane grinned, a shyness flushing her face. "I don't know why I said that. I've never actually had them before."

Elizabeth dropped her fork in mock alarm and its clang turned a dozen heads from half as many booths. Which made Diane snicker. "Well, you really *are* a Yankee, aren't you, dear."

"Told you I was. Pennsylvania and New York…City. That's it."

"I've always thought that such a burdensome state to speak of, Pennsylvania. Just so many darn syllables. And to me it always smacks of—oh, what's that place Dracula is from—?"

"Transylvania?"

Elizabeth pointed at Diane while tapping the bridge of her nose with her other hand. "Yes, that's the place! Vanna, tell the young lady what she's won…!"

She peeled back her lips to bare teeth that were enviably white and uniform, save the canines which were rather pronounced.

"I vaaaahn to suouock yuouuouh bloooood…" Elizabeth cooed in her best Bela Lugosi, though the actor never said that line in the film. Not even once. Not ever.

Diane choked down her laughter along with the soda in her mouth before it spewed from her lips like spray from a fountain on a windy day.

Elizabeth smiled, rolling her eyes at her own silliness. Mildly embarrassed, or perhaps pretending to be, she shrunk down in the booth, just a little, when two European women in an adjacent one shared what they thought of the impression. The curt response likely had something to do with the fact that they were speaking something like Hungarian. Or maybe Slovak. Hell, it might have even been Romanian—home of the Transylvania province—for all Diane and Elizabeth knew.

*And wouldn't that be some crazy, coincidental shit.*

Uncomfortable silence for a good twenty seconds. Which, if you've ever experienced uncomfortable silence, you know that's at least two lifetimes.

Clearing her aching throat, Diane sipped more soda.

"You know," offered Elizabeth, her inner matriarch surfacing. "If your throat is sore, that pop isn't going to help, hun. All the acid, you see." She waggled her fingers at her throat to simulate the carbonation. "Let's get you a nice tall glass of still water filled with fresh cut lemons…"

Diane nodded. "Well, anyhoo. This all started with me talking about home. I was going to call it Pee Aay, 'cause we never say the whole name either. But I wasn't sure you'd know what I meant."

"You're right, hun. I mean, I'm just a poor little backwoods ninny of a gal from Georgia. How *ever* would I know that Pee Aay means Pennsylvania?" She now hucked out a laugh that was such a perfect impersonation of Goofy, you would've sworn the dog (or whatever he was) was right here in Chantilly Café with them.

Now the two European ladies—let's just call them Brides of Dracula, to keep it simple—repeated their looks of disdain, even torquing it up a notch.

This time, Diane's Coke did spray from her lips. "Aaaaagghh, that burns!" She rubbed her nose, snorting, while carbonated brown liquid drizzled from one nostril.

Elizabeth wiped soda spray her face, overly dramatic and grinning. "And you think *I'm* the local yokel…"

"Oh my God, I'm so sorry! It's just that—"

"—Just that you haven't been able to laugh for longer than you can remember. Am I right?"

Diane nodded, her smile receding.

"Hey, I'm sorry," Elizabeth apologized as she reached across the table and patted Diane's hand. Or at least she tried to. At the first sense of the woman's touch Diane pulled away, hiding her hands in her lap under the table.

Uncomfortable silence 2.0.

Elizabeth cut this pause short as soon as it began. "Well, hun. You know, you Yankees don't have the monopoly on long or funny place names. I mean, could there be any more annoying than Mississippi? I've never been able to say that name in my head, not even once, without phrasing it all sing-song-cheerleadery like, 'em-aye-essess, aye-essess, aye-peepee-aye.'"

She was right, of course, which revived Diane's smile. Even though she didn't want it to.

Because deep down, she really did.

"Or, how about where I'm from," Elizabeth continued without so much as a breath: "Dahlonega. You know how that's spelled?"

Diane shook her head.

"Neither do I, and I grew up there! Isn't it Duh-LAWN-eh-guh?"

"Wait," Diane interjected. "Are you talking about Dall-Oh-NAY-Guh?" (This she pronounced to rhyme with Talladega.)

"Why yes, I am. One in the very same, my dear. Except…it's Duh-LAWN-eh-guh."

"I'm going to Dahlo—" Diane began to pronounce it the way she always had, cut herself short and restructured the word in her mind to pronounce it the way a native of the town did. "*I'm* going to…Dahlonega. Are you really from there?"

"I am. From the place with a name the way I say it at least, yes. But what brings a pretty young thing like you to Dahlonega. Are you planning to check out the Appalachian Trail?"

Diane shook her head, downing the last spoonful of grits. "To be honest, I didn't even know the trail went anywhere near there."

"Not only does it go near there, it *starts* there. The southern terminus is about twenty miles northwest of town. Dahlonega is the biggest nearby community, so that's pretty much our little town's one and only claim to fame."

"Wow. But, no. I'm visiting my uncle who lives there. Well, I'm kinda *surprising* him, actually. So, I hope he's not on vacation, or something." She paused. "'Cause I could do with crashing there for a bit. I think he'll be okay with that."

"Gosh, hun. I can't imagine he wouldn't be. I mean, how excited is he gonna be to see you! In what part of Dahlonega does your uncle live?"

Diane held up a finger while she swallowed her coke.

Swallowing sill hurt.

"He doesn't really live in town, I guess, but a ways out? He has a cabin in the woods around Blood Mountain. Creepy address."

Elizabeth laughed. "Well, hun. Like I said, you Yanks don't have a monopoly on funny names. Lord knows, we got more than our fair share of them down here. This is the bible belt, after all. We got names that can scare the devil straight and turn an angel bad.

What road's your uncle's cabin on? Maybe I'll know it."

To Diane the question felt less natural than the rest of their conversation. Intrusive. She did her best to answer without actually answering, but her nerves made her ramble on.

"Well like I said, it's out a ways. I don't think it's even near the road. From what I gather, at least from the stories he's told over the years, it's quite a trek from the road to his cabin. Down a gravel and dirt driveway, if that's what you'd call it? Or maybe it's more like a private lane? Though, calling it a lane sounds rather too grand for him, *hehe*."

Just when she realized that she'd almost said too much, Diane stopped herself from revealing anything more by adding that awkward little chortle at the end.

Elizabeth shrugged.

The silence was excruciating.

Before she knew why, Diane found herself speaking again.

"I know he's always made a joke of the fact that his address is a whole different county to his cabin. I mean, the road used for his postal address is in one county, but after you go down his drive, or lane, or whatever, his place actually sits in the woods across the line, in the next county over."

*...the Mexican Train Champion of Lumpkin County...*

She shook her head and stared at the table, feeling suddenly very tired and as if she'd given away far too much information already. After everything that happened to her, it was insane. Why was she suddenly so trusting of this woman she'd only just met?

*'I don't know,'* Doctor M. asked as she appeared in Diane's thoughts, one toned leg still rocking lightly over the other as she peered at Diane over the top of her reading glasses. *'Why do you think that is, Ms. Cockerton?'*

Elizabeth recanted, seeing so much going on behind the young woman's eyes and appreciating that they'd only just met forty minutes ago. (If you ignored the ten hours together on a bus from

New York, along with thirty-one other people, that is.) "You know what, Diane? It's really none of my business. I'm sorry. I shouldn't have even asked. You don't know me from Adam, so—"

"—Slaughter Creek," Diane heard herself blurting out, feeling equal amounts of both concern and relief that she'd done so. "He lives somewhere off Slaughter Creek."

Elizabeth paled. "Oh. My. God."

"See," Diane felt compelled to placate. "I told you it was a creepy-ass address, didn't I?"

"Oh. My. God," Elizabeth repeated, even more animated. And slower. "Your uncle is…*Eddie*?!"

Now Diane felt the blood pull from her head and begin pooling in her gut. She'd said way too much.

"H-how do you know tha—" It was suddenly an effort to breathe. "—That. How do you *know* that!"

"Because, hun, I have the same creepy-ass address!" Elizabeth nearly shouted the reply, so excited was she. This time, the two Brides of Dracula got up and relocated to another booth a good halfway across the restaurant. "Well, not the *same* address, I mean, your uncle and I don't live together. God, no!"

Feeling oddly self-conscious about the clarification, Elizabeth let loose an awkward chuckle that came across like a reverse hiccup.

"I mean, I live on the same creepy-ass road! I *know* your uncle, babygirl. Very well. My God, Eddie and my late husband are— *were*—the absolute best of friends. For years!" Elizabeth was now doing everything in her power to keep from running around to Diane's side of the booth and throwing her arms around her. "I can't believe it. You're Eddie's *Deedee*! I'm sat here, for the better part of an hour, having lunch with Deedee. And I don't even know it. Well bless my cotton socks!"

Elizabeth was so excited, she was vibrating. Literally. Diane could feel them coming off the woman in waves, a broadcast of bright, high vibrations.

"He never mentioned me, hun? Oh for Heaven's sake. God help that feeble old man. I'm *Elizabeth*. Still nothing…?"

Diane's expression remained blank. Having no recollection of ever hearing Uncle Eddie mention an Elizabeth, she was loathe to admit so. This woman had already been so kind, the last thing she wanted to do was come across as stupid, rude, or both. So, Diane said absolutely nothing at all.

Which looked even worse.

Still, Elizabeth persisted. "Are you having me on, hun? Or maybe you're just mistaken. I know it's been a long trip already, and we're only halfway there. You see, I'm Lizzie Winslow, Diane. I'm Reicher's wife…"

# 11

**E**ARLIER THAT SAME day, Detective Magdalena Romano perched at the edge of Rebecca Cockerton's hospital bed three hundred and fifty miles away. She gestured for Della to have a seat as well, but the woman remained standing at Rebecca's side, taking the mother's hand and gently weaving her fingers into hers. "...What he saw was Diane, Rebecca. Standing there. Alive and breathing. And as real as you or me."

With her head in her hands, Rebecca's sobbing filled the room as a barrage of emotions collided at the mother's core.

"Do you understand what I'm telling you, Mrs. Cockerton? Both officers have made official statements that Diane...that your daughter...stood up and walked away from that morgue."

Della dropped to her knees, clinging to the bed's safety rail with one hand, the other still clasping Rebecca's as the emotional spillways were cast wide, relieving the unbearable pressure which had weighed upon her heart. The murky waters of guilt discharged in a wave of intense energy, and though her lips were not moving, Maggie was certain she could hear Della crying out.

*No, not a plea,* Maggie decided. *An invocation.*

She could not make it out completely. Sporadic words, partial phrases. They rose and fell in a way Maggie could feel but not hear, each one a vibration of Della's silent voice somehow echoing from within Maggie's own being. They radiated outward as warm chills, the words she could not hear (but yet understood) rippling across her shoulder blades, down her spine, spreading to her arms and legs. Tingling her skin with a thousand butterfly kisses.

*...praise...child...limitations no more...behold...*

Like a blast wave, Della's every unspoken word, each syllable not articulated, struck Maggie with such intensity that for a moment the detective struggled to stay on her feet.

*...the true Disciple has come to us upon a horse of Light. And an army of Heavenly warriors rides behind Her!*

The intensity of the declaration was so powerful that now Magdalena's legs did weaken and she, too, dropped to her knees and began reciting the Angelical salutation almost as a reflex. Spiritual muscle memory from her catechism days, it came to her now as naturally as it had then. "Hail Mary, full of grace, the Lord is with thee. Blessed art thou among women..."

Magdalena repeated the prayer more times than she knew, stopping only when something soft as air brushed against her cheek. She opened her eyes to find Della's locked onto hers, the smokiest green she had ever seen, so light they were almost transparent grey. For a moment, the detective found herself entranced, even a little nervous, as though they possessed the power to see through to her very soul.

II

"I can't explain it either, Rebecca. But I'll take grateful over logical, any day." After the tears had stopped flowing and she felt her decorum was sufficiently restored, Magdalena Romano was saying her goodbyes. "And tomorrow I will stop by again. If that's alright with you? I may have some more news."

Rebecca's cheeks were streaked with salted lines, capable only of nodding in response as no words were powerful enough.

"Do we know where Diane is?" Della asked, still squeezing Rebecca's hand. A comfort to her as much as it was to Rebecca.

Maggie shook her head. "I'm sorry. We don't. And I know the officers guarding the morgue could have tried to stop her. But," here she paused, careful to maintain the decorum she'd only just reestablished, "I place no blame on them. Restraining a walking corpse isn't exactly part of their training."

Realizing she'd just referred to Rebecca's daughter as a walking corpse, she grimaced.

"I'm sorry. See? I think, yeah... Well... I think it's time I left you two alone for what's left of the day. I'll be sure to check in with you tomorrow."

### III

It was not until she was alone that evening that Maggie found the feather in her handbag. A black feather.

*A raven's feather.*

She touched it to her face and knew instantly it was what Della had brushed so tenderly across her cheek; what had broken the infinite loop of her prayer to the Blessed Mother and returned her to the moment...

### IV

"Are you sure?" Della was apprehensive but trusting. "Never mind. Stupid question, I know."

Rebecca nodded. "I am. And it's not."

She embraced Della, trying hard to ignore the pain as she stood with her friend's assistance. Thick, clotted blood pressed like cabernet pulp between the sutures that bound the incision bisecting her abdomen. Her hospital gown blossomed with more dark spots. "I'm blessed to have a friend like you."

More than just signing the DAMA (Discharge Against Medical Advice), Rebecca was required to engage in several conversations with three physicians, one of whom was a staff psychiatrist. Hers was the onus of proof to illustrate mental competence. Not only to sign the waiver which absolved Saint Benedicts of all malpractice or negligence, but also that she understood the very real, and very likely, medical risks of forsaking the hospital's ongoing care.

By nightfall, they were on the street.

"Take me home, DeLaCroix."

## V

They hailed three taxis with yellow roof signs illuminated 'FOR HIRE' before any was willing to stop.

Pointing at the blossoming crimson petals across the waist of Rebecca's fresh shirt, the driver barked: "Youstain youpay!" Running his words together in pairs, they could just as easily have been the first and last name of a compatriot from the Middle East. "Whereto? Whereto!"

"Just seven blocks from here," Rebecca answered in flawless Arabic. "Please, Amir. Alhamdulillah."

Della leaned forward between the seats and handed the driver a hundred dollar bill.

"It's all yours. Just...*smoooooth.*" Drawing out the word, she slid her hand through the air. A slow, gliding pantomime. "No bumps or sudden turns. Okay?"

"Yesyes," Amir assured and snatched the hundred from Della's fingers, popping on the overhead light and holding the bill up to it as he examined its authenticity. Satisfied after several turns through his hands and one unusual moan, he shoved it into his trouser pocket rather than the cash box.

Suddenly, the taxi was a prestige limo.

"Whereyou wantgo, fineladies." He fished through a travel cooler on his front passenger seat, offering them both a bottled water. "Onhouse. Yesyes?"

Father Gabriel was waiting for them on the steps of Saint Casimir's. He and Amir both assisted Rebecca from the back seat of the cab and up the cement stairs of the side entrance.

"Yarhamuk Allah," Amir nodded, returning Rebecca's blessing. To Della he said, "Tasharrafna." Gently taking her hand and turning her palm upward, he pressed the hundred dollar bill into it and closed Della's fingers. His hand lingered upon hers as he nodded with a deferent smile.

## VI

The church's interior was cool and dimly lit. On the chancel in front of the altar, three large candles in red glass jars flickered within a golden framework. As Father Gabriel and Della helped Rebecca to the chancel rail, one of the flames sizzled and popped before extinguishing to a thin wisp of smoke.

Rebecca knelt with a stifled cry of pain. Across her abdomen, the crimson petals had bled into one, creating a solid line from her left all the way to her right.

"Mother, are you ready for the Viaticum?"

Rebecca nodded, bowing her head and silently praying as the priest prepared the Eucharist.

He returned with a purple sash which he laid reverently upon Rebecca's shoulders. In his left hand he presented the communion wafer while making the sign of the cross before her.

"Take this, and eat of it. For this is my Body, which has been given up for you." He placed the wafer upon her tongue.

In the silence of the vast and empty nave, the crackling of the two candles were amplified by the natural acoustics, a soothing campfire sound.

Wiping a silver chalice, he presented Rebecca with the wine. "Take this, and drink of it, for this is my Blood, which has been given up for you." He placed the cup to the mother's lips and the wine was smooth and rich. Rebecca felt her body absorbing it like a thirsty sponge, and the sensation was comforting and pure.

"Corpus Domini Nostri Iesu Christi custodiat animam tuam in vitam aeternam. Amen."

*May the Lord Jesus Christ protect and lead you to eternal life.*

With this, the second of the three candles slowly dimmed. With a bright, flaring spark it popped one last time before its flame became a spiraling line of rising smoke.

Across Rebecca's forehead, Father Gabriel traced the sign of the cross with his thumb moistened by holy water.

"I commend you, my dear Mother, to Almighty God, and entrust you to your Creator. May you return to him who formed you from the dust of the earth. May holy Mary, the angels, and all the saints come to meet you as you go forth from this life."

He then signed the cross over his own chest, turned to face the altar, genuflecting before the cross. He did not wipe away the tear which slowly fell from his eye until he retired to his sacristy and wept in prayer.

"Rebecca...?" Della's voice was a soothing whisper as she placed her hands upon the mother's shoulders; kissed the top of Rebecca's head. Rebecca Cockerton did not respond. Lost in prayer, she had begun to lean more heavily into the chancel rail.

Kneeling, Delta carefully snugged up against her friend, pulling her close so that she absorbed Rebecca's weight into her own body as opposed to the cold, rigid railing.

"I love you, Mother," she spoke softly into Rebecca's ear and rested her cheek upon her friend's.

In time, the third candle died. It did so not with a pop or a spark, but simply by its flame diminishing...

...Until it was gone.

# 12

*welcome to paradise*

S TILL, NOTHING. DIANE simply had no memory of Uncle Eddie ever mentioning a man by the name of Reicher. Or his wife, Lizzie. She decided to admit it now before this ran away from her. Even if it wasn't what her new friend wanted to hear. Because that's what friends did, right? They told the truth to each other. "I'm so sorry, Elizabeth, he never—"

"Please, call me Lizzie. For heaven's sake, we're practically related."

*Well, not practically,* Diane countered but would never say it out loud. *For a start, even Eddie's not really my uncle. A friend of my dad's from childhood? You bet. A friend as close, if not closer, than any relative could be? Absolutely. But you being a friend of a friend makes us potential friends at best, lady. So let's go easy on the 'related' line of thinking. We all have fucked-up family, but I've more than enough to go around and I don't need to add anyone else to the mix just now.*

She said none of this and simply replied: "Okay, then. Lizzie, he just nev—"

Elizabeth cut her short, finishing the sentence. "—Never said much about me…"

Diane shrugged, mild discomfort shrinking her in her seat.

"We are talking about the same Eddie, here, right Deedee?

That is what they call you?"

Diane nodded, cringingly self-aware.

"Except your uncle. He calls you Petunia. Am I right? Is my Eddie the same Eddie as your Eddie? Haha, that's a lot of Eddies. But hopefully just one!"

*Petunia.* It had been so long since she'd heard that nickname. Seven and a half years, to be precise. Eddie had come to visit her at Barrow Moor. He was the only one who did. He'd brought her a leatherbound hardcover of the complete and unabridged works of Edgar Allan Poe. That, like so much of who she had been, was long gone now.

Tears welled in her eyes and she squeezed her lips closed, pinching back the cry.

It did not go unnoticed, and Elizabeth answered her own question so the girl wouldn't have to.

"I'll take that as a yes," she replied softly and again placed her hands over Diane's. This time, there was nothing tentative about the move and she only pressed more firmly when Diane tried to pull away. "*Shhhh.* It's okay, Deedee. You're not alone now."

II

The Traveler's Stop wasn't much to write home about. Two single beds with one flat pillow each. An old TV on a swivel wall mount that looked like the ones Diane had seen at Felipe's new Home Plate Grill. A sink in the bathroom with a permanent hard water ring, and a toilet bowl that dripped throughout the night.

But at least it was a place to lay her head.

"It really was nice of you to do this, Liz. I could've gotten a room of my own. I do have some cash with me." What was meant as a show of appreciation was turning out to be a snotty 'so there' kind of remark. Which was the furthest thing from Diane's intentions. "God, I'm sorry. Again. I'm so terrible at this. I guess I really do need to brush up on my social skills."

"I know, Deedee. I mean, about you having your own cash, not the social skills part. But remember, your uncle and I are friends. Long-time friends. I've heard your story for so long and so intimately I feel I've known you most of your—" Sensing Diane's unease, she didn't finish the sentence. "I just feel that I know you, hun. That's all. And it's my pleasure to do this. So stop apologizing. I mean, look around! You're actually doing *me* a favor, girl. I might need you here in case some giant cockroach tries to run away with me in the middle of the night!"

They watched 'Will & Grace' back-to-back on NBC, suffering through the television's audio that sounded like its speakers were underwater. Diane didn't make it past the first commercial break of the second episode.

For the first time in longer than she could remember, she no longer felt alone, and her rest was deep and fulfilling.

### III

The bus was underway by eight a.m. and this time, Diane and Liz sat together.

"So, have you been to your uncle's place before?"

"Huh-uh. My first time."

"Oh, well. It's beautiful there, on the mountain. Especially the fall. God, I love that time of year, don't you." It was rhetorical, and Elizabeth did not wait for a reply. "Not much for a bright young girl from the city to do around there, though. Hiking, rambling, maybe some rappelling, if you're into that. I think a couple of spots are known for being great spelunking caves. And I don't know about you but I'm definitely not into that."

"Is spelunking the thing where you explore down some dark, tiny hole in the rocks?"

"That's the one," Liz replied, again placing her finger to her nose. She almost threw out the 'Vanna, tell her what she's won' line again, but the sudden realization that she was becoming more predictable than she liked stopped her from doing it. Besides, Pat Sajak never actually said that. And Vanna White's only job was to look pretty while she spun some lighted letters around. She never presented any prizes. So, she wasn't sure why she'd become so used to using such a silly phrase.

All of this flashed through Elizabeth's mind in a fraction of a moment, and it was here she realized that she too had been alone these days more than was healthy.

"You wouldn't catch me dead going down one of those things. Or, maybe I should say, you would. Because that's the only way you'd get me into some hole...if I were dead."

"I think I agree with you. Although, I'd rather be down one alive than dead, I guess."

"Better you than me, Deedee!" She paused, imagining this. Then shivered with a funny *bwwwaa* sound. "Anyhow, I guess I'm just forewarning you that besides a lot of outdoorsy stuff, there's not much for a young woman to do around us, especially when you're so used to everything the big city has to offer."

"Uneventful sounds like heaven to me right now, Lizzie."

"Well, then welcome to paradise!"

# IV

# DECIPIO

# 13

*slaughter creek*

THE CABIN WAS nowhere near Dahlonega. In her mind, Diane expected to get off the bus in town and make her way on foot. Never one to shy from a walk and being penned up in a stuffy bus for two days, she imagined she'd be ready to stretch her legs for a spell.

She hadn't thought it through. Nor did she put two-and-two together when Liz shared that Slaughter Creek Road was a good twenty-one miles away. Worse, it was another three-thousand feet higher in elevation than Dahlonega.

Essentially, an eight-hour hike.

She eyed her rudimentary sneakers with their thin soles, realizing just how unprepared she was for 'a spell' to suddenly mean 'all day.'

"Like I'd make you walk. Silly Girl. I've got ol' Charli here." Liz jangled a set of keys as they walked across the bus terminal, which was really just the Dairy Queen parking lot with a small ticket shack at one end, reminiscent of those old standalone photo booths from the eighties. Of course, Diane had never seen one in real life. But it was the spitting image of the Fox Photo shack in the middle of the mall's parking lot in *Back to the Future*.

Charli was short for Charli Cherokee, Liz's all black Jeep Grand Cherokee. The windows had been tinted darker than Diane thought legal—or perhaps even safe—the steel wheels had been replaced with all black ones, on much larger tires, and the hood had a wide matt black stripe up the middle.

"Pretty badass. When we were in Penns–*in Pee Aay*–my mom used to have this old Chevy Blazer. I always liked that thing. And it would've looked sweet, decked out like this."

"Well, I can't take all the credit. I bought it like this from a used car dealer when it had just a hundred miles on the clock. Only thing I did was the tires. You can't live on Blood Mountain and have girlie little tires. I'd never get up and down Slaughter Creek, for heaven's sake. Especially in the rainy season. And winter? *Forgeddaboudit*, as you New Yorkers say."

In all her years there, Diane had never heard a New Yorker say that. It was just another of those things everyone thinks. Kinda like Bela Lugosi's famous Dracula line he never spoke, or the game show reference about Vanna White. Or thinking that 80s exercise guru Richard Simmons wore a headband. (He didn't.) Or that Mickey Mouse wears suspenders. (Again, nope. Just a rad pair of red Capri shorts.)

*What do you call it when society as a whole pretty much shares the same false memory? Whatever it is,* Forgeddaboudit *falls squarely in that category.*

"My house is just up there, over that bend," Liz pointed out seconds before taking a sharp right off the road. For a second, Diane was certain she'd lost control of the Jeep as they careened toward a mass of trees. Then the thick greenery seemed to just open up and there was the gravel lane. "Now you'll see why your uncle lives in another county. And why I had Charli lifted and bigger knobby tires added."

They bounced over potholes that could've swallowed a Mini Cooper; glided through puddles the size of hot tubs. Dusk had already begun to descend as they headed out of town, and as Liz navigated northeast down Eddie's private obstacle course, Diane watched with no particular feeling as the forest swallowed the sun in the rear view mirror.

The light in the woods gradually changed from crisp white to golden, and finally hues of amber, as Eddie's cabin rose into view around the final bend and Liz pulled up next to Eddie's Mustang.

On the porch, her uncle impatiently waited as the lights came on and he was bathed by an angelic, golden glow.

II

Eddie was at the Jeep and embracing Diane, almost before Liz pulled the vehicle to a stop.

"Petunia!" He needn't say any more. Diane's soul filled like a sponge that's been left in the desert then submerged in a tub of warm, soothing water.

"Oh, Uncle Eddie. I've missed you. *So* much. In fact, I've missed you rotten, to tell the truth!"

"I've missed you too, babygirl," he whispered and hugged her longer than either could remember.

"Uhhh," Liz interjected after a respectable amount of time had passed. "Hello, what am I, chopped liver over here?" It was said in her best attempt at a Brooklyn accent, and Eddie chuckled—

*Ahh, the breathless Muttley laugh!*

—as he hugged Liz, too. "Thank you, so much. For bringing her."

She waved the comment down as though it were a pesky fly drawn to her soup. "Ed, it's nothing! I told you on the phone, I couldn't believe the coincidence." She paused, thinking about it for a moment. "Still can't, if I'm honest."

"I know, right," Eddie agreed. "Crazy."

*No such thing as coincidence.*

The thought rushed through Diane's mind without warning, a shrill series of vibrations in her tummy and the words heard in DeLaCroix Laveau's lilting Creole voice. How she had loved that voice. Now, it filled her with rage, though she wasn't fully certain why. Something deep inside told her that Della was her own personal Judas and not to be trusted.

*Fuck you, Della,* she cursed, and the image of the woman shattered like cheap glass in her mind. The tinny vibrations in her gut receded to the natural growls of an empty stomach and the intense sensation of craving something sweet. "Hey, Uncle Ed. You don't happen to have any gobs, do you?"

Eddie shrugged his apologies, eyes smiling. "Sorry, Petunia. It's been a long time since I've been in Pee Aay..."

### III

*If only that were true.*

### IV

The cooler air drew in with the night as their faces danced in the flickering orange glow of the fire pit. Weightless as they nestled into deep Adirondacks, paper plates in their laps flexed from the heft of Eddie's gigantic grill-master onion burgers.

"I don't know what's gotten into me, I'm so hungry these last few days." Diane finished hers off, folded the plate and tossed it into the flames. The greasy card stock caught in an instant, and the blue flame bellowed in a way that twisted the faces of Eddie and Liz into surreal masks of shadow and light.

"It's been a long couple of days for you," Eddie remarked, polishing off his burger and tossing the plate as Diane had. Again the flames devoured the thick grease-soaked paper, morphing the perimeter of trees surrounding the cottage into a wavering, animated army of guardians. "So, what've you been doing since you were released from Barrow Moor last month? You should've called me, Petunia."

"Funny name for a guy but okay, I will, Petunia." Diane's response was whipcrack fast and for a moment, Eddie appeared taken aback as though she were mocking the pet name she'd always seemed to love. Diane said nothing to let him off the hook so soon, but her burgeoning smile gave it away and the penny dropped.

"Oh, I get it!" Eddie quipped. '*You should've called me Petunia*.'" He thought about it for a moment longer before Muttley returned, his facial features scrunching together as he chortled like an animated department store Santa.

"I should've," Diane finally answered, her tone sobering with eyes downcast. "I should've called. I guess I was afraid to."

"Oh my gosh, Petunia. Why ever would you be afraid to call me, of all people?"

She thought about how to answer this without having to lie, but also without having to tell the whole truth. The last thing she wanted was to offend him…or be shipped back to Barrow Moor for the lunatic she clearly must be if she were to believe in even a portion of what had happened in the past week.

*Maybe Doc M. was right about you. All along. But would you listen? Nooooo. Now look at you. Maybe we should go back to Barrow Moor. At least it was safe there.*

She hushed the voice in her head and carefully gathered the words she spoke as one harvests the safe mushrooms from the poisonous…*or psychotropic*…ones.

"Mom…was…um…" The words pulled at her gut, painful before they ever travelled past the raw lining of her throat. "Mom was pregnant. It was…it was…*it was*…Ian's."

Uncle Eddie's face lit with joy, only to darken with sudden realization. "*Was* pregnant?"

Diane paled. Unconsciously nodded. Withdrawing to the scene which had played out just three days ago, yet felt like a different lifetime, she took Liz and Eddie with her:

"…Mama! What happened?" I screamed as I dropped to my knees and grabber her hand. It was caked in drying blood and smelled like rusty iron. Her face was ashen. The gown clinging to her inner thighs was soddened red, dark patches that continued to grow.

"Go, babygirl," she pleaded in my ear, her words staccato and thin between the sucking hiccups of a suppressed sob. "Please, Deedee. Go. Now. Befor—"

Her appeal was clipped short because Simon Peter emerged in the cathedral's antechamber at that point. The dusky backlight glowed in a corona around my nine-year-old brother as he climbed the stairs. In his right hand, dangling by its legs like a skinned rabbit, a baby—much too small to be alive—screamed. Magnified the deeper Simon Peter moves through the cathedral, the baby's cries were a high-pitched peal that rang through the vaulted chambers to send shivers down my spine.

Still attached to the baby by the umbilical cord, the placenta dragged behind them through the grit and droppings like a sack of wet sand leaving a trail of blood-smeared mucous. It would periodically snag on the ragged corners of broken tile, forcing Simon to tug on the fleshy, twisted cord to yank the sack free.

"Thought I'd save you the hassle of coming to us. You know, seeing as I'm your half-brother, 'n all. Isn't that nice of me? So here she is—your disgusting sow of a mother."

I could tell he relished the stunned horror on my face…I could *feel* it, you know? Then he lifted the baby high above him, displaying it like a prized catch. Fighting for life, the little baby boy was still covered in a white, gelatinous film mixed with the blood of my—his—*our*—mother.

"Oh, this?" He had a depraved look of pleasure on his face, sickening every layer of my soul. "Yeah, look what we found!"

*We?*

I didn't intend for Simon to hear my thought. But you know he did anyway. He thumbed the air behind him to indicate my uncle—my dad's brother, Ian—who appeared in the massive doorway at that moment. Ian's forearms were red to his elbows. Behind him, others began filing into the cathedral in a parade of silence. Each was wearing the same white gown as my mother.

All the while, the baby's tormented wails filled my ears.

He couldn't have been anywhere close to full-term. Suspended upside-down and stretched thin, his body was still barely a dozen inches long. His innocent little face was beet red as the blood drained to his head, his mouth and fingers curling in unison as he wailed. I've never seen a thing more vulnerable. Or innocent. And I feel sick to my stomach even now, thinking about Simon Peter bobbing him up and down by ankles so small I was sure they were about to snap. Maybe they already did, because that little boy's wails had risen so high in pitch, they became a jarring whistle.

"Seems your uncle and that whore of a mother made this pathetic half-breed example of a Nephala five months ago. Twenty-one weeks, to be precise. Here, do you want to see it?" Here Simon lowered the baby as if he was going to throw him, and I was just paralyzed, able to say or do nothing. "No?" he says. "Okay then. Well, anyway. I had your uncle rip this annoying bastard from your cunt mother. Or maybe I should say, from your mother's cunt"—he really liked that wordplay and laughed, and it filled the cathedral, making my skin crawl—"not ten minutes ago. Seems the ginger slut went from *not* being able to have kids, to not being able to *stop* having them. And, well, there's just no room for another. You see, the black witch was right. I am the Alpha and I am the Omega…"

Lizzie was sobbing and made no attempt to hide it. Whether from the story itself, or the fact that Diane so clearly believed what she was saying, was yet to be determined. Its eeriness was intensified tenfold by it being so incongruous to the peace and contentment the fireside setting had exuded only minutes before.

Eddie was silent. No longer making eye contact with Diane, he stared past the pit's dying flames, unmoving.

Diane cupped her hand over her swollen throat and watched as the fire tapered away to embers. Every few moments, a rising spark would crackle mid-flight and she reflexively flinched as the popping sound accompanied the spark's deconstruction into myriad tinier ones; a miniature firework show.

So the scene remained, the escalating tension the only thing to change. The first to break the status quo was Eddie.

"You can't be here, " he first mumbled so softly that the words were barely audible. He then repeated them. More clearly. And again, so loud this time it was all but a shout: "You can't be here!"

Diane flushed, fidgeting in her blue Adirondack. "Uncle Eddie?"

He rose from his seat and squared to face her, eyes drilling into her own. "You heard me, Deedee. You cannot be here! Why did you come?" He spun to face Liz: "Why did you bring her here?"

Liz blanched. "I–I—" she stuttered, wiping her eyes and looking to Diane in amazement. "I-what do you mean? Ed! I had no idea—"

"You need to go." He stood tall, crossing his arms.

Bewildered, disoriented, Diane was unable to speak.

"Now," Eddie demanded, pointing toward the gravel drive and stepping aside to clear a path for her departure.

"Uncle Eddie? I-I don't know what's happening! Why are you saying that?" She stood and moved toward him, and he moved back by an equal amount. She stepped forward again, and he shifted back the same. "I really d-don't understand. Liz—?"

Elizabeth Winslow was wide-eyed, her lids puffy, the whites dark and crisscrossed with endless pink lines where she'd rubbed until the fine capillaries were on the verge of bursting.

"Eddie?"

He did not answer her.

"Eddie!" Liz persisted, the appeal fast becoming a demand. "Why are you doing this? That's Deedee you're talking to. That's your *niece*!"

"She's not my niece. We're not even related. Don't you know that?"

Liz shook her head, her dismay yielding to carefully governed anger. "Okay, your best friend's daughter, then!"

Eddie did not reply verbally, his answer instead coming in the form of a baleful glare on the verge of being frightening.

"I see." Elizabeth's response was monotone as she rose from her seat with a level of composure and grace Diane hadn't witnessed from the woman who had been so buoyant and carefree. She dusted off her trousers. Clenched her lips. Stepped decisively around the fire pit as its remnants sizzled and popped orange and dim yellow.

At first Eddie did not move.

"I'll kindly have you step aside, Edward," she asserted, her tone making it unmistakable that this was in no way a request. When Eddie moved aside, she deliberately turned and went the other direction around the cinder block pit. Her way of illustrating that he had no power over her, regardless of what he may believe.

"Diane…let's go."

She extended her hand and Diane accepted it, allowing Liz to lead her silently away. With every step the darkness thickened, the cold mountain air slicing that little bit sharper.

Liz did not look back as they strode with intent to her Jeep.

Diane did.

Her gut heavy and breaths short, she repeatedly glanced behind her as she followed the pull of Liz's hand in hers.

Eddie did not look at his niece, however. With eyes downcast, he scuffed his feet through the dirt and gravel surrounding the pit until they were over the small hillock and out of sight.

Through the silence came the growl of the Grand Cherokee's

engine as it fired up; the crunching of crush and run gravel beneath its knobby tires as Liz made a slapdash three-point turn. On this occasion, she cared little about the stone chips that flew up as she accelerated down the lane.

When he thought they were out of earshot, Eddie screamed. But Diane had rolled down her window. And to her ears, his was not a bellow of outrage but a forlorn, mournful cry.

V

With gravel dust billowing in their wake, they bounced along the winding drive faster than Diane's eyes were able to keep up. Navigating curves and bends as well as any rally driver, Elizabeth drove without slowing. Try as she might, she was unable to outrun the unbearable tension that stuck with them like glue. It wasn't until the long straightaway running parallel to Slaughter Creek itself that Liz finally let off the accelerator and took a deep, audible breath.

They coasted to a slow crunching stop in the gravel as the dust caught up to them and swirled around the Jeep like fog. Just yards away was the main road.

"Well," Lizzie stated in the most deadpan manner as she cast a sidelong glance at Diane. Her eyes were bright against the darkness blanketing the woods, and they glimmered in the dim yellow light of the headlights as it reflected back from the dust cloud. "I guess the night could've gone a *little* better."

And just like that, the tension shattered. Diane's discharged as a snorting roar, and that made Lizzie bite her lip as she tried not to laugh herself. It didn't work, and she began to giggle. Then cackle. Then crow as the headlights radiated in prisms off the swirling cloud that now engulfed the stationary Jeep.

They were still laughing when the windshield imploded with a rasping, heart-stopping squeal…

# 14

*the shadow*

I T DROVE ITS face through the glass, shrieking as cloven feet outside the Jeep peeled back the windshield's lamination. Thrashing with its body halfway into the vehicle's cockpit, its mouth hinged impossibly wide to emit a squeal of countless voices, layer upon disharmonic layer in a shriek so disturbing that Liz's heart gave out.

She clutched her chest, mouth twisting. Though she cried out, the last sound Elizabeth ever made was eclipsed by the demon's wail as it tore through the vehicle's glass, teeth snapping at Diane who was frozen in place in the passenger seat.

The shot rang out in the moment the demon's head burst apart, a barrel flash of light visible from beyond Liz's open window as rancid meat and something like cartilage imploded. Deconstructing in slow motion, each piece sizzled and vaporized, nothing more than soot by the time it drifted to the dash, the console, the seats. Black snowflakes, they simply evaporated and were gone. Still clawing at the hood, its feet, wings and tail writhed like a snake after losing its head. Fiercely animated, death traveled down the creature's body the way carefully laid dominoes tip one after the other.

Flitting away in the breeze, the soot left only a scorched silhouette in the hood's paint as if the vehicle had been left outside and its paint blanched from years in the blazing sun.

And the scratches.

*Deep, clawed scratches.*

Spattered with black vaporizing ash, Diane's scream finally surfaced as she swatted manically at her face, hair and clothes. Over and over, her vocal cords were pushed to their limit as Eddie pulled her from the Jeep and into his arms…

# 15

*now and then*

HOURS PASSED BEFORE Diane was capable of speaking without crying; breathing without her lungs pulling too short, too long, too fast or too slow. When Samuel Hill, the Sheriff's Deputy for this part of Blood Mountain, appeared on the front porch, Eddie suggested Diane get some rest and escorted her to the couch in the den.

"Hey, Ed. Sorry to bother you so darn late. But we had a call from a concerned citizen."

Eddie held up his index finger, left to close the door to the den, then returned to the deputy standing awkwardly on the porch swatting at mosquitoes.

"A Mr. Williams, not from around here, I gather, heard the crash as he was driving by. Said he seen something odd, too. Not sure what that means really, but I reckon a lot looks odd to folks who aren't from around here. 'Specially so late at night."

To this Eddie nodded in agreement.

"Anyway, Mr., uh," Hill looked at his notepad again. "Um, Mr. *Williams* figured he'd be a Good Samaritan card and give us a call."

"Absolutely. Don't blame him."

"Mind if I come in and have a quick chat? Just to cross the I's and dot the T's?"

"Of course not, Sam. Come on in. Just—" He pointed at the

closed door to the den and placed his index finger over his lip. "*She's resting*," he added so softly it was nearly a whisper.

Hill nodded. "*Sure thing*," he whispered back.

The Deputy listened to the account of what happened then drove back out to the end of the lane with Eddie in the police cruiser's passenger seat. After a cursory look at the Jeep, he found nothing that contradicted Eddie's statement: It was clear that, yes, a deer had indeed leapt through the vehicle's windshield.

*And who could blame any driver, let alone Eddie's niece who was new to the area, for being so upset.*

He'd seen plenty of men, and twice her size, too, just as shook up, sometimes even more, when a buck committed *hara-kiri* through their pickup's windshield. He couldn't imagine what emotions it wrought from a twenty-two-year-old from the city.

"Sure did a number on your hood though. Hooooeey! Look at them scratches."

Eddie shrugged. "It's only things, y'know?"

"Still. I don't want you stuck with that repair bill. Or that young woman in there stuck with some I.O.U. to her uncle on her first day visiting us here on Blood Mountain."

"I sure do appreciate that, Sam." Eddie pumped the deputy's hand a good half dozen times.

"I'll write it up that you were driving, and you can submit the official report to the insurance or whatever you want. 'Kay?"

It didn't hurt that Eddie played pool with Sam most Thursday nights at Smokin' 19. And those evenings always began the same way: with Eddie greeting the Deputy by joking, "Who in the *Sam Hill* thought it was a good idea to give you a badge…and a gun!"

Eddie would then buy the first round. The truth was that he liked Sam, and twenty bucks a week was nothing between friends.

But you also never knew when you just might need a Sheriff's Deputy in your corner…

Sleep was out of the question. As opposed to literally everything else in Diane's life right now which was *in* question.

"I don't even understand," she rasped, pulling out a kitchen chair. "And is Lizzie dead?" Though her chest pulled tight, there were no more tears to cry. Still, Diane shook. Her face ashen.

Eddie slid a tumbler of whiskey across the mint green Formica top of the kitchen's small midcentury table. "It'll help."

Trembling in her hands, she emptied half in two gulps that burned like swallowing fire. Not at first, but moments later.

"And yes, she is," Eddie finally confirmed, the words more surreal given the delay.

"W-What was that t-th-thing...?"

Eddie pulled out one of the steel framed chairs and its legs squealed as it scraped across the floor. He flipped it around, straddling the seat with his arms over the backrest.

"It was a demon, Deedee."

*Silence.*

"A low-level demon. But a demon, nonetheless."

No longer aware of the heat that swelled and bit the back of her throat, Diane gulped the rest of the tumbler. She did not wait for Eddie to offer another, pouring it herself instead.

He waited in silence as she emptied most of this one, too, before responding to her uncle's matter-of-fact statement.

"What the fuck is *wrong* with you?" The question wasn't rhetorical, and Diane pushed away from the table, chair squawking as she stood. "Lizzie just died out there. Some rabid fucking backwater bumfuck of a mountain creature attacked us. And you're making sick, stupid jokes?"

Serious and resolute, Eddie rose from his seated position. Diane drew back. She couldn't imagine him ever hurting her. But then again, she'd thought that about a lot of people. And 'once bitten twice shy' was a hard habit to break.

He swiped the whiskey bottle and poured himself a double, shaking his head as he pointed at her chair.

"Sit down, Diane."

She edged away a few more inches.

"Sit the FUCK down Diane!" Eddie stood so quickly, his own chair went tumbling, and Diane's heart pounded as a wave of acid welled from her belly; feet frozen to the spot.

He lunged. Grabbed her wrist.

She twisted aside and he caught a fistful of her hoodie's sleeve. Still frozen, her eyes wet and wide with alarm, Eddie released and righted his chair, sitting back down.

"I'm—" he freed the breath catching in his throat. "I'm so sorry, Deedee. Please..."

He gestured toward the table, and she pulled her chair a little farther away, still twisted to the side as she slowly, nervously, also sat. But just beyond her uncle's reach. She was fully aware that she may not be able to defend herself against a man his size and weight, but from here the door was a clear shot—ten or twelve feet away—and if he came at her again, she would charge it.

She crossed her arms, her sidelong glance shooting bullets.

"Deedee," he repeated, softening his tone. "I'm sorry. Genuinely, babygirl. I shouldn't have touched you. I won't ever touch you unless you say it's okay."

Her eyes bore into him.

"But here's the truth: There's a lot more going on than I think you realize. And I really don't understand why that is." Here his own gaze fell to her exposed wrists and the wounds Diane had forgotten about and still had no idea what had caused them. "Unless that place, Barrow Moor, really did more of a number on you than I ever expected them to."

Tugging at her sleeve, Diane attempted to cover up her wrist. She immediately changed her mind, instead hiking it even higher to expose her full forearm. After all, she had nothing to be ashamed of. "What do you mean, they did more of a number on me than you *expected* they would? How does that place have a single goddamn *thing* to do with you, or any expectations about it? You didn't even visit me!"

This wasn't true, of course. And the leatherbound Poe compendium had been evidence of that. Sadly, it too, like so much else, had been taken from her life and was no more than a fading memory.

Eddie took another slug of whiskey.

"Eddie?"

No response.

"Uncle Ed…?"


*…the thing in the cowled robe is my dead father, and he slowly tilts his head. First one way. Then the other. It's the detached curiosity of a hyena watching the life drain away from the convulsing hare beneath it.*

*I am fifteen again. It's impossible to believe that it's actually Thanksgiving. And here I am, my life unraveling as I lie on the floor of my room on the Upper West Side, my dead father the one who is pulling at its last threads.*

*Everything's out of focus. Spinning into dark.*

*Then the ribbons appear.*

*Far from ebbing away to nothingness, an inner spark of light wisps from my mouth. Growing into a wave, it flows and dances like colored smoke in the air. Every hue I've ever seen swirls around me, but mostly deep blues, indigo and violet. And then the white. So much bright, crystal white! A calm like none I've ever known wraps around me like a blanket, eclipsing the searing pain in my chest and the thrumming which has begun to cycle at the back of my skull. None of it seems to matter anymore. Not even the cowled, rotting shell of my father overtop me.*

*Until Daddy's mouth draws impossibly long, shrieking while the jawbones unhinge in a series of snaps like fresh kindling on a campfire. Uncoiling his snake-like tongue, he spools my ribbons of light from me like cotton candy round a stick. They are drawn into the black void of its mouth.*

*And I am falling.*

*Deeper.*

*Faster.*

*Into darkness.*

*No...not darkness. Emptiness.*

*Serenity strips away to expose cold, slicing fear. I am becoming nothing. All that I am, or ever could be, absorbed into the putrid thing writhing inside the body of my dead father. I thrash and struggle to hold onto the final threads of my life but feel them unravelling, just beyond my reach.*

*Consumed.*

*The last thing I sense in this moment is a yelping laugh that gurgles up into my Daddy's blistered and peeling throat...*

*"MY GOD! DIANE!" The voice is faint to me, though I can tell it should sound loud and brusque. I think it's my mother's.*

*I open my eyes and the light is so bright its whiteness blinds me. But I am too afraid to close my eyes again. Or maybe they're frozen open, so I can't? It feels like I'm turning my head away. But I'm not sure if I really am.*

*"Come on, baby! Wake up! Breathe!"*

*A slap. A shake. A pressing sensation on my chest.*

*I suck in air with a sudden and violent gasp, my back arching.*

*Now I'm blinking; it's a spasmodic fluttering of my eyelids. I'm groggy and confused as the blaze of white light slowly softens to the warm, overhead light of my brothers' room. Shapes and colors slowly appear and a face, mere inches away, is blurred and weaving like I'm seeing it underwater through a strong current. Or the way movies always show the world through a drunk person's eyes.*

*A moment later, I recognize those pleading eyes.*

*I clasp my arms around Mommy's neck and start to bawl, rivers of tears wetting my face.*

*Hours later, I'm on the couch. From the kitchen, voices ebb and flow. I can make out the odd word here or there. But truthfully? I'm afraid to know how they fit into the rest of the murmured conversation. Because the ones I can decipher are lots of 'un' words: like 'unsettling' and 'unstable.' Most of these are in my mother's voice, which sounds panicked and fearful. Some are in the vaguely familiar voice of our occasionally seen neighbor from the eighth floor, Dr. Patterson, reiterating that he's found nothing of concern about my physical health, then, almost reluctantly, adds something about a 'voluntary admission' just before lowering his voice to a near-whisper.*

*But the one 'un' word I hear that scares me the most is spoken by Uncle Eddie:*

*"Unsafe."*

*I think there's a question mark at the end of it, but I'm starting to cry so can't be sure. Even through my hiccupping tears I can still hear his flat and authoritative tone repeating my brothers' names. That, and the awful sound of my mom quietly sobbing in reply...*

"NO!" Diane screamed and kicked the table to get away from him.

The whiskey bottle tumbled over, spilling half its remaining contents. Eddie simply watched as the rest gurgled from the glass throat and pooled across the mint green tabletop.

"You did that to me, Eddie? YOU DID THAT TO ME!"

"Deedee, there's a—"

"You had me put away! My God! You had my mother lock me up in a psych hospital for the criminally insane. For eight. Fucking. years! How could you *do* that to m—" She could not go on, her words choked out by the tears that again rushed from her soul and caught in her strained and swollen throat.

"I did it to protect you, Deedee. It was the only way I knew to keep you safe. And you were. For eight years you were out of harm's way, in a place where they couldn't reach you. Why did you leave, Diane? *Goddammit*, why did you leave!"

He reached for her. She flinched away, eyes darting; pacing like a caged animal. Suddenly finding herself racing for the door, she burst outside and into a night as black as space, skidding to a stop on the cabin's front porch. She screamed as long and hard as her throat allowed before bending down to clasp the back of her knees, panting.

Eddie appeared at the screen door, watching. Not Diane, but the darkness beyond. Analyzing the degrees of shading. Scanning for movement. Far below the cabin near the creek, a Screech Owl's chilling warble sliced through the night and Diane straightened, backing toward the cabin door.

Eddie opened the screen without saying a word.

### III

"Do you remember what happened that night?" Eddie's question rang with such absurdity that he hated to ask it. But it was the basis for everything, and her answer predicated just how much he could, should, or would share.

"Simon killed Andrew." Diane's response was deadpan, all the emotion—of the memory and in this moment—sucked from her.

Eddie poured the coffees and the steam swirled in mesmerizing patterns as what had been the black square of the kitchen window lightened just barely to grades of deepest purple.

The ticking of the antique pendulum clock was the only sound for a solid minute or more until the gong struck once for the half-hour, announcing that it was 6:30am.

"Yes," Eddie finally agreed, and it was only in this moment that Diane caught a glimpse of the moisture in his eyes. "Simon Peter killed Andrew."

"But why!"

Eddie sat, cupping his hands around the mug as though needing its heat.

"Why does a housecat kill a mouse?" he replied. "It isn't hungry. It doesn't need to rely upon hunting for its survival. Awaiting its return home is a bowl of kibble fashioned into cute little fish-flavored triangles, just begging to be eaten."

"Then why!"

"Instinct, Deedee." Eddie paused before choosing to add: "And because it can."

These four words weighed heavy in the air, and even the steam from their coffees wafted in an odd direction and lower to the table as if the atmospheric pressure in the room had increased.

"How?" Diane asked before her thoughts would take her to a place they could ill-afford to go, for another chink in her armor might be the last. "How could he? How *did* he? He didn't touch Andrew. Not once. And Andrew was a smart boy. He wouldn't just do that because Simon said so."

*...Simon says: flwy Andwew, flwy...*

"You know how he did it, Deedee. You've always known."

*So, here's the thing. I should tell you that every once in a while, I get this weird, random information. From the Universe. It's like something deep inside me just sits there, idle, not really making itself known most of the time. I can tell it's there, but I've learned to ignore the white noise of it humming away in the background. Then without warning, it'll whirr to life and interrupt whatever I was doing. It's like some hidden part of me is the same as Uncle Ian's desktop computer we sometimes play games on. It just sits there, quietly purring away, not knowing when it's going to get any data. Then... ZAP... a floppy disk slides into that slot and we're off and running. That computer has no idea when it's going to be fed, or what the data is going to be about. It doesn't care if it completely interferes with what you might've been right in the middle of doing. It just gobbles up that info it's mysteriously been given and spits out the results on your monitor. How you handle that, or what it all means to you, is for you to figure out.*

*That's how it is with me.*

*I've started writing down when it happens and figured out that the Interruptions I get from the Universe fit into three basic types: I can feel something about my life right now; I feel something about my future; or I feel something about somebody else's life.*

*My bestie, Crystal, says that what I have is supernatural, like I'm a kind of psychic or something. But that girl wouldn't leave her house before reading Madam Starry's horoscope in the newspaper back in Pee Aay.*

*I don't know if what happens is something from the spirit world, like Crystal says, but I can tell you it definitely used to freak me out.*

*I'm starting to roll with it a little more though, now, and even working on how to control it a bit.*

*Sometimes, I almost can.*


"So, you do remember them. Your Interruptions." Eddie was already pouring another coffee.

*Have I been gone in the memory that long?*

"Just a few minutes," Eddie answered audibly, though the question had been posed to herself. And only Diane's own mind. "I was worried those witch doctors in Barrow Moor had worn you down until you'd have no recollection of them at all."

Diane pressed back in her chair, widening her eyes as if to discern which reality she was currently experiencing.

*So, you can do it, too?* She asked him in thought—a test, if you will—and Eddie replied in kind.

*'Yes, Deedee. Me, too. Just like your father. And your Uncle Ian.'*

*'Don't call him that.'*

*'But why? He is... is he not?'*

"Because I hate him. He killed m—" She cut herself short, remembering the truth. Remembering what really happened. Remembering that it was she who pulled the trigger and took her father's life.

"Oh, Di. Do you really think that?" It was the first time in her memory Eddie called her by the same pet name her father had. The name her mother could not abide because it sounded just like the word 'die.'

He sat and the sound of his spoon against his mug as he stirred was calming. Comforting.

"I don't know what to think."

"I know, Petunia. And I'm going to help you change that."

Eddie patted the chair next to him, an invitation for Diane to sit closer if she wanted.

She thought about it for a moment, started to rise, then decided to slide just a little closer instead, keeping one chair still between them. Doing so made her feel safer.

At least for now.

"I am so, so *very* sorry that you've thought that—any of that—for all these years. But It's time to make it right, and the truth known." Here Eddie swallowed, hard, as if sharing what came next were too much to pass from the place where it had been held for so many years. "What if I were to tell you that it was neither your uncle Ian nor you who pulled the trigger...?"

# 16

*the mentokinesis*

Y OUR FATHER WAS killed by that shot, Diane. That much is true. But what if I were to tell you that it was your father himself who made that happen?"

There was a time when this would have shocked Diane, rocking her to her very core. Now she merely listened.

"Someone would be taken that day. You see, they were owed a seventh. He knew that sacrificing himself was the only way to save you."

"They?"

Eddie nodded. "Oh, Petunia. In the past four days you've forgotten more of the knowledge of the mysteries of this life than most will ever be blessed—or perhaps 'cursed' is the more appropriate word—to acquire. But it's time to bring those memories, and you, back into the Light.

"Bryan, your father, channeled his abilities through you. It was he who ensured you spun that gun from under the brush; made certain you drew upon powers you didn't even know you possessed to use only your mind to pull that trigger. And though it wasn't planned, your uncle Ian then offered himself to it—*to them*—in place of you."

This part rang familiar upon her ears, except the words she heard were again in a soothing southern drawl.

'Yes. Della,' Eddie confirmed in thought. *'You're starting to remember.'*

"Remember what?"

Eddie slid his coffee mug aside. The pendulum clock read 6:43am. What had been the dark purple square of the kitchen window was now blood orange dissolving to the color of fall pumpkins. He reached across the small table and moved Diane's mug aside as well.

In the silence of dawn, only the ticking of each second as the pendulum swung left and right, a metronome marking the endless passage of time…

…Also drawing her closer to the place and event from which she'd detached in favor of the comforting blankets of numbness.

Tick…

  …Tock.

tick..

  ..tock..

*tick.*

  *.tock*

*tick*

  *tock*

The kitchen of Eddie's cabin was no more. Instead of the small midcentury table and steel framed chairs, she was perched on a hard wooden pew. With her was DeLaCroix Laveau, the woman's once beautiful smoky green eyes now clouded white and sunken. Della has the most magnificent raven by her side, and he squawks so sharply at Diane's recognition that the caw reverberates through the empty cathedral like a full treachery of ravens.

*Poe! Diane acknowledges with a joy she did not know she'd lost, or even had to begin with, for a bird which until now she had forgotten even existed. She extends her arm and Poe leaps from the back of an oak pew to perch upon it. Hopping down its length toward her hand, Poe stops at her wrist and gingerly pecks the skin there. The pain of the weirdly inflamed wound he's drawn to is like a cattle brand pressed to the supple skin of her wrist and she shrieks.*

*Poe pecks it again and this time the broad head of an iron mallet peals in metallic, ear-splitting chimes as it slams against a rusty nail as thick as a railway spike. Again Uncle Ian raises the hammer high above his shoulder. A dozen faceless people in white gowns are holding me down, laughing and sneering as they pin my quaking forearm to rough-hewn timber I can feel but not see.*

*Recognition shocks me fully awake as I realize the sounds of the chains and deafening boom that had filled the cathedral are linked to the sensation of wood I now feel beneath my blood-soaked arm.*

*They've lowered the life-size cross to the pulpit.*

*And I am stretched atop it.*

*Hulking and unwieldy, the cross pitches at an uneven incline upon the riser, it's long vertical post dropping at an awkward angle down the half-dozen stairs. I kick to free myself, but a multitude of hands squeeze my ankles together like a vice.*

*Ian brings down the hammer a third time and I scream in agony as the crude iron nail slams further through my wrist. Blood spritzes my uncle's face, the ferrous tang on his lips and in the air as the spike drills through muscle and tendon. Another strike and it embeds into the wood beneath my arm as I cry in unimaginable pain. One more hit and the bones in my wrist snap as the wide head of the stake burrows beneath my skin, pinning bone to bone.*

*My face and chest are covered in vomit. Blood pours over my eyes as someone loops a cat o' nine tails of barbed wire into a series of bands and presses it into my scalp. The barbs burrow under the skin of my forehead. Through an eyelid. They bite into the bone at the rear of my skull as my head is slammed against the timber to secure the torturous headdress in place.*

*I hear the sickening sound of the bones in my feet breaking as Ian pins them together to the wood, my knees bent at a forty-five-*

*degree angle. I do not feel it, however, as my body has exceeded its faculty for a neurological response to pain. I sense only the shudder as each clout of the mallet travels through the timber in a wave, all the way to my head.*

*And the unnatural way my legs bend as Uncle Ian breaks them just above the knee.*

*The cross is tugged upright and begins lurching toward the ceiling. Notch-by-notch, the ponderous chains are hefted ever tighter until I am hoisted high above the altar. Swaying in the air as the chains are secured, the cross is a massive pendulum tracing slowly back and forth. Back and* forth.

*Back.*

*And forth.*

*back*

*and forth*

*tick*

*and forth*

*back*

and tock

tick

and tock

Tick...

...Tock...

Diane vomited as she came out of the mentokinetic trance, the unimaginable pain as real as it had been four nights ago but now with the inexplicable sense of violation of someone else having been inside her mind.

When she was finished being sick, Eddie prepared her a dense sugar water and carefully folded a kitchen towel on the table as a small pillow, resting Diane's head upon it. He draped a thin blanket over her shoulders. And when her shivering subsided to the occasional tremor, he carried her to the spare room...

# 17

*the truth*

**S**HE AWOKE IN the middle of the night to a silence so complete it was a sound in itself. A quiet like nothing she'd experienced since she was a twelve-year-old girl, back in their old house in their tiny Pennsylvania neighborhood.

*Their neighborhood at the edge of the Little Woods.*

Sweating to the point of drenching the sheets, she threw off the covers and swung her legs out of bed. Throbbing and thick, her head was in the jaws of a vice grip and the room momentarily swam on her first attempt to stand. Once the spinning slowed to the leisurely rotation of a merry-go-round in the park, she tried again.

Her rubbery legs barely held her weight as she fumbled her way across the room illuminated only by shimmering reflections of the moon which shone in gold and silver points across every part of every wall. She found the switch by the door, slapped on the overhead light and squinted in the harsh light. When she opened her eyes, the walls were covered in hundreds of crucifixes.

Large and small. Gold, silver, brass, wood, resin. Lord knows what else. They blanketed every available space on each of the four walls. Even climbing the vaulted ceiling to come together at its apex.

"Jesus…*Christ.*"

Diane stumbled to the center of the room, landing awkwardly on a faded rag rug as the moonlight played over the crosses between rippling shadows. A silent flash of summer lightning brightened the distant sky in a burst, only to restore the darkness as swiftly as it had been fractured. The momentary silhouette it created of the trees made them appear like the skyscrapers she had become accustomed to: some tall and grand, some grouped in clumps like a distant city center. Others sporadically spaced but all the more dramatic for their isolation.

*What the fuck is this?*

Another flare. Another silhouette. This time a soft rumble, long after the night sky returned.

The overhead light flickered, a brief stroboscope that made the crosses on the walls come to life, the Christ figures all moving—

*writhing in pain*

—before the bulb fizzled and *popped* and the room went black.

Diane scrabbled to the door on her hands and knees, throwing it open and lurching into the corridor. She blundered down the unfamiliar steps, following the diminishing darkness and muted sounds of activity until the soft glow of light drew her to her back to the kitchen and her uncle standing at the stove, his back to her.

"You're hungry," he stated without turning, his voice monotone. It wasn't a question. "I'm about to throw on some bacon."

She must've slept only minutes, for the kitchen window was still black with night.

*But hadn't it been the first hues of morning, last time she looked?*

"You've been asleep almost twenty hours," Eddie answered and laid a half dozen fatty strips into the cast iron skillet. "It's the early hours of Wednesday morning. August third."

She'd arrived in the evening of Monday, August first. The night the three of them had laughed and talked around the fire pit. The night of the demon. And Lizzie's heart attack.

*The night she remembered what happened.*

It was all too surreal and she wanted to question it, but was so tired of fighting what, deep down, she'd always known was true.

She pulled a chair from the table with a squeak and sat as the antique clock chimed four times; soft, resonant *gongs*.

"You need to eat. You'll feel better with something in your stomach."

II

"Elizabeth was Reicher Winslow's wife." Eddie voice was monotone, his demeanor deadpan. As if he were repeating something so obvious to her that it barely merited mention. "I know that means absolutely nothing to you, though I'd venture that Elizabeth probably thought it did."

He fished the rashers from the skillet and flipped them over to a fresh sizzling static.

"Reicher and I were very close. I came to know him when I moved here at a very young age, and we've been friends ever since. That was, gosh—" he stroked his chin as he did the calculation "—a good twenty-eight years ago. At least. It broke my heart the day he and Elizabeth revealed he'd been diagnosed with an aggressive and inoperable tumor growing quickly inside his cerebellum. By that time it was already stage four, and the prognosis was six to twelve months."

He slid a plate of bacon and eggs across the table and joined Diane momentarily.

"I know you think this is pointless info and what you really want to know is why you're here. *How* you're actually here. But, this matters. Oh, I forgot the orange juice."

Eddie poured two glasses and returned to the table.

"You need the glucose. Please drink it."

"I really don't lik—"

He stopped chewing and tilted his head to the side, eyes boring into her the way her father used to do when she would complain about the cauliflower she didn't want to eat.

Diane took a sip. Then another. The juice was cool and felt like pure energy as it was absorbed into the very cells of her body. In three more gulps she finished the glass with a reflexive *'ahhh.'* Eddie nodded toward the carton and she poured herself a second.

"He was a writer. A novelist, actually. Thrillers, horror. Dark stuff. The problem is, he started to believe the scenes he was seeing in his head. The tumor fucking with his reality, y'know? No longer satisfied to simply put it on paper, he was seeing this stuff come to life before his very eyes."

"And this is relevant because…?"

"Because he called me ten years ago screaming, telling me Elizabeth was dead. I drove over there so fast I can't even remember the drive. I expected to pull up to red flashing lights washing over their house. Instead, it was dark and silent."

"What happened?"

"He was beside himself, pacing and wailing. 'Lizzie caught her hand in the food processor,' he repeated over and over, saying he didn't mean to do it. 'It's our anniversary, I was just being silly,' he kept telling me. I asked him where Lizzie was, and did he call nine-one-one, and he couldn't tell me."

Eddie glanced away, staring up and to the right, and Diane could tell he was looking at nothing in the room. In his mind, he was back in the Winslows' house.

"He was in such a panic, Elizabeth didn't know what to do. I wanted to call an ambulance but the mere suggestion of it sent Reicher into a rage, and Elizabeth herself feared that if he were to go to the hospital that night, he'd never come back home."

"So, what did you do?"

"I got him calmed down. Eventually. And around three in the morning I came here, back home. I didn't get more than a handful of hours' sleep before the phone woke me. Elizabeth this time.

Reicher had gone in the night, and she had no idea where." Eddie took a deep breath and returned his eyes to Diane. "She never—we never—saw him again. That was July, ninety-five. Over ten years ago."

Diane was silent as she took this in, processing what he'd just shared; processing that the new friend she'd just made was now dead, too. Processing the thing that had come through the windshield. Processing what had happened in the cathedral only five days ago. Processing Della's role in her murder. Processing the eight years in Barrow Moor before that. Processing Andrew's death that Thanksgiving night.

*Processing the darkness that was Simon Peter.*

"I know you're wondering how that ties into your situation. Right here. Right now."

Diane looked into Eddie's eyes, her own glistening with more pain and confusion than any one person had the right to bear.

"Did you know about the boy who went missing from the old Pee Aay neighborhood when this all started in nineteen-seventy-seven? The boy everyone presumed was the seventh innocent child killed that summer? Jimi's brother, the boy named Jack...?"

III

Eddie explained how it had all come to light after seven years had passed and Reicher never returned. Elizabeth was making the arrangements for a funeral service of sorts and collating the legal documents required in order to procure Reicher's death certificate. Among these was one revealing that Jack legally changed his name shortly after his eighteenth birthday, back in nineteen-eighty. The Winslows, who Liz always thought were Reicher's parents, were actually his distant great aunt and great uncle. It was their house at 66 Slaughter Creek which had been left to Jack after their passing, and which she now called her own.

"The truth is, I think Reicher was the one who went to that bar in Manhattan back in ninety-five and shot the place up before taking that shotgun blast himself. I don't have any proof, but my gut tells me it was him. I knew Jack back then. Back when we were kids. And that was one fucked-up teenager. Him and Stu Klatz, both. What they did to the Chauncey boy was–was—"

He couldn't go on. And didn't.

Instead, he retrieved a white, sealed envelope from a kitchen drawer. "The police classified it as a random crime of passion by an anonymous perpetrator. But I think—no, I *know*—different. Suffice it to say, it was that incident that brought your uncle Ian back home. And sadly, you know what happened from that point onward…"

He handed the envelope to Diane.

"I'll come back and talk to you after you read this, Petunia. All will soon be revealed. I promise." His eyes were downcast. He took a long, slow breath. "As you're reading this, just know that I love you, Diane. You are not alone."

In tidy cursive on the front was written her name. Underneath this, the words: 'The Truth. The Light.'

It was dated four days earlier, July 31st. The day she walked away from the morgue and found herself on a bus to Georgia.

*A bus where she had coincidentally met Lizzie.*

Eddie walked away with the envelope flitting lightly in Diane's quivering fingers while more frequent flashes of lightning blanched the colors of dawn breaking through the kitchen window. She sat this way until long after he was gone, to where, she neither knew nor cared.

Her only care was this envelope.

*And that handwriting.*

When the distant, hollow peals of thunder rang out, Diane carefully peeled open the envelope, steadying herself for the storm she knew was finally approaching…

# 18

*the letter*

To my sweetest Diane.

I know you don't understand anything right now, sugar, and will probably want to tear this letter to pieces.

But I have every faith that you will not.

I beg that you do not . . .

While I can never express my sorrow for having put you through so much pain, I also cannot tell you how much your life will soon mean to the world. A meaning which in time I know you will come to understand, too. You are the one Light and the one Truth. Diane, and all of mankind will be drawn to you.

For your deliverance is our final salvation.

Once this has become clear to you, I pray you will bestow your forgiveness upon me, your most humble servant. The path ahead of you was always yours to travel, and all of humanity shall follow the trail you blaze as you lead us to redemption with the one Holy God and our Universe of Light.

If achieving that, however, means I am to be reviled and unforgiven, then I am willing to accept that price for the part I have played.

My only regret is not having the chance to hold you one last time before I left this earthly life.

I love you, Diane Cockerton.

I always have. And I always will.

Your Mother,

Rebecca xox

# 19

*the storm strikes*

THE MORE SHE read the letter, the more she wept. Initially Della's voice in her head, it was her mother's she should have heard all along. She read it again, this time with her mother's voice wrapping around her soul like a blanket on a chilly night. She did not stop reading until the tears no longer flowed.

"I'm so sorry, babygirl."

"My mama's, d-d-d—?" She could not finish the word. Her mouth would not allow it. "I-I-Is that t-true?"

Eddie peered over the top of his readers, at a loss for words. It was an answer in itself.

"I loved your mother, Di. I can't begin to imagine the pain, the excruciating suffering, you both endured."

Diane only stared.

"But here you are, Deedee. You were able to walk away, even after what they did to you."

Again Diane threw up what little food she'd managed to keep down, and Eddie made no attempt to clean it. "Everything is starting to come to a head for you, I think, babygirl…"

II

He bit his lip, horror-stricken but not showing it as he examined

Diane's injuries while she lay on the sofa covering her bare body with a sheet. The amount of trauma that had been inflicted upon her was inconceivable. There were signs of her skin having been torn in jagged strips from her back and sides by a cat o' nine tails fashioned from barbed wire. The same wire looped into a series of bands had burrowed through the skin of her forehead, and numerous small scars were visible if you looked closely enough. Her right eyelid showed evidence of being pierced through. The back of her scalp was bruised and still raised in a lump where they had repeatedly slammed her head against the timber cross. Just above each knee, a knot in the muscle and tendons betrayed the location on both femurs where her legs had been broken by a mallet so she would no longer be able to support her weight. Doing so meant that her rising ribcage would pull at her lungs in an endless cycle of rapid, shallow inhalations without matching exhalations.

In essence, drowning in air.

Then there were the obvious wounds: Diane's wrists and feet run through by nails akin to railroad spikes.

He refused the natural reaction of shock and overwhelming emotional dismay as he applied antiseptic salve where the tell-tale signs of threatening infection had appeared; a mix of menthol and wintergreen oil gel over much of the rest.

"It really doesn't hurt. Hardly at all, to be honest."

How could it not? Eddie couldn't imagine. But then, he also couldn't imagine how Diane was even here at all.

He *understood* it.

He even *expected* it.

He just couldn't *imagine* it.

Swiping the moisture from his eyes while she changed in the bathroom, Eddie pulled a rucksack from the closet. He spoke loudly enough for her to hear behind the closed door.

"We can't stay here, Di. When you've changed into those new

clothes, I want you to run upstairs and grab whatever you need from the bedroom. You can throw it in this bag. I'll leave it out here."

"Uncle Eddie?" she cracked the door just enough to peer through. "Can *you* grab my stuff please? I just can't go in that bedroom again. I'm sorry. It just really creeps me out. What's the deal with all those crosses…did *you* do that?"

Eddie's only confirmation was the sound of his footsteps as he climbed the staircase, the creaks and moans of the old treads blending with the layered rumbles of approaching thunder.

She pulled a new hoodie over her head with care. Still, the material was as coarse as straw despite the softest of cotton linings gliding gently over her skin, her abrasions and pale purple bruises more sensitive than she'd admitted. Contrary to this, what had been an unkempt tangle of a hairstyle was already regaining its luster. Its color was now much closer to the strawberry-blonde that had been her mother's natural hue and head-turning trademark than the dirty-dishwater-blonde bird's nest Diane had suffered all her years at Barrow Moor.

Gathering it together in the mirror, she swept it back into a modest ponytail while her free hand searched the cabinets for any kind of hairband. Why she thought her uncle would have one, she could not fathom.

*But still, you never knew, right?*

Eddie was a good looking guy for his age. He surely had female company around the place from time to time. And ladies were wont to leave the occasional accessory now and then when visiting a new beau. Especially if they had intentions of returning.

But there was nothing in the mirror cabinet.

She scoured the vanity drawers.

Still nothing.

Into the kitchen, then. Everyone has a junk drawer. And whose doesn't boast a tangle of rubber bands buried somewhere at the back? Worst case scenario, she'd make do with a twist-tie. Not very glamorous, but it would do the job for now.

On the ceiling, Eddie's footsteps paced back and forth as she continued to hold back her hair with one hand while delving into kitchen cabinet drawers with the other.

The snub nose pistol was in the second drawer she opened.

Next to it, a dense foam base of hollow-point shells stood proud like individual soldiers at attention. Behind these, a spray bottle lying on its side rolled forward and back, a clear liquid inside and the word 'sanctified' written in blue permanent marker by what was clearly a man's hand.

For a moment, the footsteps in the room above her halted.

Diane held her breath.

With a creaking of old floorboards the thumping footsteps resumed, moving to the far corner of the ceiling then back again.

She let go of her ponytail and picked up the revolver. Its metal was cool in her hands, and she turned it over in her palm, its feeling unlike anything else she'd ever held. The cylinder spun smoothly, quiet clicks announcing its rotation, and five bullet tips were visible from the front of it. They weren't the same as the ones in the little foam base in the drawer, though. *Similar, yes. But not exact.* These seemed to have some kind of opaque glue over their tips—*maybe a wax of sorts?*—sealing off the hollow indentation. One of the slots in the cylinder was empty.

*The single round Eddie had shot the other night?*

She returned the pistol to the drawer and picked up the small spray bottle, righting it and giving the red trigger a little squeeze. A clear mist expelled in a small cloud, and she dared to move her nose toward the vapors.

To her they were odorless. She sprayed again, this time spritzing the countertop, and swiped her index finger through it, rubbing the liquid between her finger and thumb. It wasn't oily. It wasn't thick. She sniffed again, but could smell nothing.

She tasted the tip of her finger...

*Water.*

'Sanctified,' the bottle was labeled.

*But, didn't that mean holy?*

She dared to spray the tip of her tongue. A mild tingle, an unexpected warming sensation. But no flavor whatsoever.

*What was Eddie doing with Sanctified water?*

Overhead, the footsteps stopped again.

This time, there was a scraping sound. Something being pulled across the old pinewood floor above where she stood: Above the kitchen, in the corridor to the guest bedroom.

*The bedroom with the crucifixes.*

She carefully placed the bottle back in the drawer the best way she could recall finding it, then edged toward the rickety old staircase.

Peering around the banister and up the stairwell, she listened.

*More scraping. Something heavy being dragged.*

*Then silence.*

Lightning strobing beyond the windows lit the downstairs in blinding, jittery light.

Then came the rain, the pattering of thick drops against the tin roof panels a soothing audible backdrop to the morning that had begun so bright but now was saturated with clouds. If she didn't know better, Diane would be forgiven for thinking it was still the middle of the night.

"Uncle Ed?" she called up the stairs and listened for his response as the rain shower intensified to fill the house with deep brown noise like a heavy surf. "Eddie...?"

She edged up the steps, gripping the banister with both hands as she craned to see around the dogleg landing at the top.

"Eddie." This time, not a question but a statement.

Still no answer.

"Eddie!" she demanded, her voice sounding foreign to her own ears as it came back from the walls so sparsely decorated. "EDDIE."

The growl that answered was low. Long. Guttural. So subtle it could easily have been mistaken for the rolling thunder as it descended from the mountain top to wrap itself around the isolated farmhouse. Which is exactly how Diane rationalized it in her mind.

"I'm coming up, Eddie. So, if you're half-naked or something, *heeehee*, I'm giving you fair warning right now." Her smile was broad and genuine, for the sibilating Muttley laugh was sure to be his only rebuttal. Eddie never could resist a saucy, or sophomoric, joke. Once she had learned this growing up, it made him easy pickings. Need a Cheer-Me-Up? No one could be unhappy when Muttley joined the party. Not only did he sound like him, Eddie and Muttley shared basically the same body shape. Add to this the way Eddie lowered his head when he laughed, placed a hand to his mouth and shook like a bobblehead, and he was the spitting image of the cartoon dog. Give him a matching red scarf and aviator's cap, and you'd be hard pressed to tell the difference.

All you had to do was tell a fart joke, penis joke, sex joke. Anything that was off-color, and the kind of line a sixth-grader would find amusing, and there you had your Muttley.

And a good time was had by all.

Diane's beaming, expectant smile dimmed by degrees with every second the Muttley laugh did not answer by way of reply. As the lightning grew nearer and thunder grew louder, she inched her way up to the second floor, the old house shaking with every third or fourth pairing of light and sound. The storm was so near now that there was no delay between the two, and her eyes and ears were being assaulted in unison. A dizzying, disorienting onslaught.

Her blood froze cold when the lights fizzled and popped as she rounded the second floor landing and the house fell to a darkness like deepest night, now fully enveloped by the summertime storm.

"*Eddie?*" she whispered as she palmed her way along the wall.

The deep, bestial snarl in reply came as a billowing waveform through the dark. A lion-like sound that in Diane's mind had the predatory big cat watching her every move, stalking her, while she herself remained blind to its position. Her thoughts careened through a maze of nightmare scenarios, each more terrifying than the last as white hot panic threatened to hijack her amygdala.

*Remember, you know how to do this,* she reassured her racing mind and took a breath deep into her nose, holding it for three full seconds before releasing it slowly from her mouth. Already, the oxygen to her brain was diverting the freight train of debilitating panic and she mocked herself for being the scaredy-cat she'd always abhorred in horror movies.

Then a burst of lightning blanched the house with such brightness that the second floor lost all sense of dimension and she shrieked, pinching her eyes shut. A snapshot absurdly over-exposed, the upstairs became variations of brilliance. Walls, floor and ceiling blended into one as she stumbled forward, shielding her eyes. Dazzling spots saturated her vision, shimmering black patches slow to clear.

She opened them a moment later to a lightless void.

"D-don't come any closer, b-babygirl," Eddie's voice stuttered, from the shroud of darkness, nothing like the authoritative and confident Eddie she knew. It knotted her stomach.

Another pulse of light outside the window and Eddie's figure was revealed stock-still in the center of the crucifix room, rigid with terror. In a millisecond, he was blanketed in artificial night.

"Uncle Eddie?" She stepped forward, hands feeling the air before her as she moved into the room.

Lightning roared overhead, shaking the house as the room was lit brilliant white to expose Eddie adorned head to toe in dark liturgical vestments. A priest's full-length black tunic flowed from neck to toes, secured at the waist by a corded ligature of braided rope. A purple sash was draped over his shoulders; white clerical collar tight around his stocky neck.

The room fell to darkness once more.

"What's going on, what are you weari—"

"—P-Please, Deedee. Go!"

Now came the sound like a motorcycle engine firing up. It ticked over four times before catching, rumbling at the side of the house as the electricity strobed on then right back off. In the far corner of the room, a small brass lamp without a shade fizzled weakly to life. Its deep golden Edison filament brightened, dimmed, snuffed out, then ignited again in repeated cycles with the rhythmic rise and fall of the generator's choppy idle.

This macabre dance of amber light revealed Eddie's face ashen, his wide eyes exposing white all the way around his irises. Yet with pupils so grotesquely dilated they absorbed all but the thinnest ring of their hazel color. His right hand was clenched tightly around the index finger of his left, arms extended far in front of him as a child eager to share something during his turn at Show-and-Tell.

The color draining from her skin, Diane backed away toward the door.

"STAY!" Eddie demanded in a voice that was not his own, but the striations of a dozen others at once.

Behind its sheer curtains yellowed with age, the room's sole window flared white and Eddie's form twisted and rippled, becoming each of the beings to whom they belonged. When the thunder roared and the glare sizzled away to the flickering amber bulb in the corner, it was again Eddie who was standing before Diane.

Behind her, the door slammed itself shut with such force that splinters of wood sprayed from the casement.

"Let's play a game, Deedee," the voices offered from lips that moved without a change to the frozen horror on Eddie's face as he listened to the words he was not speaking yet were voiced from his own mouth. "You've always prided yourself on being so observant, my precocious little girl."

To emphasize the latter part of that statement, the voices came together in unison to perfectly impersonate her father's.

*...my dad used to listen so intently when I'd tell him all my elaborate stories. Then he'd ruffle my hair and kiss me on the forehead, smiling as he called me 'precocious.' That made me happy, after I looked up what it meant...*

Eddie's mouth laughed as the memory formed in her mind, so tangible that for a moment she was again that innocent fourteen-year-old.

"Yessss, that's right. So much to live for and not an ounce of pain ahead." Her father's voice *tsked* thrice, becoming the many by the time the third was uttered. Coming from Eddie's own lips while his head remained incongruously still and his unblinking eyes transfixed upon her, the expression was beyond gruesome and made her blood run cold. "Remember your 'people watching' from the fifth story window and your aspirations of becoming a writer? Let's put them to the test, shall we? Just stay right there if you want to play!"

*NO*, Diane screamed inside and turned for the door.

Except she didn't.

Her feet had become encased in invisible concrete, her arms weighted with unseen bricks. She and Eddie had become two paralyzed individuals merely feet apart, staring at one another. As the Edison bulb continued to flicker and pop in the corner, their shadows played eerily across the walls plastered with glimmering amber crucifixes.

"Oh, good! Then let's begin! If you win, we'll let your pig of an uncle go." Now the voices had unified to become Simon Peter's, and Diane could see her little brother as he had once been, an innocent child jumping up and down with delight. The vision occurred within her uncle, as if his body planted to the spot had become transparent and a two-year-old Simon Peter were inside, wearing Eddie like a costume.

Still, Eddie was motionless with his arms extended and stiff as he grasped his index finger so tightly that it was bloodless from the knuckle down, his right hand turning red from the exertion.

"First question, my dearest Diane: Is your uncle Eddie a priest in the Lithuanian Roman Catholic Church?"

*Of course not,* Diane's mind responded on autopilot. Yes, she had only been 15 years old the last time she'd seen Eddie. And admittedly, visits were only on some holidays and special occasions. But wouldn't she have known? Then again, did she ever ask, or even think about, what he did for a living?

Her mind a whirlwind, she projected her answer to the things holding Eddie hostage before she could stop herself from doing so. God help her, she hadn't intended it. But she was now playing the game.

"Thank you for accepting our invitation, Petunia! But I'm afraid that's incorrect." While the many voices spoke, nothing but Eddie's lips moved…except for his eyes which grew impossibly wider, their whites exposing his terror in the flickering amber light. His voice now took on the air of a game show host. "That's one point for Team Edward. Show the man what he's won, Vanna."

Trembling as he fought against them as hard as he could, Eddie was unable to resist. He bent his left hand index finger back until it snapped like a wishbone at Thanksgiving dinner.

Screaming in his own voice louder than Diane had ever heard anything come from his mouth, only Eddie's eyes expressed the pain that was not permitted to register upon any other part of his countenance.

With his finger lying against the back of his hand like a rubber prop, Eddie moved with surety to the next digit, again wrapping his right hand around it the way a baby instinctively latches onto a finger it is presented.

"Your uncle Eddie *is* a Catholic priest, Diane. He always has been, since the month of his twenty-fifth birthday. His way of finding peace, and hopefully offering penance to the Big Guy upstairs for what he did. Sadly," here the things that were Eddie unclenched his fingers and held the back of his mangled hand to his mouth in the fashion of sharing a secret. In a hushed voice it revealed, "Sadly, and don't tell Eddie this, but his strategy hasn't worked. The Big Guy says Eddie's all mine. *Shhhhhhh!*"

The Eddies laughed, a morose sound so at odds to the pain and horror in her uncle's eyes that Diane felt the bile rising in her throat.

"Now, let's find out just why that is! Question number two, my deliciously nubile goddess." They made Eddie lick his lips and emit a lascivious slurping sound. "*Hoooeeey!* That's some Grade-A pussy meat, right there. *MmmMMMM*. But, I fear we digress…"

They now made Eddie mime the act of stroking his cock and his broken finger dangled as his arm moved stiff and unnaturally the way a mannequin's might.

"Hehe! Anyway, good ol' Uncle Ed here was such a prince to share the history of Reicher Winslow, his best pal, with you. Because Reicher Winslow was that Jack kid from back in your father's day. Right? The one that got away, as it were."

Diane's heartbeat was a hard, quick pulse in her throat. *I'm not playing. I'm not playing!*

"Oh, that's too bad then."

Shrieking in pain so intense that Diane felt it, Eddie slammed his middle finger back. This time, the end of the Proximal Phalanx bone burst the skin and a warm red mist spritzed Diane's face.

Eddie now gripped the ring finger of his left hand as the voices demanded an answer from Diane.

"Okay, okay!" The metallic tang of her uncle's blood on her lip. "Yes! Reicher Winslow was Jack!"

The Eddies laughed, a grotesque mechanical facsimile of mirth they could not know, and therefore could not replicate. Slowly, and by the smallest degrees, Eddie bent his ring finger back and the repulsive laughter morphed into a squalling cry of torment that seemed to beckon the very thunder. It again shook the house as the room blanched white, every crucifix gleaming. Eddie's third finger snapped not once, not twice, but three times. Silently. The sound masked by his screams and the bellowing thunder.

"That's Team Edward, three—Team Diane, *nil poi*, as our friends, the Frenchies, say. Looks like Uncle Ed's having all the fun."

Eddie's mouth turned down at the corners in an exaggerated clown frown while his eyes pleaded for my help.

"I thought you'd be so much better at this game, Deedee. I really did…" The voices sounded genuinely disappointed, and the hairs stood proud on the back of Diane's neck. She began to shiver, her skin growing clammy. "Think now. THINK! You know this answer, Di. C'mon baby—" (now her father's voice from Eddie's mouth again) "—what was Jack's last name? You heard it when you re-experienced my game in the Little Woods, the start of everything. You knew it, when you were in the cathedral with Della just a few days ago and the columns turned into trees. Remember, Di? C'mon baby, you know this. Think!"

Their impression of her father was so close to the voice in her memory that tears welled thick in Diane's eyes.

*…Craig Dalton,* she found herself dutifully recalling, *big Dan Mercer…Stu Klatz…Jack and Jimi—Jack and Jimi—Jack and Ji—*

The realization stole her breath away and Diane fell to her knees, the paralysis gone.

"Yessssss," the Eddies confirmed and relished horror the horror her understanding brought. "Jack and his little brother Jimi, who was led to his death in the Beechnut. Jack, who laughed and played the flute as Jimi fell twenty feet and was impaled. Jack, who along with Stu, then dragged Woody into the swamp to drown him in the mud and brackish water. Jack—"

Now every crucifix in the room began vibrating, a chorus of tinny, metallic ringing. Flapping against the wall in the tumult, Eddie's Graduate degree from Saint Casimir's Seminary dislodged itself and flung to the floor, spinning to a stop before Diane.

In the year of our Lord
Nineteen-Hundred-Eighty-Seven
Master of Divinity (MDiv)
is Hereby Awarded to
JACK EDWARD RAKER

"—Jack. *Edward*. Raker," Eddie admitted, and this time it was his own voice. Resisting. Breaking free one final time. "I tried, babygirl. God help and bestow his mercy, I tried. To fight it. To make up for all I've done. I tried, Petunia! Tried so hard to—"

Then he was gone, the others within Eddie again becoming the voices, his face again an expressionless mannequin.

"—I tried so hard to serve my master. And it was so deliciously easy for us to manipulate Reicher. After we'd planted the cancer, of course. A story of Eddie's youth here, a tale of what we'd done there. *Et voilà*, between his weakness and illness, Reicher soon enough came to believe that it had been *him* in the woods as a boy that summer; *he* who had perpetrated such atrocity. Yes, Reicher Winslow was a friend. He was also a pawn who died as a hero, a glorious mercenary of Darkness. He went to that bar because the master grew impatient of waiting for your uncle Ian's return. So, we—Eddie—made it so. And now, your uncle has delivered you, unto us. The One True Lamb."

Diane's cry eclipsed the clangor as hundreds of crucifixes of every shape and size shuddered against the walls and ceiling in a violent storm. Matching her outcry, the more she screamed, the more they shook upon their hooks and hangers.

"NO. NO. NO, NO, NO NO NO NONONONNONO! I TRUSTED YOU! YOU WERE MY LAST FAMILY!"

The first crucifix pulled from the wall with such ferocity, when it came free it was barely visible as it flew across the room. It embedded in Eddie's side, the arms of the cross and the Christ's head were all that visible outside her uncle's torso.

The things that were Eddie shrieked, and Diane felt a power pulse through her like the deepest bass vibration. It felt *good*. It felt *strong*. It felt like she was *free*.

She sent another crucifix flying. This one struck Eddie's arm, running it all the way through. Eddie yowled, a pitched animal cry, and Diane sent three more. These embedded in his leg, his abdomen. His groin.

Then Diane sent them all.

And the cry of the voices became jeers of real laughter as every crucifix shot from the wall, a hailstorm of projectiles that impaled Jack Edward Raker, skewering the priest like a pincushion.

Diane's uncle fell to his knees, his life's blood pouring from his body as his niece ran.

### III

She took Eddie's car and did not stop driving until every ounce of gasoline was used up, the tank having nothing more to give...

# V

# INSTIGO

# 20

*the end begins*

# 11 days before the end | halloween 2011

THE END OF it all began on the woman's front porch, seventy-seven minutes after dark. Responding yet again to the door chime's jangling vibrato, she leapt from the couch with a giant pumpkin candy bowl in hand. It did not escape her attention how thrilled Dr. Pavlov would've been to witness such a prompt and obedient response.

*Who's a good girl.*

She pasted on her best smile, the fake display feeling foreign and unnatural as she swung open the door. So far tonight she'd welcomed gaggles of wee Wonder Women, Glee Cheerios galore, Iron Men aplenty, and even one pint-sized Lady Gaga, meat dress and all. Gathered 'round her festive doormat, they always pointed and giggled at its cartoon ghost, the mouth of which was in the perpetual oval of a scream as though it were terrified by the very sight of *them*. They would then erupt in a raucous chorus of voices sing-shouting 'Trick or Treat!' In this mass ultimatum, one child would invariably lag behind, and their voice, now the only one, would subsequently trail off in embarrassment. Then, like the hungry mouths of colossal baby birds, the openings of a half-dozen gaping plastic sacks would be thrust her way, eager to be fed snack-sized chocolates or sweets.

But there was no one on the porch.

Instead, sitting on that doormat was a box.

Wrapped in plain brown kraft paper, across the front someone had handwritten her full name in a crisp but casual cursive that smacked of intimacy between sender and recipient.

*Red flag #1.*

For a start, since when did the post office deliver this late? But more noteworthy was the fact of her very Catholic middle name being penned across that package. Because she had never shared it with anyone. *Ever.* Not even those in her small but steadfast circle of friends.

By contrast, where the sender's address and at least their last name should be written, was only empty space.

She examined the remaining sides.

Nothing.

*Red flag #2. One more strike and you're out.*

While she couldn't quite put a finger on it, there was something familiar about this moment that began to gnaw at the back of her mind. Grasping for what it might be, she stood motionless in the glowing doorway with the plastic pumpkin candy bowl balanced in one outstretched hand, mystery parcel in the other. If you had happened upon her silhouette at this moment, you'd be forgiven for thinking her mimicking the 'Bird Girl' statue made famous by John Berendt's iconic novel, *Midnight in the Garden of Good and Evil.* One of her favorite books, she was amused when she recognized the unintended likeness, and the smile she'd feigned for the benefit of the kids actually brightened her eyes for the briefest moment.

When a blast of frigid air snuck up from behind, it extinguished that flicker of joy as quickly as it had come. For on that gust rode a random memory. In it, her late husband's booming voice was calling out to her, pleading for her to 'close the goddamn door and stop letting all the store-bought heat out!'

When a second blast struck, this one more blustery than the

first, a whirlwind of leaves blew deep into the foyer and dashed even this mixed sentimentality beneath the sadness in which she now so often dwelled.

*Goddamn it*, she cursed to herself as leaves whorled throughout the entry hall. With every change in the wind's direction, more were deposited across the brownstone's polished tile floor.

*And Goddamn you too, Carlo, for always being such a cheapskate. And a blowhard.*

"I didn't mean that," she relented immediately, staring into a place that did not exist. "You know I don't mean that, Boo." A moment later she added: "But Goddamn you for leaving me. And that I do mean."

Now the wind blew the heavy oak door like a sail tacked unchecked. It slammed so hard that the small, coiled doorstop gave out with a *thwaaang* as the wrought iron handle sunk into the century-old plaster wall. There, the door remained pinned as the outside world continued to bombard the inside.

With pumpkin candy bowl and mystery box still occupying both hands, Retired Detective Magdalena Romano stretched as far as she could toward a small table in the entry hall, just beyond her reach. Doing her best arabesque with one leg extended horizontally behind her, she hooked her foot around the edge of the door while lobbing the parcel toward the tabletop and hoping for the best. Straining to free the door from the wind's grip, it suddenly tacked in the other direction. Choking the growling wind to a shrill whimper, it then slammed shut with an earsplitting bang as candy flew from the pumpkin bowl she still clutched in one hand.

Leaves in the hall blew upward, wafting in the warm 'store-bought air' which now circled back into the foyer. They cycloned round and round in this manner before drifting to the floor like soot from an extinguished bonfire.

Surprising even to Maggie, with a *thud* the parcel also hit its mark. The sound blended with the slamming of the door so that both echoed through the vast, high-ceilinged foyer. Where the door had a jamb to stop its momentum, however, the package had only a decorative glass bowl. Spinning across the table, the parcel struck it like a hockey player checking his opponent. Maggie's keys, a handful of loose change, and at least one car wash token from an establishment long out of business, all jangled as the mystery parcel came to a stop with the heavy glass bowl pressed halfway over the edge.

Maggie breathed a sigh of relief and shook her head. Frankly she was amazed the package not only landed on the table, but hadn't destroyed the glass bowl.

*What had she been thinking?*

It wasn't that she treasured the bowl so much as she didn't feel like tending to a thousand shards hiding among the leaves she already had to sweep up. Shards that could slice and penetrate and bury beneath skin, the smallest able to cause the greatest pain for the longest time.

*And wasn't that just like life?*

In the past twelve months since Carlo's death, Maggie had come to realize it wasn't so much the big and dramatic things as the smallest and most frequent that caused such pain.

Things like Carlo shouting for her to close the door. Like making fun of something on TV but with no one on the couch to share the joke. Things like spotting something beautiful in the world and turning to share it with your person because their joy in it will only amplify yours. Except no one is standing beside you anymore, and that tightness in your chest returns. Your gut fills with familiar heaviness and dread. And what you thought was beautiful just a moment ago decays before your eyes. Rotten fruit filmed in a time lapse.

*'Whether 'tis nobler in the mind to suffer the slings and arrows of outrageous fortune'*—Hamlet had asked—*'or to take arms*

*against a sea of troubles, and by opposing, end them?'*

Magdalena had come to recite Shakespeare's quote with such intensity and regularity these days that it had become a mantra. Was it better to move through life suffering a constant barrage of pain and sadness, or was Hamlet correct that the best option was to take arms against it in the only way possible…by ending it all?

*Stupid glass bowl.*

She cursed it for making her go there again. Tonight, of all nights. Maggie had promised herself that she wasn't going to allow that pain in.

*Not tonight, demons.*

And she sure as shit wasn't going to let it get the better of her. No. Tonight she would let herself start to experience the world again. Even if only for one night. Perhaps her last night. Good, bad or ugly, what would come would come. Because Carlo wouldn't want her to suffer like this.

*She* didn't want to suffer like this.

*Anymore.*

Maggie touched the tip of her finger to the bowl so precariously balanced on the edge of the table. Its side was thick and cool and firm, with a wonderful texture that felt stimulating. Even soothing in a way. It was an unexpected sensation, and she looked up with a flash of accidental joy across her face and urged Carlo to feel its magic too.

"Hey Boo! Come feel thi—"

She cut the bid short, Carlo no longer here to heed it.

Yet again, conscious thought had taken a moment to catch up to the emotive. It had been exactly twelve months to the day.

And still, Magdalena would find herself forgetting.

She again placed her finger against the bowl, slowly pressing until it slid past its tipping point. Maggie then watched in numb silence as the floor deconstructed it into a million glass shards…

# 21

*carlo*

# 5:05pm | the halloween prior

CARLO PROMISED HE would be back in time, then laughed. It was loud and real. Carlo's joy was *always* real. "Me, miss Halloween? You *are* kidding me, right Mags. Have you been smoking crack from one of your drug busts again?"

Though she never told him, Maggie had always been envious of how unfazed he seemed by life when she, herself, found it so unnatural. Lord knows, she tried. It wasn't that she was unhappy. It was just that some people's resting countenance was always a smile. Others, not so much.

Carlo paused at the front door. "I'll be back in time. I promise."

How on earth they could forget to buy the candy was beyond her. It was their favorite time of year, after all. Well, to be completely accurate, it was Carlo's more than hers. She'd always liked Halloween. But yeah, she loved it now because Carlo did.

"Be safe, Boo."

This was something she always said when they parted. And she always meant it. Being a detective with the NYPD had a way of revealing so much of the filthy underbelly of life that sometimes it was hard to see anything above it.

Carlo rolled his eyes, winked, and blew her a kiss.

The door closed with a conclusive *thud* and she was alone.

Maggie plugged her phone into the speaker Carlo bought for her birthday. She loved music. It was possibly the only thing she was more passionate about than he was. And he wanted that joy for her. Because *her* joy increased *his* joy in music even more. He guessed enthusiasm was just kinda contagious that way.

It was still incredible to Maggie how you could just buy and play whatever you wanted, right from your phone. Gone were the days of stacks of CDs and huge stereo systems taking up a good portion of one living room wall. Now an entire world of listening entertainment was available on the same thing you grabbed when you wanted to call in your pizza order.

Though the foyer table was rather too small, Maggie wanted the fun holiday music and spooky sound effects to fill the house with Halloween spirit before Carlo got back. The entry hall had incredible acoustics, and from here the music would rise and resonate as though they'd commissioned the bands themselves to come perform just for them; beseeched the moaning ghosts to become their own personal haunts.

She placed the speaker and her phone on the table, ever so carefully moving the beautifully decorative glass bowl to one side. The bowl had such a nice look and feel to it, she would hate if anything were to ever happen to it. Which was funny, because she couldn't even remember exactly where they bought it. She found herself distracted from putting up the remainder of the Halloween decorations while she racked her brain to try and remember exactly when this bowl had become an integral part of their world.

*I wonder if everyone has one of these?*

The question was poised only to herself inside her head.

*Okay,* she admitted, engaging in an earnest conversation with the voice, *so maybe not everyone's is an actual bowl. But I bet they have their own version. You know, that thing you simply had to have from that forgotten vacation years ago. That thing you purchased despite the price tag that in normal circumstances would have you running, not walking, for the exit. But not that time. No sir. Because it was 'just so beautiful and perfect, and price aside, it would always remind you of _____.'* Maggie's voice continued speaking to her as though she were addressing an audience of many. *Feel free to finish that sentence by inserting any vacation destination of your liking.*

She smiled at her own wittiness, eyes bright and full of life as she opened the phone's music app. Without hesitation, the bubbling of chemicals in lab beakers and rattling of ghostly chains filled the foyer, the sounds rolling across the ceiling and down the Navajo White walls. And just like that, the brownstone was audibly transformed into a mad scientist's lab. When the first musical bars of the 'Monster Mash' then sprang to life, Mags was utterly giddy with excitement and sang along.

"—Late one night—my eyes la-la la la-la sight…la la the mash!"

She spun around in circles and laughed at how perfect everything was.

*God, Boo's SO gonna love this!*

### III

The last of the decorations were being hung and positioned, and not a minute too soon. Any moment now, Boo would be returning home with bags and bags of candy in bite-sized portions. All the good stuff. Trick-or-Treaters would get no cheap knockoffs at the Romano household. Not on Carlo's life. Though, with it being the eleventh hour, so to speak, Maggie did have to wonder if this year would be the one time he would actually make an exception.

She chuckled out loud, imagining Carlo handing out those generic peanut butter kisses. Despite their name, were neither a delicious Reese's nor Hershey's treat, but taffy-like candies wrapped in plain black or plain orange waxed papers…

*Ewww*, Maggie thought, wincing.

…Black licorice…

*Nope. Carlo would rather chew off his own arm.*

…Those small waxy pop bottles with barely a drop of colored sugar water inside…

*Pointless,* she thought and actually shook her head. *Other than their first-time novelty value for a five-year-old. Maybe. And even then, did you ever find yourself clamoring for more?*

…Or, God forbid, 'circus peanuts.'

*Those orange foam-like whatever-they-weres? Just…no.*

Huh-uh. Wasn't gonna happen. If the nearest store were out of snack-sized versions of brand name bars, she knew Carlo would go to another store. Then another. If he still couldn't find any, he'd just come home with armfuls of full-sized bars—even if it cost him an arm and a leg—and that would be alright by Maggie. This was his holiday. His Superbowl. His time to shine. She wasn't about to piss on his parade over a few measly dollars.

Now, the one treat Mags and Boo did disagree on, and this was known by all their friends as it invariably became one of the hottest topics of the season amongst them, was *Candy Corn.*

Maggie loved it.

Carlo would rather eat worms.

"Fine," Maggie remarked to herself aloud as she now tossed a palmful of those tri-colored sugar kernels in her mouth. A waxy, chemical taste reminiscent of honey, butter and vanilla coated her gums as she tried to remember the dance steps of 'Thriller' which was now pulsing big from the foyer. "Enjoy your delicious worms, Carlo."

# 22

*candy corn*

# 11 days before the end | halloween 2011

S HE STARED AS the leaves lilted to the floor. It was almost peaceful as they settled in silence over a spray of glass shards, a dozen or so chocolate bars, and several snack bags that had sloshed to the floor from the big plastic pumpkin bowl still clutched to her bosom. She wondered why—*how*—she managed to close that huge oak door with one foot while also successfully tossing her new mystery package onto the small foyer table.

She could have just put down the candy bowl, placed the package on the table, then closed the door.

*Like any sane person would.*

But the truth was, Magdalena knew full well why she hadn't done that. Because that stupid pumpkin bowl, and the candy it held, were in so many ways all she had left of her Carlo.

It was a stupid thought. She realized that.

This bowl of candy was no more her late husband than it was a bowl of gold bullion. For a start, the chocolates in it weren't part of the small stash they'd already had in the house last Halloween. Even if they'd still be edible a full year later, it wouldn't matter. Because those chocolates, like so many other things (including the speaker Carlo had given her and most of his prized Halloween decorations) Maggie had thrown away in the days following what happened. Nor were these candies from the supply Carlo had gone out to buy that night. Because, like him, those chocolates had never made it back home.

No...this candy—half still in the giant pumpkin bowl and half now strewn across the floor—was purchased by Maggie only a week ago. It had absolutely nothing to do with Carlo.

*At all.*

But yet somehow, it had everything to do with him.

Among the scattered pieces were several treat-sized bags of Candy Corn. Boo would be turning in his grave if he knew she were handing them out along with the Snickers and the Reese's and the Twix.

She plucked one of the packages from the floor and ripped it open, funneling a half-dozen fake kernels into her mouth. Their distinctive taste and scent triggered her memory instantly.

Overwhelmed, she slumped against the stairs.

*I miss you, Carlo. God, I miss you so much—*

Now she openly wept.

*—I miss you TOO much.*

She did not leap to her feet the next time the door chime jangled. Or anytime again this night.

Even when her tears eventually subsided, Maggie remained numb and silent upon the entry hall stairs as group after group of trick-or-treaters rang the bell. Some expressed their disappointment with passive moans; a few, a childish outburst. Most merely walked quietly away. One chaperoning adult, however, made it a point to inform Maggie of her annoyance by decrying through the door, just loudly enough, "Wow, how self-absorbed can you *be*, lady?"

# 23

## 6:13pm | the halloween prior

MAGGIE KNEW IT would take him longer than he claimed. It was Halloween night, after all, and there weren't that many shops nearby that would still be open.

Sure, they lived in New York City. But that was the point: They lived in the city. And Halloween night surrounded by ten-million-plus people, many of whom are running around in masks, isn't always the safest place if you're a small shopkeeper. Over the years, the department had arrested so many rubber-faced Billy Clintons, Dick Nixons and Ronnie Reagans for armed robbery that the uniformed boys had begun to call it President's Day.

So, unlike the claim made famous by the song, it *was* possible to find yourself in a New York City that *did* sleep.

Sometimes.

And tonight was one of those times.

Which is exactly why Maggie doubled how long Carlo had anticipated he would be. She figured at least the first two stores on his list were probably already closed, grates locked. Which made Pepperdines the next available one, a good twenty minutes away. And it would be packed. But that was fine by Maggie as it gave her a rare opportunity for some alone time (always a nice thing) and the chance to finish putting up the rest of the decorations before the first revelers of the season arrived.

At first, she'd been all but bouncing off the walls. Having torn through all the Candy Corn, she now had energy to burn. Singing along to the playlist blaring from the speaker in the foyer, she danced around the house with herself.

After an hour, she called Carlo's cell, anxious for him to join her. It rang once. Twice. Three times. A fourth.

Voicemail.

*'Hey, this is Carlo.'* Forgetting that the speaker was still attached to her phone, his voice boomed larger than life. *'Go ahead and knock yourself out—leave a message if you really want to. But honestly? I probably won't call you back.* Here the greeting paused. *Unless you're Maggie. In which case yes, I'll definitely call you back, babe.'* He then pretended he wasn't aware the greeting was still recording, and his trailing voice muttered, *'Like I'd dare NOT call her back. I mean, the chick knows how to use a gun...'*

Always the joker.

Singing along to 'Werewolves of London,' Magdalena hit redial.

It rang four more times and clicked over to the greeting.

Now the feeling that something wasn't quite right grew cold and heavy in her gut.

She pressed redial again.

But this time, she hung up before it connected a third time. Carlo would already see the first two missed calls. He would call her right back. He always did. But if he were to see three, he'd drop everything (maybe even the candy) and be back in the car and heading for home before she could even answer the call herself. The whole night would be ruined. And all because she was being overly anxious. Carlo was a capable guy—he knew how to take care of himself. Besides, he was probably just in the store and left his phone in the car. Maybe he'd been paying at the register at that exact moment. Or had armfuls of candy and couldn't get the cell out of his pocket in time.

She forced herself to wait two full minutes before calling again.

This she knew because she'd timed it. And every one of those seconds ticked by slower than they ever had in her life. At precisely the one hundred and twentieth, she called again.

*Same outcome.*

Her pulse quickened; chest tightening. Heartbeat trying to keep up with the glucose and anxiety spurring it on like a greyhound chasing a fake rabbit. She began pacing, staring at her phone. Checking the ringer was on. Turning the music off in case it might interfere with receiving an incoming call. Turning it back on when she realized that was ridiculous.

*You've got to cool it, girl. You're going to give yourself a heart attack. Then Boo's gonna come home, laughing about some silly something-or-other reason for his delay, only to find you collapsed on the floor. Then you'll not only be dead, you'll have ruined his Halloween, too.*

The idea of which would upset Carlo more made her chuckle a little, and it felt good to let that mirth push its way in front of the nervous energy. Half of overcoming a panic response was simply being conscious of the fact you were having one. Something to do with avoiding an amygdala hijacking.

She took a deep breath, pulling it through her nose and filling her lungs until she could feel the air inflating them all the way to their lowest point in her body.

*One-one-thousand.*

*Two-one-thousand.*

*Three-one-thousand.*

She released the air slowly between her lips, already feeling calmer and more clearly able to think. Repeating this several times was the self-imposed requirement before she would allow herself to pick up the cell phone again. When she finally did, her rational brain was able to make the decision not to further feed the panic, and she put the phone right back down.

*Carlo was safe,* she reassured herself. *He had a flat tire, or something equally innocuous, and his phone battery had died.* He was always forgetting to charge it, so that last part was as good as fact in Maggie's book, and that made her feel more comfortable. Any moment now he would be standing in the entry hall with bags galore and blurting out, 'Babe, you won't believe what just happened...'

II

The phone's Halloween playlist was already on its second run-through when the old door chime jarred to life, piercing even the resounding music from the foyer.

Maggie's concern melted as she rushed to the hefty oak door to let Carlo in, bags and bags of candy undoubtedly draped over his person and struggling to open it. "Coming, Boo! Hang on...!"

Eyes alight with relief, she swung open the door.

"TRICK OR TREAT!

—ICK OR...*uhh........treat...*"

*(Always that one trailing voice.)*

With bags open and held high, three Spider-Men stared up at her with those blank Spidey eyes.

Maggie's heart sank, the cold weight in her gut returning.

The pint-sized Spider-Men stared at her, hungry bags secured by both hands at arms' length. After an uncomfortable silence, one drew attention to his bag by rustling the opening just a little and moving it a hair closer to Maggie. Like maybe she hadn't noticed it. Or perhaps she just didn't understand her role in the process here.

Apologizing as she darted behind the door to fetch the giant pumpkin bowl, Maggie threw not one but handfuls of chocolate in each sack.

"Actually, you know what? Here—" She swept the plastic bowl over the three open bags, pouring out its meager contents until it was empty. "—Happy Halloween."

"Sweet," the sack shaker declared and nudged his two partners as his way of gesturing that they'd better skedaddle before she came to her senses. "Thanks, lady!" He was already off the front porch and heading down the sidewalk, his cohorts close behind.

The first trick-or-treaters of the night, and Boo wasn't here to greet them. He *always* greeted the first. And the last. And most of the others in between.

Carlo was missing Halloween.

And that began to scare the shit out of Magdalena Romano.

III

"Screw this Zen bullshit." While she did appreciate the grounding techniques the occupational therapist had taught her—and, truth be known, had found some real benefit in them after the charges were brought against her—now just wasn't the time.

Already punching up her phone's contacts, Maggie tapped the little green phone icon next to the one labeled DESK SERGEANT.

She immediately recognized the voice picking up the other end of the line. "Frank? Hey, this is Detective Romano..."

The sergeant ran through the reports occurring within a three mile radius of her home in the last 90 minutes. Two petty thefts, one infraction. Vandalism of a local store run by a nice couple who'd recently emigrated from Afghanistan. A handful of your basic noise complaints. "Oh, and one trespass," he added.

"Trespass? Tell me about that one."

"Caller said she had a grown-ass man prowling around the perimeter of her home dressed like—are you ready for this—dressed like a devil."

"The devil? Like, bright-red-skin-horns-and-pitchfork devil?"

"Not *the* devil, no. *A* devil, Detective. Y'know, like a demon. At least I guess that's what she was trying to describe. Whatever it was, she said it freaked her out, so she thought she should call."

Romano was silent before adding, "Halloween, huh? Brings out all sorts of nut jobs." Whether referring to the perp, or the lady who called in the trespass, was unclear. "Thank God it isn't a full moon, to boot."

"Got that right."

"Hmmm."

"Oh, she did say something that seemed odd." The sergeant rustled through some papers on his desk, in his lap. "But then again, just sorta confirms the whole Halloween thing..."

"Yeah? What did she say?" Romano's blood began to run cold, feeling her jaw tightening, throat constricting.

"So, while this gal's on the line, she's describing this guy who's actually milling around in her front yard as she's speaking. He isn't casing her place, so much as he seems to be watching what's taking place across the road."

"Across the road, Frank? What's across the road from this caller's home?"

"Some kinda grocery store, I think. Hang on a mo'..."

More papers rustling.

A profane exclamation as a coffee was nearly toppled.

Audible relief when it wasn't.

The sound of the phone's receiver brushing against the sergeant's uniform as he clenched it between shoulder and ear.

"Okay, got it here. Sorry about that. Looks like it's one of the Pepperdine locations. The one over on Goudy and Thirteenth."

The air sucked from Maggie's chest.

The sergeant heard it. "You know that one, Detective?" Then: "Oh hey. Yeah. I see that's not *too* terribly far from you." Chuckling a little nervously he added, "Hey Maggie, your hus—"

"It's Detective, Sergeant."

"Sorry?"

"It's *Detective* Romano. I'm still on the force, Sergeant. I haven't gotten the boot. Not yet anyway."

An awkward pause. "Right. So, um, *Detective.* Um…Carlo…he's not out raising hell dressed as a demon now, is he? Hehe."

After the mild reprimand, his delivery was stiff and uncertain. The joke fell flat and just lay there between them as the line clicked with gentle static.

Maggie cleared her throat. "Uh, no. He isn't. What else did she say, this woman who called in?"

Reading the metaphorical room, the sergeant stopped swiveling in his chair, sat upright, and took the phone from his shoulder to hold it properly. "Right. Um, well…she said this demon-dude was pacing back and forth near the sidewalk like he was anxious or something. Then he just crossed in front of a tree and was gone."

"How? He was gone *how*?"

Though the gesture wouldn't be seen, the sergeant shrugged. "Just gone. Crossed in front of a tree and some kid came out the other side."

"What do you mean, a kid?"

"Just what I said. A kid. Ten years old, she said. Maybe twelve. I mean, it's Halloween, y'know?"

Magdalena spoke carefully to mask the apprehension crawling through her nerves like a nest of spiders that had been disturbed. "What was this kid's costume, Sergeant?"

"Some kinda zombie. And a really good one, too…for a kid. At least, that's what she told us."

When Romano did not respond, the Sergeant took it as a sign to elucidate. "Said his makeup was the real deal. Face looking half sunk-in, one eyeball hanging out. And he was all burnt. She said the kid's costume made him look like a human shish-kabob."

"Jesus." The image made her queasy and only more tense.

"Right? I'd love to find out where his parents got that fake skin stuff. Like, was it makeup, or a mask, or some kind of latex?"

*God help me, another horror fanatic, just like my Carlo.*

"Anyway," the sergeant continued. "She said the freakiest thing was the way the kid's head kinda bobbed to one side. Like his neck didn't work quite right. Now *that* trick I'd definitely like to learn how to do. Badass stuff, that." At his desk, he returned the phone's receiver to his shoulder, lilting his head to the side as he assumed the classic zombie stance with both arms straight out and stiff. "Hehe. Kid's parents are rock stars. I'd love for one of our Uniforms to pick him up, just so I could get his folks to tell me how they did it. Hell, I'd beat it outta them if I ha—"

The words hadn't fully passed his lips before he realized. Maggie did not respond. In the silence, the natural static of their connection crackled and hissed.

"Hey, I didn't mean nothing by that, Detective. I know those charges of yours were dropped and I was jus—"

"Was there anything else you wanted to share, Sergeant?"

He sat back up in his chair, straightening his shoulders. Cleared his throat before gulping down some water from a cheap bottle that crackled as it emptied. "Only the clothes the kid was wearing, I guess."

"Not the usual ripped t-shirt and old jeans rubbed in dirt, I'm guessing?"

"Hell no to the tee-and-jeans. Hell yeah to the dirt. Woman told me this kid looked as if he'd stumbled straight outta the nineteen-seventies…and clawed his way from his own grave. Like some undead kid from one of those old scary movies. You know, like the old Hammer House of Horror ones?"

No, Maggie did *not* know. Carlo definitely would, though. And he was gonna get a kick out of this whole part of the story when she relayed it to him later that night over a whiskey and shot of tequila. But she replied to the sergeant by saying nothing at all.

"Anyway, the caller, she said this kid was even wearing a little suit. Like the kinda thing you never see a kid wearing unless it's a wedding…or a funeral." He hesitated. "*His* funeral, is what I'm sayin', Detective."

"Yes, Sergeant. I got that. And the color? Did you think to take that piece of information down—or were you too distracted by her description of the awesomeness of his zombie makeup?"

If the jab landed, the sergeant didn't let on.

"Royal blue. Big brass buttons. Down the front and on the cuffs. Oh, and *big* lapels." Here, the sergeant pretended to brush down his own invisible lapels, a smarmy look across his face. He then cupped one hand to his mouth as if calling out to someone. "Hey! Nineteen-seventy-seven called. It wants its zombie-kid back. Hehe. Really gotta hand it to his folks' attention to detai—"

A click.

"Detective?" He tapped the receiver. "You still there?

Dead air.

"Well, okay then. You're welcome for the information…*Maggie*." He whipped his middle finger at the phone before dropping it on his desk.

IV

She called Carlo's cell with the sergeant's words still ringing in her ears. This time, it didn't go to voicemail.

"CARLO?"

The line fizzled and popped. Just as it had done all evening.

"Carlo! You *there*, Boo?"

From somewhere far away came…*something*. Not quite a voice. But not quite *not* a voice. A faraway cry buried in a deep grating, like river rocks dragged across the top of an empty wood barrel. Magdalena shivered, a chill materializing between her shoulder blades. When the sergeant had first mentioned the zombie kid, her anxiety was as palpable as if she'd just disturbed a nest of spiders. Now that mass of pulsating eggs had burst, a thousand freshly-hatched arachnids scurrying down her spine.

"...*Boo*...are you *there*, babe...?"

As if by way of answer, the interference in the line immediately cleared, its reception crisp and bright. Even Carlo's breath had become audible, to the point that Maggie could almost feel it brushing the hairs at the nape of her neck.

She spun around, expecting to find that her husband had somehow snuck back into the house, and this was all just one of Carlo's stupid Halloween pranks.

Then came the voice she would never forget.

*A child's voice.*

Except, with no innocence to brighten its timbre, it oozed dark with hatred and venom. It pronounced her name slowly, savoring the sound, the way you might describe the best night of your life to your friends: *It...Was...Soooo...Good.*

"Mag...Da...*Leeeee*...Na."

The tongue, black and rotted, slithered from the phone into Maggie's ear with a stench like roadkill.

Screaming, she jerked away and threw her cell across the foyer. It slammed against the music speaker on the hall table, its touch screen cracking as a wave of shrill distortion tore through the house. As the volume bars pegged solid red, the pitch rose to an ear-splitting howl that shredded the air like a thousand flutes, each out of tune with every other.

"MAGS—" Now Carlo's voice. Struggling to be heard from somewhere beneath this audible hellscape.

"CARLO!"

Magdalena twisted round and round, clapping her palms to her ears and screaming her husband's name until the foyer began to spin, its walls wavering. Ceiling rising. The room darkening.

In this abyss grew reds. Yellows. Crackling oranges and flashes of brilliance.

*Fire.*

No longer in the brownstone, Maggie was in a wooded enclave

engulfed by flames. At its center, a massive oak where there was a boy—

—swinging by the neck. Twisted and beaten, his head cants at a sharp angle as his spine bulges the opposite side of his neck. Stretched tight, the skin threatens to pop.

But still, the boy twitches.

Beneath him, other boys, *his friends*, are dancing around the flames, chanting what can only be gibberish amidst howls like wild hyenas after a kill.

And in the flames at their center, a shape.

*Something rising.*

It is the image of personified evil beyond her comprehension.

Maggie begins screaming over and over as the twitching boy's eyes set upon her. At this moment, the limb from which he hangs cracks with a flame that licks up from the oak's trunk. The limb jerks downward half a foot and one of the boy's eyes is forced from the socket that can no longer contain it.

*Help me!* he cries, though his mouth is an impossible oval, his lips black, swollen and unmoving. *HELP ME!*

But it is not a child's voice…it is now Carlo's voice coming from that mouth of horror.

*MAGGIE HELP ME!*

Parading around the flames are no longer children, but adults cloaked in crimson, their cowls deep to hide faces alight with excitement as they chant. As though they are manifesting its very existence, the image rising from the fire is an abomination that owns all the pain and darkness of the world. The cloaked figures stretch to touch it, to be part of it. Now it becomes the dangling boy once more. The cloaked figures tear at his clothes, peeling them from his body as charred skin flays from muscle and his body writhes and kicks and flails.

*MAGGGGGGGGS!* Carlo screams, for it is his flesh being stripped away, his body twitching from the noose.

Maggie lunges toward the flames, the heat searing. "NO!"

Bursting through the ring of figures, she calls her husband's name again and again. She leaps but cannot reach him, cannot even touch him, cannot free him from the noose or the flames that lick up his body, hungry and unrelenting.

*CARLOOOOO*, she screams as—

—her cell phone rang, and the woods imploded to become the foyer once more. On her knees in the center of the entry hall, Maggie stared in shock at the Navajo White walls enveloping her.

*A second ring.*

She felt the cold sensation of the polished slate floor beneath her prone body. And the leaves which had been scattered by the wind. Hundreds of leaves. Spread far into the entry. Strewn among them were packs of Candy Corn and chocolate bars...and a spray of glass shards. At the source of this plume of destruction stood the entry hall table. Upon it was no longer the speaker that was Carlo's gift for her birthday. In its place sat a package about the size and weight of a ream of paper, wrapped in plain brown kraft paper. Next to this box was nothing. Yet, this is where their decorative glass bowl should be. They'd purchased it on an island vacation, Carlo insisting they take it home despite its exorbitant price. Maggie didn't argue. She knew it would always remind them of that week—the week when they decided they should marry.

*A third ring.*

And now the package did not exist, the music speaker sitting atop the hall table as it had since she'd placed it there at the start of the night. Glass shards did not litter the entry hall's polished tile floor, the bowl still intact next to the speaker. There were no leaves strewn there; no chocolates; no packs of Candy Corn. For none of this vision would become reality for a year yet. Most importantly, there were no woods on fire. And no dying boy.

*A fourth ring.*

Maggie crawled across the foyer, searching for her cell phone which she'd thrown while trying to understand anything at all that was happening. Last she remembered was a conversation with the Desk Sergeant.

Her heart sank as she recalled the reason why: because Carlo had gone out for more candy and still had not returned home.

*A fifth ring.*

Maggie found her cell phone not on the floor, not thrown, not broken. But lying neatly on the entry hall table alongside the speaker to which it was still connected.

*But hadn't she just been speaking to the sergeant, and of course disconnected it?*

Its playlist was paused, the incoming call taking priority as the speaker echoed each ring through the house.

*A sixth.*

She lifted the phone, foggy and unsure. On its screen was a photo of Carlo holding her tight as they were enraptured by an island sunset. Across the top, big letters declared: BOO CALLING.

A flood of adrenaline coursing through her, Maggie's trembling fingertip glanced across the touch screen. She had to tap several times before the phone would recognize her input and accept the call. When it finally did, the line crackled to life.

And so did Carlo's voice.

It was mixed with static and wind and the road noise from the Jeep's tires. But it was definitely her Boo's voice: "Mags, I'm on my way home. Jesus, what a madhouse it is out here. You will *not* believe what I've been through. Actual Hell."

Magdalena pulled the phone from her ear and cupped her hand over her mouth, quelling the gush of relief.

"Maggie, you there?"

Shaking, she cleared her throat and took another deep breath through her nose.

"*Mags...?*"

"I'm here, Boo. Sorry about that," She coughed to disguise the hiccupping sobs. "Drink went down the wrong tube, is all."

"On the sauce already, huh? Lucky you. Anyway, can't wait to get home. To you...and those TOTs!"

Carlo first abbreviated 'Trick-Or-Treaters' years ago. Though it hadn't quite landed for Maggie, she certainly appreciated its brevity. Her mind just always rewound any sentence in which he used it and inserted the word 'TATER' in front of it.

"Me too, Boo. Hurry. Okay?" Her voice cracked. Just enough.

Carlo picked up on it. "You sure you're alright, Mags?"

She cleared her throat and again inhaled deeply, feeling more grounded as the breath carried the tension away with it.

"Fine, babe. Really. Just eager to have you home."

*Fine...? How could she* say *that, after the near mental break-down, or whatever the fuck it was, just happened?*

And yet it was true, the past few hours—even the last few minutes—seeming to wash away to this restored normality.

"Me too, Mags. We have any TOTs yet?"

For a moment, Maggie considered lying to spare his feelings. She seriously couldn't remember the last time he'd missed the first TOTs of the night, and the truth was gonna sting. But there was already enough weird, ugly juju swirling around without her feeding into the bad karma even more.

Maggie nodded. "I'm afraid so, babe. One group. More coming any moment." She peered through the curtains of the sidelights flanking the front door. Several groups were making their way up the street, methodically stopping at each house along the way. "And before you ask: Spider-Men."

"And...?" Carlo prompted. "...You said group, not single. What were the others?"

She laughed. It was genuine joy. Or maybe just the sweet

release of the night's unimaginable tension. "Spider-Men."

"*All* of them?"

"All three." She paused. "It was actually kinda adorable. But I wasn't really feeling it, y'know? To be honest, I was starting to get a bit worried…"

"I know, Mags. I'm sorry. Phone died. I had to run all the way to Pepperdines. And when I tell you what was going on there, I don't think you're going to believe it."

"Well, I think I'd believe anything right about now. I'm glad your phone is finally charged enough that you could call. Where'd you get the cable?"

Carlo chuckled. "How'd you know I forgot my charger?"

"Really, Boo. You have to ask?"

"Yeah, OK. You got me there. I had to buy the fucking thing. Pepperdines. I couldn't let another half hour pass before letting you know I was okay. I had a feeling you'd already be crawling out of your skin, as it was."

"I was starting to, not gonna lie."

"You know, Mags. That job of yours has such a huge impact on your outlook. Sometimes I wonder if it's even worth it anymore."

Though Maggie didn't respond, she found herself silently nodding. And that, she didn't expect. Because in Maggie's mind, she couldn't even picture a life where she was no longer a detective; no longer on the force. Despite what had happened, even with the charges they had brought against her—and dropped just as quickly—she loved that place. And those people. Even goofy Frank, the desk sergeant. So this little unconscious nod of hers was perhaps the biggest indictment Magdalena could imagine.

"Well, anyway, I'll be home in no time." Carlo reached down to tap the screen of the charging phone wedged at an awkward angle below the Jeep's console. 8:33 flashed on the screen. "Holy shit, just kill me now. Is that really the goddamn time?"

At first Magdalena didn't respond. She had no idea what time it was, but also had a feeling she shouldn't ask. Which, of course, made no sense. It was just one of those instances where an odd vibration passes through you and feels like something trying to communicate. But you don't understand the language—and probably wouldn't believe it if you did—so you let the message go, forever discarded into the ether of life. Which, for Maggie, would become one of the Universe's ironic, sick and twisted little jokes. For in a moment, she would forever wish that she had listened to that intuition. And while she had no inkling what time of night it was—nor did it matter, now that she knew Carlo was safe and on his way home—that meaningless information was about to become three numbers she would never forget.

But Magdalena, of course, was aware of none of this. And figuring it might be nice to know just how long the hellish weirdness of this night had kept her in its clutches, she chuckled at the intensity of Carlo's rhetorical comment by simply replying, "No idea, Boo. What time *is* it?"

Just to be sure he had seen it correctly, Carlo reached for the phone again. This time, when he tapped the screen, the phone twisted from its haphazard perch and slid from view between center console and passenger seat.

"Fuck *meeeee*." He tugged on the charging cable and began coaxing the phone toward him. "C'mon, baby..."

"Carlo?"

"Oh, the stupid phone slid down between the seats again. I really gotta get myself a phone mount or something. Hang on a minute, babe."

"Carlo, just leave it. It really doesn't matter."

"No, no. I got it." Grunts. A few more choice words. "Gotcha, you little bastard. Wow, so it really is eight thirty. Nothing I can do about that now. At least I'll be home in just a few min—"

The sound of the crash through the phone was sickening.

You always imagine a huge, resonating explosion. But for most people in a head-on crash, life ends not to a dramatic Hollywood sound effects track, but to an impossibly dull, metallic *THUD*. It's the melee of horror sounds which follow that actually makes us believe otherwise.

For the end of Carlo's life, these were the screeching of rubber tires as the two vehicles spun each other across the cold, uneven blacktop. The wrenching of metal twisting and coiling into metal. Redlined engines screaming. The sound a skateboard makes as it boardslides atop a metal railing (this being Carlo's Jeep as it ground across the guardrails).

A *PUUUFT* sound like a vacuum cleaner choking out on a rug.

Then the screams that would tattoo themselves upon Maggie's memory as what had been two distinct vehicles just moments before were now a single, indistinct mass. Teetering over the guardrails of the third street bridge, flames crackled as they licked up from the engine compartments. Intensified by gasoline and oil, they tightened and burned nearly white, bellowing the thickest of black smoke.

With the seatbelt he wasn't wearing now bound around his neck, Carlo dangled outside the open-sided Jeep. He kicked and spasmed as he swung like a human pendulum. Slicing into his throat, the belt's polyester webbing peeled the skin upward, tightening around his esophagus as his weight stretched his spinal column.

He was still conscious as the flames began to feed upon his clothing smeared with gas and oil and grease that acted like napalm. Every nerve felt the searing pain as his polyester pants and long sleeve shirt began melting into his flesh. He was fully aware as he tried desperately to strip them from his legs, chest and arms.

He did not stop. Not even when his melting garments fused into his skin and both peeled away in long, jagged strips.

Capable in this moment of any self-mutilation if it promised even the whisper of a chance of escape, Carlo continued to thrash and strip away flesh and fabric as they fused into one. Exposing fat layers and slick muscle like a plastic anatomical model, the fresh oils and protein only strengthened the flames as the fire methodically devoured him.

*"MAGGGGGGGS..."* A low, guttural cry, it was the last time her name would ever cross his lips.

"Carlo! Hang on baby, hang on!" She fumbled with the phone, attempting to reach 9-1-1 without disconnecting the call from her husband.

She failed at both and the cell went silent, her home screen wallpaper registering that she had now left Carlo to die alone.

Furiously jabbing the touchscreen with hands that shook to the limits of her control, Maggie paced in tight, frantic circles as the call to the emergency number connected. Terror ran cold through every cell of her body as she somehow managed to provide her best estimate of Carlo's location.

V

She would later remember very little of that call.

*And none of the one she made next...*

VI

*'Boo can't come to the phone right now, Mrs. Romano.'* The voice that answered Carlo's phone was akin to a child's but woven from a darkness that stole Maggie's breath.

Then the boy giggled, the sound wet and bubbling up from a throat clotted with moist rot and things that crawled. Buoyant with delight, he began jumping up and down on the side of the road as he watched the flames licking up Carlo's torso. Their flickering orange light was reflected in the brass anchor buttons which adorned the boy's mud-encrusted blue suit; danced in his single milky eye.

Tossing Carlo's phone onto the burning heap, he clapped with vigor as Maggie's husband writhed and screamed until his lungs collapsed, riddled with heat-blistered perforations. His spasms lessened, the kicking and clawing slowing.

Then Carlo Romano was no more.

Through the growl of consuming flames now inching toward Carlo's phone, Maggie could hear the approaching drone of faraway sirens. As their shrill, cyclic pulse grew, the boy who rejoiced over Carlo's corpse pulled something from his own charred and shredded suit jacket. Breathing black tendrils of air into a cheap wooden flute, he mimicked the rise and fall of the sirens until they overlapped in a perverse chorus.

On her knees and with the foyer beginning to spin, Maggie could no longer govern her breaths. They came fast and shallow as the disharmonic minor chord that was both the wail of the sirens and the shrill cry of the boy's flute became the hiss of the brownstone's cast iron radiators. As steaming water expanded to push shrieking air through valves, all three nightmare sounds filled Maggie's head as one. They cut to abrupt silence when Carlo's melting cell phone went dark.

And Magdalena's consciousness did the same.

VII

From his bed in their Pennsylvania compound, Ian Cockerton sat up as the baseboard radiators in his childhood room began to…

…*whistle*…

# 24

*mind games*

# 11 days before the end | halloween 2011

T HE LAST TRICK-OR-TREATERS of the night had come and gone as Maggie lay sprawled across the bottom of the stairs. While she knew it would never be possible to completely shake the memory of that night exactly one year ago, still she prayed every day for a diluted version: the abridged *Reader's Digest* edition, if you will. Of course, this would do nothing to assuage her loneliness. Or the isolation and abandonment that scraped her hollow on a daily basis and consumed so much of her emotional real estate. But it would be a mercy to no longer hear the sounds with such intensity; to not imagine the scene quite as vividly. And in some ways, this prayer was coming true. Recently, Maggie had come to realize that some parts of the memory had begun to waver, like reading a page from a book by viewing it through a glass of water in your hand. The images and sounds still pulled at her stomach, but at least this easing off was a start.

Now, there *was* a part of the memory Magdalena's mind had suppressed completely. And that was the fact that after she spoke to the emergency operator, she did call Carlo's cell. For Maggie, that call, and everything she heard in it, had simply never taken place. She therefore had no memory of hearing her husband's last breaths before his lungs blistered. She did not hear the macabre whistling of the sirens and the flute. And most importantly, she never heard that child's voice, his exuberant cheers or perverse laughter as he rejoiced in spectating Carlo's torture through one clouded eye.

But deep down, Magdalena always sensed there was something more to Carlo's accident than her memory would allow. Something that, if she were unable to bring herself to remember, would very likely mark the beginning of her inevitable end...

# 25

*the package*

It was well past one in the morning before Maggie was able to leave the emotional cocoon she had fashioned upon the foyer stairs. Shuffling in her stocking feet across a floor littered with chocolate bars, candies, shredded leaves and shards of glass, she plucked the mystery package from the table. It had been the initial retrieval of this package which had caused her to be abducted by the memory she would've given anything—*absolutely anything*—to have forgotten.

Now, having no more emotional currency to invest, she studied the box with an eye of disaffected interest.

She spun it between her hands, gauging its heft as the corners made small pink divots in her palms.

Its fare through the U.S. postal system had been satisfied by a row of seven limited-edition stamps, each meticulously affixed so that its edges were perfectly square with the stamp adjacent to it. Issued the previous year in commemoration of what would have been the 200th birthday of Edgar Allan Poe, they were unusually gothic and quite beautiful for something from a federal agency.

Again, she noticed that the sender's name and address were conspicuous by their absence. In fact, having been plainly wrapped in brown kraft paper, five of the six sides were impressively devoid of any markings at all. Her name and address were handwritten across its face in that smooth, intimate cursive.

The sender used black ink, not blue.

There were few smudges.

The lettering itself wasn't overly fussy, and perhaps even bordered on casual...for cursive. Other than its unexpected beauty in a day where longhand is short on style, nothing else in particular stood out about this.

Examining the postage stamps more closely, even these seven cawing ravens refused to give up the ghost about their master. Blurred beyond legibility, the postmarks identifying city and date of the package's origin were all but useless black smudges. It could have been mailed from somewhere across the country or from across the street.

Maggie took two steps back. In her socks, she half-glided to not slice open her feet upon a sliver of unseen glass.

*The Stingray Shuffle*, she commented to herself and again only in her mind. *Isn't that what they call it on Florida beaches? Or maybe it's closer to MJ's moonwalk...?*

Having conditioned herself over the past year to no longer share such casual observations aloud, these internal monologs spared her the pain of receiving nothing but silence in return.

Silence that reminded her of her loss.

Proof in point: the reason she was having to do the Stingray Shuffle in the first place.

From this new perspective a few feet away, Magdalena no longer eyed the box with indifference, but with suspicious curiosity. How could it be, in this day and age, that the Post Office had accepted a parcel where the sender's credentials were missing? She couldn't imagine it, let alone the idea of them processing and actually delivering it to an unsuspecting recipient.

Yet here it was, a plainly wrapped box from an anonymous sender. Contents unknown. Motive uncertain. And she'd brought it into her home. Without even thinking twice.

*How effortless it had been to penetrate her sanctuary.*

Then she'd tossed it halfway across the entry hall. This box that could be anything.

*God help me, I fucking threw it!*

Maggie had long ago earned the reputation of being a staunch guardian of her personal information from the clutches of the public domain. That vigilance had only grown in recent years, and this was largely a direct response—and in equal proportion—to the rise of the Church of the New Apocrypha.

Some had thought her caution obsessive. Even bordering on the verge of extreme. But to Magdalena Romano, it was the most rudimentary of safeguards. And then last year happened. Carlo happened. And so, for the most part, those detractors were apologetic.

Now, a simple kraft-papered package had infiltrated her safe place. Silently mocking her, it was proof that even her most strenuous efforts had been in vain.

*Score one for Team Detractors,* her inner voice scoffed while tracing an invisible tally line through the air and ignoring everything telling her not to do what she did next…

II

Protocols had been put in place for situations exactly like this and their dictates couldn't be clearer: she was to immediately vacate the premises, call the NYFD with the code 'Red Crater,' then inform her District Captain once she was safely out of harm's way. Well, at least that's what she was supposed to do when she was still on the force.

Now, she imagined, her reliance would have to be upon that highly sought-after asset we like to call 'Wisdom.' Little more than the time-earned memory of lessons learned the hard way, it was no less forthright and insisted Maggie remember the pipe bomb that took the lives of two fellow officers, and the sight of a third, just the year before. Not to mention the anthrax-laced letters which had terrorized an already reeling nation in the months following 9/11, not yet a decade past.

Choosing to ignore both Protocol and Wisdom, then deciding she might as well throw Better Judgement under the bus while she was at it, Maggie Romano let out a resigned sigh and snatched the package from the table in hands that trembled despite her best efforts.

*Gentle now, Romano,* that inner voice cautioned. *Easy breezy, light as a butterfly.*

In her mind, she conjured the image of a golden Monarch. With effortless agility it flitted upon the breeze, lighter than air.

The scene was calming.

For a moment.

Then her mind blew the insect to smithereens, its wings, delicate as tissue paper, becoming a cloud of yellow confetti.

Though wincing at the imagined destruction, she remained stubbornly undeterred. Turning her face from the package she held at arms' length, Maggie squeezed her eyes tight. Held her breath…then gave it a light, little *shake.*

The percussive, flesh-singeing explosion—

—never came.

Instead, the muffled thump of a single, hefty item sliding inside the box was an anticlimax that released the breath from Maggie's chest. It came out as a loud chortle of relief that echoed across the entry hall and sounded awkward, even to her.

Continuing to tilt the box back and forth with significantly less concern, she noted how the weight shifted each time.

She gave it three quick sideways shakes. Moving faster than the contents within, it took a split-second for the momentum of whatever was inside the box to issue another muted thud.

Still no explosion.

So, clearly not a bomb.

Well, it's *probably* not a bomb.

*Maybe it's not a bomb.*

In fewer than a matter of seconds, her inner voice had successfully belied the confidence she'd feigned up to this point. Deciding that perhaps this voice of reason was worth heeding, she was more careful as she ran one blade of the scissors through the packing tape and unfolded each side flap of the kraft paper like petals of a brown origami flower.

Unlike the stark and pragmatic nature of its wrapper, the wooden box she coaxed from within was anything but. Ornate and beautiful, every one of its six faces was intricately carved in a series of arcane celestial and spiritual images.

As the kraft paper drifted to the floor, Magdalena placed the wooden box back upon her entry hall table.

Slowly, with both hands, she opened the hinged lid.

A studious but attractive man peered up at her from a grainy black and white photo on the back of a used book. Tattered and worn, the hardcover's white dustjacket was yellowing to the color of cream. Its once crisp pages had been thumbed-through so many times that their edges had begun to soften and wear thin. And from them, a rainbow array of sticky notes protruded from both top and side.

Magdalena turned it over to see the title, *The New Apocrypha* by R. Bartholomew, PhD, emblazoned across the front. Beneath this, a black notecard had been taped. In silver ink, and the same handwriting that had penned Maggie's address, it simply read:

*...from an old friend*

# 26

*a portent*

# 10 days before the end | Nov 1, 2011

Maggie slept. When she awoke, she decided not to open the book yet. Instead, she busied herself around the house, occupying her time with chores that had been neglected during the week. She turned on music, hummed as she distracted her mind with the mundane. Watched a rerun of a home renovation show.

Anything but face what was waiting for her to face.

Only when she felt the pull of the book stronger than the pull of literally everything else did Magdalena return to the couch with a coffee in one hand, the wooden box, book and kraft paper wrapper balanced in the other. As was her practice each day, she made a conscious effort to block out the rest of the world—if but for a few seconds—and exist only in this moment as she took the first sip of her sweet cream latte.

Denying the nervous energy beginning to drone behind her thoughts, she took one more sip before staring unblinking at what to most would seem an innocuous, if strangely niche, gift. While she would agree that it was oddly specific, if not bordering on downright academic, it felt anything but benign.

The heaviness welling in her stomach concurred with what her intuition had already begun to decipher: that far from being harmless, the book's arrival was a portent of something dark and unimaginably disturbing on the horizon.

She continued to stare, not moving, not blinking.

The book stared silently back. *Go ahead*, it smirked. *See who blinks first. I've got all day…*

"Fuck you, book."

She spoke it out loud, her voice at first cracking and sounding timid in the silence of the space.

*For God's sake, you're a seasoned detective, Romano! You used to eat bad guys for breakfast. What the hell are you so scared of?*

She spoke it again, louder. Angry that she'd allowed it to get so inside her head. "FUCK YOU, BOOK."

This time it was a shout. No, not even that. It was a *command*, assertive and strong. A mechanism to quash any trepidation before it could dig in, she'd employed this tactic for years. Just replace 'book' with whatever it is that's got you feeling cornered. But you have to believe it. And you have to channel that anxiety into anger. Forget everything you've ever heard the Jedi say. Anger is a great tool. It's hard to be frightened when you're angry.

*And when you're fearless, you're unstoppable.*

Brushing the kraft paper aside, she yanked the book onto her lap and all but slammed open the cover. A hundred pages or more fanned open with it, the momentum carrying them to a spot where a feather, so glossy black it was iridescent, had been tucked into the gutter between two pages.

*A raven's feather.*

Despite making every effort for it not to, the feather trembled noticeably in Maggie's grip as the light played over its surface. A thousand barbs, each as fine as baby's hair, shimmered purple, blue, violet, then radiant black once more. Beautiful and hypnotic, the hues washed over her in a way that was both comforting and unsettling as Maggie's mind now took her back to that place where her life—*everyone's life*—had changed forever…

It should have been just another muggy morning in the city. But on that particular one, Magdalena was in the hospital. Not for her own care, but for the care of two women with whom she had fashioned a strong and instant bond. Standing at the foot of a bulky bed covered with wires and sensors that made official-sounding noises, Maggie would taste that room's sterile odor for as long as she lived; see the stark blue-white illumination if she blinked hard enough.

It would not be until she was alone later that evening that Maggie would find the feather that had been secretly placed in her handbag. A black feather.

*A raven's feather.*

Touching it to her face, she had known instantly it was what Della had brushed so tenderly across her cheek, breaking the infinite loop of Maggie's prayer to the Holy Mother Mary.

She returned to the women that next morning, but there were no uniformed officers standing watch; the room itself empty and being prepped for its next patient.

While it might be cliché to admit it, Maggie had been overcome with a bolt of panic that something she couldn't bear to imagine had occurred overnight. Her relief had been palpable when the nurse so casually informed her that Rebecca had merely discharged herself. *Against their better advice*, the young man had added after a moment's hesitation. This he had accentuated with a small but clearly derogatory shake of his head—one of those 'poker tells' he had no realization he was doing—as he continued wiping down the gurney with a rancid disinfectant Maggie could not imagine anyone ever getting used to.

And so, with the nurse proffering nothing more, and with nothing else for Romano to ask, she had simply turned and left.

The book dropped to the floor as Maggie leapt from the couch, a cold tingle down her spine. Landing squarely on its covers spread wide, the hardcover remained open to the pages the feather had been used to identify.

She ran to Carlo's study and tore through stacks of books piled in the most disorderly fashion in and upon the bookcase in the corner. Stashed somewhere amongst these was an heirloom King James bible. Maggie hadn't read a page of it in five years—not since the night she had dreamt of being in the desert with Christ. That dream had divulged to her that the man at the makeshift camp outside the Cockerton residence on West 93rd Street—the man calling himself Simon Lepros—was, in fact, Greer Eliason. He was also the most likely perpetrator of the Clive Astor murder.

Given Astor's repugnant past, however, and the fact that Greer himself had essentially fallen off the face of the earth, the murder was duly assigned cold case designation and any new resources spent upon it were ceased.

Maggie found the bible tucked behind an old dictionary along with several other nonfiction books on Billy the Kid, Carlo's passion project on which he'd been formulating some rather intriguing theories. The King James was covered in distressed black leather with worn edges and faded dye on the corners. The spine had been creased almost to the point of breaking, the outcome of countless generations opening and closing, bending and dog-earing it each Sunday and every holiday for over a hundred years. Until, that is, it came into Maggie's possession.

There, the  tradition stopped dead in its tracks.

She brushed the dust from its cover and opened it to the teachings she had once honored with every fiber of her being, but could no longer bring herself to do so. Snugged away on a pair of random pages in the 'Book of Revelations' was a feather.

A black feather.

*The one from the hospital that same July.*

She held this feather in her left hand and compared it to the one in her right, the one she'd just found in the mystery book.

The two were nearly identical.

On the original feather, the finest markings lined up perfectly with those on the new one. Their lengths were the same. Their widths were the same. Even their bald quills were all but identical in size, shape and girth.

"Oh my God! This package was sent by *Della*…"

Unlike so many others these days, this observation Maggie spoke aloud. Like the sweet taste of honeysuckle to an adult after years of dismissing such uncomplicated joys, the name of her long-lost friend upon her lips was bliss. For she had never seen or heard from Rebecca or Della again.

*Until now…*

IV

Back on her couch and with her sweet cream latte going cold, it was hard to imagine that the last time she'd seen either woman had been six years ago. Nor could she wrap her head around the fact that she had never again experienced the comforting, inexplicable glow that had emanated from Rebecca Cockerton. Some called this the aura of the soul. Others, the spiritual energy. Whatever you labeled it, it had been as clear and welcoming to Magdalena Romano as a fireside's warm glow. This energy was all the more glorious given the fact that Rebecca had endured unimaginable suffering at the hands of her own brother-in-law. Tortures commanded by the woman's very own son.

Maggie forced herself to repeat that last thought. Because it was beyond her comprehension that a child, a nine-year-old no less, could orchestrate the sadistic mindfucks Simon Peter had.

And yet, six years on, the sixteen-year-old was revered by far more of the world than he was reviled.

*Simon Peter, the one true Prophet, come to make us whole again.*

*Simon Peter, come to restore our bodies and cleanse our souls.*

*Simon Peter, who will lead us to all we ever wanted...if we but denounce the false god we have proclaimed for millennia and follow Him, our new savior, from this, our misguided path on which we tread.*

Creating an immortal deity from a mere boy took far less than you might think. A perceived miracle on live TV. A reprobate proclaiming his born-again status. A small core of individuals whose vulnerability and desperation made them only too eager to declare their loyalty.

And that was all she wrote.

Soon, this small core of followers had become an assembly. The assembly, a multitude. The multitude, a crowd. The crowd, a throng. The throng, a horde.

*The horde, a flock.*

And the flock did not see the forsaken and persecuted sibling Simon Peter had nailed to a cross of cathedral timbers. They did not witness the mother with the glow of a saint whose unborn baby boy had been ripped from her womb...by the baby's own father and the only man left on earth who still shared the DNA of Rebecca's deceased husband. They did not see the innocence of a boy so cruelly beguiled to his barbaric death from a fifth-floor window on a bitter Thanksgiving night.

All the flock saw, all they had ever seen, was the cage of their own misery. And here had come an answer, sent to make everything that was wrong about their world right again; a boy who was a fisher of men, casting his golden line of promise into a sea of self-absorbed misery.

And the whole world had taken the bait.

*Hook, line, and sinker...*

# 27

*the compound*

# 1 year, 11 days before the end | 2010

THE CHURCH OF The New Apocrypha was the fastest growing spiritual doctrine in human history. In just five years, New Apocryphals outnumbered Jews by forty to one worldwide, while converts from Christianity knocked the single largest religious demographic in the world to second place behind Islam. With an estimated six hundred million followers, this also meant that Simon Peter, now fifteen years old, had more devotees than there were people in the United States.

Almost double.

June 27th, 2005, was the day the world witnessed Simon Peter resurrect a dead man on live TV. In just four weeks' time, over ten million people from all around the globe had donated to the newly formed church. By the end of July, Ian Cockerton was able to announce their imminent move from the Upper West Side streets of Manhattan's Central Park to a permanent, custom-built campus out of state.

In the twenty-eight years following the summer of '77, the community that was once the Cockerton family's idyllic Pennsylvania home had become known as the Cursed Neighborhood by all in the region. As a consequence, all other families who lived there were either unable to sell and essentially held to ransom by the place they had once so loved, or had simply abandoned their properties and walked away.

The latter were left to fall into disrepair as the ravages of Pennsylvania winters froze pipes and cracked roof shingles. While the blazing P.A. summers nurtured mold and rot in moist, airless houses. The result was a median property value that consistently and significantly lagged behind both national and area averages.

*For decades...*

It therefore took less than two percent of the church's tax-free donations acquired in that very first month to purchase each and every one of the thirty houses in the old neighborhood.

Most were more than eager to sell, and several would have taken far less than they were offered. Another ten million dollars purchased the woodland itself, at the edge of which the neighborhood was nestled. As the Little Woods was becoming known by more and more people throughout the world, Simon Peter officially declared it the holiest of places for New Apocryphals.

He broke ground on the Church's new campus in the woods by the end of August that same year. The breathtaking steel and glass cathedral known as the Mother Church, as well as his own residences, were erected in the enclave where the Father Oak had once stretched its vast limbs. The carved tree stump on which Bryan Cockerton and Jack Raker had once stood as they engaged in team selection for their annual game of War, was now consecrated ground. The altar of the Mother Church was designed in a way to be built around the stump without having to move or disrupt it...and the stump itself was now a pivotal aspect of the church's most sacred of services.

The neighborhood and the homes therein were for the use of the Church Elders and the support staff it took to run the sprawling campus. Around the thirteen thousand linear foot perimeter of the campus, a ten foot fence had been erected. On this, thirty-three individuals Simon Peter called Watchers would walk its circuit day and night to secure the wellbeing of everyone living on, or visiting, the campus.

In 2007, two years after Simon's live television resurrection of Antoine J. Washington, June 27th was announced as an official government and national holiday known as Novus *(Latin: 'revival')* in the U.S., Canada, Mexico, Australia, the United Kingdom, and seven countries of the European Union. In reality, Novus was celebrated by many more than the six hundred million New Apocryphals, as this count was only that of followers who claimed the church as their official religion on formal documents or by verified, tax-deductible donations. Unofficially, hundreds of millions more leaned toward the church's popular, humanist-driven doctrine, and so Novus was, in many ways, becoming even more popular than Christmas.

While Simon Peter openly acknowledged Christ's existence and enlightenment, the worship of him as the Son of God was denounced. Indeed, it wasn't long before the life and teachings of Jesus would become seamlessly integrated into the new Church's doctrine. Though declaring him mortal, Simon Peter would ultimately go so far as to call Christ one of the first New Apocryphals. In the boy's own words, Jesus was a trail blazing prophet, come to set the stage for himself, the one true Savior who, two thousand years later, would set free a beleaguered people and thereby lead them to final Redemption.

Any celebration of Halloween was entirely dismissed, however, as All Hallows Eve stems from the Roman Catholic observance of All Saints Day on November 1st. With all traditional forms of Christianity and Judaism fast becoming reviled for their pagan worship of a false deity which had subjugated Man for far too long, any holiday connected to the honoring of those who had been 'sainted' by the Catholic heretics had no place on the calendar of a *true* New Apocryphal.

As the top-ranking Cardinal in the new church, Ian Cockerton could have commissioned the construction of the second-finest residence. Instead, he chose his childhood home in the sector of the campus which had once been the old neighborhood.

Simon Peter strolled through the modest 1970s split-level ranch house for the first time in four years. Not since the completion of his estate in the style of a *palazzo* of the Augustan Empire, replete with three-story fluted columns and arches of marble, had the teenager graced with his presence the former home of his mother, uncle and half-sister.

He swiped a finger across the top of the television, a meandering path of flat black plastic trailing through the dust. "You need Facilities to come on at least a weekly basis, Ian. They go through mine *daily*. From reliquary to rafters."

"I really don't need them, I'm fine handling it on my own."

The fifteen-year-old shot him the cynic's side eye.

Ian ignored it.

"It's not demeaning to them, you know. It's an honor. For the facility pigs, I mean."

"I wish you wouldn't call them that."

"What would you have me call them, then, Uncle?"

"How about, 'people.' Or, 'individuals.' Or," here Ian shook his head, "at the very least, 'staff.' How about any one of those?"

Simon Peter shrugged, already deaf to the advice in favor of thoughts of his own next statement. "And the stress relief? I trust it's satisfying your needs. After all, the role of the Archcardinal in the Church of my father is a demanding one. You deserve some down time. With everything your heart desires at your beck and call, I will always expect your service to me, and thereby to our Father, to be your best."

It did not escape Simon Peter's attention that the two women getting dressed in the next room were an athletically-built woman with flowing strawberry-blonde hair, and a light-skinned African American with short hair and green eyes so pale they were almost grey.

He *tsked*. Breathed in. Let it out in a long, dramatic exhalation of disappointment.

"You really are *so* predictable, Uncle. Out of anyone in the world, these cheap dollar-store knockoffs of my whore of a mother and the Voodoo bitch are what you choose?" He observed their age. Late thirties. Maybe early forties. "And by the way, you know that age is no limit. You can have something with a nice tight engine that hasn't been broken in yet. You don't have to settle for these old secondhand cruisers."

Ian did know, and it made him sick to even hear the offer put so casually. As if what Simon Peter was offering were just another option on a menu. Like avocado toast instead of English muffins at your favorite breakfast joint. "Didn't you reward Greer Eliason to eliminate Clive Astor for that sick fuck's past indulgences in the very same?"

Simon Peter snorted with derisive laughter. "Oh my, Uncle. Aren't you the paladin in shining armor... Perhaps I shall instruct the parishioners to no longer address you as Archcardinal, but rather, 'Ian the Pure' from here on out."

Simon Peter lingered in the doorway as the woman with the strawberry-blonde hair began to dress. Noticing the spiritual leader watching her, she hesitated. Cast him a bashful glance. Then continued to get dressed...but turning to face him while she did so, softening her movements to a lithe and provocative dance.

"I gave the lemmings what they wanted." Simon Peter barely looked at Ian, his focus held by the woman. "Greer and Clive, I mean, that day in front of the apartment building. The throng needed an obvious antagonist. And an obvious protagonist to reap the rewards of my Father's grace. Did you really ever doubt it was any more than that?"

The thought made Ian feel sick in his stomach. He said nothing. Instead, he yanked the door to the bedroom closed, leaving the fifteen-year-old and he alone in the narrow upstairs hallway with the muted giggles of the two women clearly audible through the cheap wood laminate.

"You really are a buzz-kill, sometimes, Ian. Why my Father allowed you to tag along is entirely lost on me. Speaking of which, is there any news of my miraculous half-sister?"

"I'm working on it."

"It's been five years—more, actually—since she thought she'd be a clever clogs with that whole carpenter boy act. Thankfully, she had no audience. 'Cause, as we know, if you want a starving dog to follow you, just give it a whiff of a nice bloody steak. It'll walk into traffic for even the chance of a nibble. To the weak-minded dogs you all are, her little stunt may have seemed like USDA Prime. I'm sure she thought it was good."

"Wasn't it?"

"Ha! To me, it was canner grade chum, at best. Remember, I was at the O.G. And while I couldn't stand the guy, you had to hand it to him—what he endured was pretty fucking impressive. And through it all, he never once recanted his whole 'Son of God' act. Gotta give him that much, at least."

"Maybe that's because he really was."

Simon Peter scrunched his face, clenched his fists below arms held rigidly at his sides. The skin across his face rippled, the boy's countenance appearing as if he were under water.

"Take that back, Ian!" he shouted, his voice filled with the schoolyard fury of a child who has just been called a 'poopy pants.' "Take that back right NOW."

The voice was no longer a child's. No longer even human.

Shrieking as the door to the bedroom flew open, the two half-clad women reflexively covered themselves. They dropped their hands, giggling with relief when they saw it was the boy prophet and his Archcardinal at the threshold.

Simon Peter said nothing, merely sweeping his hand from one woman toward the other. Without hesitation, the Rebecca lookalike obediently but unconsciously threw Della's double onto the bed, tearing the panties from her pelvis. She buried her face into the woman's groin and Della's double overcame her initial shock to arch her back in pleasure. Throwing back her head with laughter, she butterflied her legs wide as mirth became moans.

The Rebecca lookalike lapped at her furiously. Insatiable, she pressed harder, faster.

"*Hey, easy—*" Della's double whispered, wincing with mild discomfort but not wanting to displease her Savior.

Now Simon Peter flexed his fingers to take on the shape of a mouth full of teeth. He opened and closed his fist, faster and faster, and the Rebecca burrowed into the Della's groin in rhythm.

"Hey, I said take it easy," the Della demanded now, no longer concerned whether the boy prophet and Archcardinal heard. She grabbed the woman's head and tried to push her away. Not only did the Rebecca not budge, she clamped on even tighter.

And began biting.

"OWW! Godddamnit! Get off me!"

Harder. Faster. Deeper. Gnawing.

Specks of red began to dapple the Rebecca's face.

Ian stepped into the doorway. "Simon, that's enough!"

"Then take it back," Simon Peter rasped in a voice resonant and layered with dissonance.

"Just stop it, Simon!"

The Della screamed, striking and twisting with manic fear, stripping great clumps of hair from the Rebecca's scalp as the woman's face was painted thick with the Della's blood.

Unrelenting, and now with the bestial cackle of a hyena, the Rebecca pinned and ripped and tore at her prey until the Della's screams merged into an inhuman wail of pain.

"I take it back, I take it back, I take it back! Now stop!" Ian ran toward the women but was halted mid-step, his feet locked in place. Just feet away, the smell of wet rust filled his nostrils and he had to look away, retching.

Simon Peter waited a moment more before bringing his show to an end. Opening his hand, the fingers that had mimicked teeth were splayed wide as he waved the Rebecca off her victim.

She pulled herself from Della's pelvis, kneeling upon the bed in confusion and horror as the Della shrieked and the blood sprayed and poured. The Rebecca vomited.

Then Simon Peter brought both hands together. A conductor readying his orchestra for their first uniform note, he swung his arms in the upward sweeping motion of a percussionist crashing together his two cymbals.

Both women were flung into the air.

Their heads slammed into one another, skulls depressing before they fell lifeless to the blood-saturated sheets.

"The witch lookalike was gonna die anyway," he informed Ian with no emotion as he released the man's frozen feet. "And the other one? She'll have wanted to die after this. Trust me. I did the whore a favor."

Simon Peter turned to walk away.

"Oh, and Ian? You're right. He probably was..."

Ian had nothing to say to this as the fifteen-year-old hopped down the half-story steps to the formal living room Veronica Cockerton had never allowed him or Bryan as young boys.

Turning the corner, the prophet shouted over his shoulder: "Have Facilities clean up that mess. Unless you're fine handling it on your own, as you say." Now out of sight, he bellowed up the stairs, "And find me that Counterfeit Christ of a half-sister. Now!"

"I'm getting closer," is all Ian could reply as his gut emptied.

Before the Church's sprawling Pennsylvania campus ever existed, even before it announced its planned relocation from the street congregations growing outside his Upper West Side apartment, Ian Cockerton was arrested.

Miraculously, Diane Cockerton may not be dead after all, but Clive Astor sure as shit was. And Magdalena Romano wasn't prepared to sit idly by as the elders of the new 'church' not only stood above the law but flaunted their seemingly untouchable status.

Unfortunately for Maggie, the suspect at the top of their list, Greer Eliason, had gone AWOL. And with no evidence of any other individual's participation in the murder, and with no member of the congregation willing to speak out against Simon Peter or the Elders, the only way to get Ian Cockerton off the street and in her interview room was the enforcement of New York City Penal Code 240.10.

"You don't have to answer my questions, Ian. But it sure will help you in the long run if you do."

Ian scoffed, pushing aside the crime scene photos of Clive Astor's body drained of blood inside his tent. "In the long run? This is a joke, right? You mean, if I do hard time for Unlawful Assembly? That's what Code 240.10 is. Isn't it, Detective?"

He smirked, crossing his arms and settling back in his chair.

"And if we're going to chat awhile, perhaps I'll be more forthright with information if the coffee you offered was even one step above this crusty percolator sludge. How about a nice Starbucks?" Here he locked onto Maggie's eyes. "A nice sweet cream latte for us both, perhaps...?"

Magdalena bristled.

*How the fuck could he know that?*

Internally, she felt the threatening rise of panic. Externally, her stare hardened.

After a long silence in which she felt every grueling beat of her heart, Ian simply grinned.

"I'm sure it was just a lucky guess, Maggie."

"It's Detective Romano to you…" she was ready to put a period on that sentence. But then found herself adding, "…asshole."

Ian nodded with a twisting grimace.

"Sure thing. But, if you don't mind a little constructive criticism, you really could do with polishing up your interviewing skillset, *Detective Romano*. Didn't your mama ever tell you? You get more bees with honey than you do with vinegar."

"And didn't yours ever teach you about common decency? That's a man who's been drained of just about every ounce of blood that was in his body." She tapped the photos spilling from the folder on the table. "I'm merely asking for your help. After all, this occurred in your so-called congregation. And essentially on the steps of your very own apartment building. And yet, you apparently could care less."

"I think you mean to say, I *couldn't* care less. Because I do care. I care a lot. I think it's awful. I think it's sad. I think it's gruesome."

He paused once more.

"I also think it's deserved. You do know what Clive Astor was, don't you, Detective?"

Magdalena crossed her arms. Leaned against the wall. Mindful not to avert her eyes from his stare. Not even for a split-second.

Ian shifted in his seat. "And we both know you didn't really drag me here for help, or to slap a pathetic Class B Misdemeanor charge on me. You want to intimidate me."

Yes, she knew it was a long shot. But hey, they nailed Al Capone for tax evasion, didn't they? Got him behind bars for *something*. So, at this stage, anything was better than doing nothing. It was at least worth a shot. And surprisingly, Unlawful Assembly was punishable by up to three months in jail and a fine of up to $500.

If Magdalena could separate the man from his creepy-ass son, nephew, or whatever-the-fuck the Simon kid was, for even a week or two, perhaps that would buy enough time for something to come to light.

*Or a mistake to be made.*

After all, it wasn't just Clive Astor. Antoine J. Washington was now missing, too. And though Diane Cockerton was not dead, the atrocities perpetrated upon her would carry a life sentence. Not only for Ian, but for several in the top tier of the new church. Essentially, they could shut it down before it had the chance to gain any more traction…if they could only find the Cockerton girl.

Ian sat upright. He plucked the wallet from his jeans pocket and whipped out six one-hundred-dollar bills.

"There you go, Detective. That'll cover the fine. With an extra hundo in it for you." He winked as Benjamin Franklin's grinning visages spun across the table. "You know, for your troubles 'n all."

Maggie punched him in the face.

IV

While Ian Cockerton walked out of the police station, it was Maggie Romano who was detained in another interview room on the grounds of Second Degree Assault. It was a sentence that, if found guilty by a jury of her peers, came with two to seven years in prison. And of course, the striping of her badge.

The Manhattan District Attorney's office convinced Mr. Cockerton to drop any charges against Detective Romano and they, in turn, would do the same. Bribery of a New York City Public Servant, Penal Code 200.04, came with a sentence of one to three years in prison. If Ian agreed, they'd basically offset the 'infractions.' No harm. No foul.

He agreed. As long as Maggie attended mandated counseling.

# V

That was five years ago.

As the Archcardinal now sat upon his bed in the room that had been his as a child, he thought about Magdalena. To his mind, it wasn't likely that the detective would just walk away from the truth as she knew it to be.

In Ian's experience, you could separate the woman from the mystery, but not the mystery from the woman.

And hadn't Della proven that point, so many years ago? A complete stranger, she had been led to Bryan and him—and the Little Woods—all the way from New Orleans.

*...I'm from a place called N'awlinz, sugar.* He could hear her round, lilting voice to this day. As clearly as the first time he ever had, fifteen years ago. And it was still as captivating as it was then. *Don't know any place by the name NEW or-LEANS...*

Her entire life to that point had been a series of choices that would make the intersection of their lives happen. Whether of her own free will, or fate in the guise of it, none had known it at the time, but now they all understood why. A threat who could have been a powerful ally, she had then been hunted by the Shadows. Blinded by Ian and hidden away, to a place where they would not feel her energy pinging like radar. And still, she had found her way back to Diane a decade later, the two gravitating to one another on the streets of New York as if nothing could keep them apart. She had led the Church of the New Apocrypha to his niece, that much was true. But in doing so, what they hadn't foreseen was that Della had also set in motion Diane's transformation from disarmed dissident to malefic martyr.

To destroy everything, all it would take was an audience.

*And Diane figuring that out was just a matter of time.*

The way he figured it, which he now understood is what Simon Peter had recognized all along, was that the first to get to her, won.

That simple.

And if he couldn't find Della, or count on her even if he did, then Ian would have to get to Diane through someone else.

*Through Magdalena Romano.*

And that would start with breaking her down. Destroying all she held dear. Starving her. Then dangling a nice bloody steak in front of her as she walked willingly into traffic for the chance of just a nibble.

So it was that on this particular Halloween, 2010, Ian sent the Shadows for her beloved Carlo.

After that, he'd steal what little would remain of her stability.

Dropped or not, after the criminal charges five years ago, it wouldn't take much more in the way of dwindling dependability for the department to prefer that Magdalena simply, and quietly, tender her resignation.

With no husband—whom she adored more than anything in her world—and then no career, Ian would yank out from beneath her all that Maggie believed herself to fundamentally be. Her isolation and vulnerability would be complete.

Magdalena would then be ripe for the picking.

*Forbidden fruit that would lead him to Diane...*

# 28

*back in the saddle*

## 4 days before the end | Nov 7, 2011

**M**aggie had been poring over the hardcover for days, finding it challenging to take it all in. Not only was it written at an academic level for a scholastic demographic, but what was being theorized was a mix of ideas so far-fetched that unrealistic was a serious understatement.

And yet, somehow, Bartholomew's ideas also seemed so painfully obvious at the same time.

*If you believed in the whole Heaven and Hell thing, that is.*

And if what happened to Diane was a legitimate miracle as opposed to some freakish biological anomaly, well, then Maggie was about to jump off the fence she'd been straddling for a very, very long time.

"What most people don't understand," Bartholomew wrote, "is that it was not Satan who placed the demons among us...but God. He did this when He banished all Watchers to remain forever earthbound. And so, we find the following overlap between the Book of Enoch and the Book of Revelation provides the key to our terrifying and fateful new reality. And that reality is this: that the demise of Mankind comes not by the hand of Satan...but by the hand of God Himself."

What Maggie couldn't understand was why no one else besides this R. Bartholomew guy had connected the dots before now? His theory was that the Watchers in the ancient Hebrew Book of Enoch were sent to earth by God, their role to watch over and protect God's greatest creation, Mankind. Their leader, known as Azazel, was beautiful and filled with Light, but became envious of God's love for Man, believing that this love now eclipsed His love for the angelic Watchers.

Maggie continued reading what Bartholomew had to say about unholy dissonance and treachery. A rebellion, the result of which caused the Watchers to be banished from Heaven to reside forever on earth. But they were now split into two factions: the Shadows (the fallen ones) and the Shadow Watchers (the minority who defied Azazel and still pledged their unerring love and loyalty to God).

Humans were subsequently corrupted by the Shadows to learn of hate and how to covet and wage wars. And when the Shadows propagated with humans to create their own perverse offspring known as Nephilim, this was Azazel's ultimate slap in God's face: a creation of beings that were neither angel nor human but caught somewhere in between.

The text continued to share Bartholomew's hypothesis that the seven-headed Beast foretold by Saint John in the Book of Revelation, and the archdemon Azazel, leader of the Watchers according to the Hebrew Books of Enoch, are in fact one in the same Presence of Evil. Long ago banished by archangel Gabriel to its place in the wilderness, upon the Day of Judgment the archdemon shall be unleashed with his army of Shadows. Per God's holy plan, they will no longer be governed by the Shadow Watchers. Free to mock the seven archangels by feeding upon seven innocents, the Shadows will then fulfill all prophecy by propagating the most perverse Nephala of all...

...the Dragon Lamb of Satan.

"The most critical mistake of Mankind is to view the Book of Enoch in terms of an ancient and irrelevant past," Bartholomew cautioned. "And the Book of Revelation as an absurdly surreal prediction of the future. For in terms of pure mathematics, when negative one and positive one (past and future) are offset, they cancel out one another. What we are left with is then the present day. Make no mistake, God's strategy for the end of days is already underway, and will have begun in the least likely of places. It will come to fruition when a new prophet comes in the guise of an innocent, an archdemon cloaked in the embodiment of a child."

This part in particular Maggie had read numerous times for three days straight, and it sent shivers down her spine each time.

*A new prophet… in the guise of a child.*

To Maggie, Simon Peter had always been a sick soul. But a soul, nonetheless. A desperate soul in need of help.

Now she feared she had never been more wrong in her life.

*If you're going to believe this whole R. Bartholomew schtick,* a clinging inner voice of doubt insisted.

And if she were truly honest with herself, Maggie would admit that she hadn't yet made up her mind, one way or the other. One minute it seemed like a bunch of hooey. The next, the most sane thing she'd ever heard.

Ultimately, what her spiritual brain and logical brain could agree upon was that it wasn't important whether or not Maggie believed any of it. But whether the rest of the world did…

II

She was on her third coffee of the morning when she spotted it.

*The underlined words.*

She'd seen them throughout more than three hundred pages of text, information Della had found pertinent and subsequently underlined with a pen. But what Maggie noticed today was that most of these were in red.

*Most.*

Of the hundreds of passages underlined throughout the text, a very few exceptions were underlined in black. Moreover, the markings appeared to be in the same smooth-inked pen with which Maggie's name and address had been handwritten on the package's wrapper.

She nuked her coffee, readied for the long haul, and opened the hardcover to the beginning. Page by page, she meticulously scanned its pages for the excerpts underlined in black only. Each one she found, Maggie saved by taking a picture with her phone's camera.

After a good hour, Magdalena opened her photo gallery and started reading the lines in each of the seven photos she'd taken:

1 ...carloads of documents...

2 ...Nadab slain by his own...

3 ...the Hebrew church a millennium before Christ...

4 ...those manuscripts, written of the Apocrypha by Enoch...

5 ... consider the repercussions one must ...

6 ...that each one correlates to find the others...

7 ...Acts 19:27, of the great goddess Diana to be despised...

She read them over and again, swiping from one frame to the next so many times that every picture swam into each of the others. Meanwhile, none of them made much sense to her at all. What she had hoped for was a clear indicator that her instinct had been right—that there was meaning to the difference in underlining color.

Of course, there was always the possibility Della had simply grabbed different colored pens as she read Bartholomew's book. But Maggie didn't really believe that. Otherwise, what was the point of Della sending it? No other message had accompanied it. No explanation for its arrival. There had to be a message hidden in there. Somewhere. Maggie was sure of it. She just needed to get her detective's brain back in gear after such a long hiatus of mindless television and even more mindless social media.

She looked over the seven excerpts again and began dissecting their meaning. 'Carloads of documents could be referring to just about anything. There was nothing else to find in that passage as far as she could determine.

Maggie then googled King Nadab. His father had been King Jeroboam, chosen by God to lead Israel after King Solomon reverted to worshipping false deities in order to appease his many wives. In return for Jeroboam's loyalty, God promised the new king the world.

*Kings 11:38: 'By obeying my decrees and commands, I will build you a dynasty as enduring as David's, and I will give Israel to you.'*

But turning away from God, Nadab's father only led Israel deeper into the wilderness. When Nadab then inherited the throne, instead of making his father's wrongs right, he continued to walk in his wicked footsteps. As a result, Nadab effected his own assassination.

The third passage Della had underlined wasn't even a complete thought, giving Maggie nothing to explore.

The fourth Maggie believed she already had a pretty good understanding of, having read Bartholomew's book from cover to cover over the past week. Essentially the Apocrypha were teachings not condoned for inclusion in the formally accepted Scriptures. Of these, Enoch's books foretold of a fallen angel, Azazel, and the division of his Watchers into two factions of Dark versus Light.

The fifth and sixth passages were incomplete sentences and did not even offer a subject that could be researched.

Number seven, however, Maggie was able to look up in her leatherbound King James bible: 'The temple of the great goddess Diana should be despised, and her magnificence destroyed whom all Asia and the world worship.'

Apparently, the goddess Diana was also worshipped by the Greeks in the form of Artemis. To the Ephesians (those residing in Ephesus, in the modern-day country we now call Turkey) Diana was a queen of heaven, a deity of fertility and the protector of childbearing...although she herself was a virgin. Her elaborate temple in Ephesus was considered one of the Seven Wonders of the Ancient World.

Was Della trying to warn her about Diane in some way?

If so, her cipher was so oblique it was going right over Magdalena's head. In which case, what could it all mean?

Scrounging through Carlo's desk drawer, Maggie found a pad of paper on which she began writing out the underlined passages, word-for-word, in one long run-on sentence. She wanted to see how they sounded when she read them all together:

*carloads of documents...Nadab slain by his own...early Israelites, the church a millennia before Christ...those manuscripts, written of the Apocrypha by Enoch...consider the repercussions one must...that each one correlates to find the others...Acts 19:27, 'of the great goddess Diana to be despised'*

While it wasn't especially smooth, more than ever Magdalena now believed a meaning was buried in there somewhere. She began rewording it, scribbling frantically on her pad, stream-of-consciousness style.

*FIRST:*
*Carloads of documents could mean proof. Lots of proof.*

*SECOND & THIRD:*
*Nadab was a bad guy from another bad guy. He was also the third ruler in a row to disappoint God by turning away from the Father. Della's third underlined passage then correctly links with this second one, in that Nadab's rule was, in fact, nearly a thousand years before Christ.*

To Maggie, this wasn't as much a part of the hidden message as it was intended as a validation from Della to let the retired detective know she was on the right track.

*In that case, is this really a comment on Simon Peter: A bad guy from a bad guy? If so, there are plenty of bad guys—and just as many slayings—mentioned in the bible, in both the Old Testament and the New. So the reference to Nadab and the fact that he was the 'third' in a row to disappoint God must be important!*

*FOURTH, FIFTH & SIXTH:*
*The Apocryphal Books of Enoch mention Azazel and the Watchers and that there will be consequences. Will these spur on others, like dominoes falling? Or maybe she means these repercussions will lead to a trail of new clues—once you find the first, more will be revealed?*

*SEVENTH: The acts of Diane are/will be despised.*

Having 'translated' the seven, Maggie crudely linked all of her thoughts together by writing her own plain-English paragraph:

*There's proof aplenty that Simon Peter is a bad guy, perhaps three degrees from God? Enoch's books on Azazel and the Watchers will expose repercussions, consequences, or clues, many we don't even know yet. And in some way related to all of this, Diane will ultimately be despised.*
*…But by whom…?*

III

Not only did the passages underlined in black all link together, but once the semantics were modernized, they did so in a way that very much felt like they were starting to make sense.

If this were coincidence, the odds were astoundingly slim. She immediately dismissed this for the Imposter Syndrome it was. Magdalena had been a detective, and a damn good one. Della knew this. She had counted on Maggie to spot the patterns—or the disparity in them—to not only *find* her message but to possess the skillset to be able to *decipher* it.

Above all, the fact that Della had gone to such lengths to hide information she could have easily provided in a myriad of other ways told Maggie this message was something Della wanted to be very careful about sharing only with her. And in a way that was least likely to be spotted by others.

It now made complete sense why Della had omitted her name and address from the parcel. And this, in turn, made Maggie ponder the ink of the postmarks which had all been smudged in transit.

*So odd, that they'd all been smeared beyond legibility.*

She rushed to the recycling bin, never in her life more relieved to have (once again) forgotten that yesterday was Saturday. Carlo had always been the one who put out the bins. And in all the ways Maggie had adapted after her husband's death, this was one of her most lingering frustrations.

After pealing some mozzarella from the kraft paper—

*See? What's a pizza box even doing in the recycling bin?* She reprimanded herself. *Carlo was forever reminding her that food polluted all the other paper, making them unrecyclable.*

—she laid the wrapper on the dining table and smoothed away the wrinkles, breathing a sigh of relief that the cheese oil had saturated the paper only where there were no markings.

Investigating the postal marks much more closely, she began taking pictures with her phone, pinching the images wide until they were as large as she could make them.

And there was her answer.

They weren't postmarks at all, but black marker smudged to appear as if they were. Della's package had never been posted.

Which meant it had to have been delivered in person.

Maggie's legs weakened.

There was now zero doubt that the patterns she was finding were intentional. Her heart raced as she analyzed the stamps, flipping feverishly through the pages of the hardcover book, fingers trembling.

*C'mon, c'mon, c'mon, I know I saw it in here somewhere…!*

She was looking again for the one page on which Della had circled not just a few of the passages, but the entire page.

*In black ink.*

Other than an interesting observation, it meant nothing to her when she'd first read it. Now, it took on an entirely new meaning.

After three passes through the book in each direction, she found it:

*… God holds a book in his right hand which is the start of the* SEVEN *year tribulation that will be the end of days. It is a scroll with* SEVEN *sacred seals that can only be opened by the Lamb who, 'had been slain, having* SEVEN *horns and* SEVEN *eyes, which are the* SEVEN *spirits of God sent forth to all the earth.*

*When the final of these seals is broken,* SEVEN *trumpeting angels shall herald destruction upon the earth. Upon the sounding of the final trumpet, Satan shall make war with the saints but be cast from Heaven, whence he shall summon the Beast at his right hand to deceive all the earth to worship him.*

*We are then warned in chapters twelve and thirteen: 'For I saw a beast rise up, having* SEVEN *Heads. Upon each was the name of blasphemy. And its feet were as the feet of a bear. And the devil gave it his power, and his seat, and his great authority…*

At the bottom of this, Della had scribbled two things which also had no particular meaning to Maggie at the time.

The first was the name of a place: *the Little Woods*.

The second was a year: '77.

Beginning to shake as adrenaline coursed through her, Maggie counted the number of stamps.

SEVEN.

She also noticed that each was worth a dollar. Had the package been mailed (as it was made to appear) rather than delivered by hand, the book would have classified as media mail and cost far less than seven dollars to send.

More than the stamps being added to the package as part of its camouflage, they must be an integral part of Della's message...

IV

A long-neglected steam iron tucked away at the back of Maggie's closet softened the stamps' adhesive. She peeled them from the kraft paper with great care...and revealed a faintly written letter on the paper beneath each of the seven.

C  A  S  I  M  I  R

*Was it an anagram—a word jumbled to avoid detection?*

After numerous attempts, the only word Maggie could make by rearranging *most* of the letters was 'RACISM.' While this was a matter of relevance at any time, she didn't feel it was pertinent to Della's specific message.

She mentally chewed on the anagram until it became a blur of letters, questioning what meaning it could possibly have. Then it came to her: Casimir wasn't a word at all.

*It was a name.*

In a flash she remembered seeing it a day or two earlier in

Bartholomew's book.

*Such an unusual last name. Very eastern European.*

Again, she flipped madly through the hardcover but found nothing. She returned to the table of contents, only to find nothing there, either. As a last resort, she scoured the appendices.

The third page of credits was dedicated to the images the publisher had reproduced amongst Bartholomew's text. One in particular had thanked a Catholic Church for their permission to use a black and white image of a fifteenth century Lithuanian Prince. A prince by the name *Casimir*. According to the painting's caption, the prince had been canonized in the First Roman Martyrology in 1583 and was now officially *Saint* Casimir.

What was most interesting was the fact that the painting had been lent to the publisher not by any church, but by Saint Casimer's Lithuanian Roman Catholic Church.

*In Pittsburgh, Pennsylvania.*

Now, Magdalena summarized what had become a two-part message from Della. She did this in bullet points scribbled beneath her previous plain-English translation:

- *Simon Peter is not the savior the world thinks him to be;*
- *He has something to do with Enoch's demonic prophecies;*
- *There will be consequences, including many unknown;*
- *Diane will also be despised, but by whom is uncertain;*
- *Saint Casimir's Lithuanian Roman Catholic Church;*
- *Pittsburgh, PA*

She was so close to the complete message, a wave of energy rushed through her. It may have been the adrenaline of being back in the detective's saddle, as it were. But it felt like something more to Maggie than mere anticipation alone.

It felt like a connectedness. It felt like her friend were actually here, with her.

There was still something missing, though. Maggie had found and decoded two components of the message. But didn't things so often come in threes? And wasn't three also a spiritual number? Bartholomew had mentioned it several times, comparing the coming of the Dragon Lamb of Satan to the coming of Christ.

*"The Holy trinity was Father, Son and Holy Ghost. The unholy trinity was a mockery of the same."*

There must be a third and final part of the message.

Out of hundreds of pages, Della's message was based upon just seven underlined passages. So again Maggie read these, this time looking at them not from a grammatical perspective, as she had already done, but from a numerical one.

Apophenia, or the natural human tendency to spot patterns or meanings in unrelated pieces of information, was a highly evolved instinct for Maggie, more developed than most. Throughout a career of evaluating evidence, if there had ever been a truth hiding beneath layers of the obvious, Maggie was the cop to find it.

She now stared at the seven passages she'd first written down, those which she had scribed exactly as they had been underlined, with none of her subjective translations to tarnish them.

Reading them over and over, they steadily lost all meaning until, ultimately, what Maggie saw was no longer the words constructed by the individual letters of the alphabet, but merely the characters themselves and the way the passages flowed geometrically.

She had taught this technique to rookies from time to time, only if she deemed them worth the effort.

"Have you ever repeated a word over and over so many times that it begins to lose its meaning and become nothing but a sound?" she asked them. "It's like that. Or, like those magic eye puzzles where you never see the real image hidden within the abstracts until you relax your mind…and your eyes. Then *bingo*, suddenly it appears."

She did this now, allowing the lines to become fuzzy, wavering, no longer seven strings of sentences but seven patterns merging into one flowing, oscillating shape.

*Seven patterns.*

*Numerology.*

*Three.*

*Three degrees from God.*

*Numbers.*

*Patterns.*

*Numbers.*

And there it was! The key now rose in her mind as clearly as a submerged ball rises in a pool.

*The seventh word.*

*In the seventh passage.*

The one word which held the most meaning. It couldn't be mere coincidence that its number in the excerpt matched the number of the excerpt itself.

For that word was 'Diana.'

Maggie pressed her shaking hands to her temples, trying to still the frantic thoughts racing through her mind as she hurriedly highlighted each word corresponding to the number of the passage it comprised—the first word in the first passage, the second word in the second passage...

1...**CARLOADS** of documents...

2...Nadab **SLAIN** by his own...

3...the Hebrew **CHURCH** a millennia before Christ...

4...manuscripts of the **APOCRYPHA** by Enoch...

5... consider the repercussions one **MUST**...

6...that each one correlates to **FIND** the others...

7...Acts 19:27, of the great goddess **DIANA** to be despised...

**"Carloads slain** by **church** of the **Apocrypha. Must find Diana."**

But had Della really meant 'carloads,' meaning a bunch? When Maggie focused on that word, specifically its first five letters, she discovered that what Della was really saying to her was…

*…CARLO.*

Magdalena's breath vacuumed from her chest as she stumbled from the papers scattered across the dining room table. For over a year she had been plagued by nightmares she could not understand. Gruesome and debilitating terrors where Carlo's death was not an accident. Where his life, and that of the other driver, were not curtailed as a consequence of Carlo taking his eyes off the road, but because of something malevolent. Something malicious. Something vengeful.

Now those fears had been confirmed, and her world had been turned upside-down again. Somehow, the Church of the New Apocrypha was responsible for Carlo's death. And while much of her life over the past year had felt beyond her control, that was a thing Maggie was more than ready to do something about.

Tearing the paper from the pad, she read it one more time before tossing it into the fireplace along with the hardcover book, the kraft paper wrapper, the stamps and every random scribbling she'd made over the past six days.

*Carlo slain by church of the Apocrypha. Must find Diane. Saint Casimir's Lithuanian Roman Catholic Church, Pittsburgh.*

Magdalena struck the match and watched it all become nothing but energy—heat-giving fire releasing all its impurities through the smoke—as the message disappeared up the chimney and into the cold November sky.

Then she packed her bag. Her car. And her gun…

# 29

*watching*

## 2 days before the end | Nov 9, 2011

IT HAD TAKEN a full year. Longer than Ian had anticipated. The torments through which the Shadows had been putting Retired Detective Magdalena Romano had been brutal; the pressures more than the average person would be capable of bearing. It hadn't been enough to merely take away her Carlo; they'd made certain to participate in his torture through the guise of dead little Matt Chauncey. Maggie had known nothing about the boy, or what had taken place in the summer of '77. But his appearance at the moment of Carlo's death, and that unmistakable voice in Maggie's ear, had been a harrowing knell meant to imprint upon her day and night. Unfortunately, it had been so unspeakably macabre that Maggie's consciousness had merely shut it all away, then locked the subliminal door.

Next came the nightmares. And the constant uncertainty. The *almost* innocuous noises in the house, one after the other. On their own, each was nothing—a bump here, a footstep there— but together they were an unnerving, incessant and unrelenting auditory assault. Then came the smells that would remind her of Carlo. The scent of his favorite leather jacket she'd long ago donated, or his pipe with the French vanilla tobacco she'd thrown away. Finally came the visions: A glimpse of movement out of the corner of an eye; a blur in the background as Maggie walked by.

The sleeplessness stole away her focus; the exhaustion, her peace. Before long came her superiors' hints at retirement. Soon, these hints became suggestions. Suggestions, an official recommendation.

Ian's plan was isolation to the point of breaking, at which time Maggie would either kill herself or go in search of the answers for the only case of her career which remained unsolved: the mysterious deaths and missing people surrounding the Church of the New Apocrypha.

Maggie Romano had chosen to dig in, becoming housebound to the very precipice of agoraphobia.

Ian's plan was backfiring.

Then Della, who like Diane had also disappeared, inserted herself once more into Maggie's life. Desperate for help but determined that only Maggie learn of Diane's soon-to-be whereabouts, Della had engineered an elaborate trail of clues that few besides Maggie would be able to decipher.

And at last, Magdalena Romano had begun the search.

II

Knelt before the stump upon which his brother and Jack 'Eddie' Raker had once selected teams for their game of War, the Archcardinal couldn't imagine a more apt place to learn the news. Filled with a deep, thrumming energy that saturated him in the warmth of darkness like a blanket, he watched through the eyes of the ever-present Shadows. Silently, he commended Maggie for the deductive reasoning that had built such an illustrious career, and thanked her for allowing him to see it in action right now, through her own eyes.

*Saint Casimir's Catholic Church, Pittsburgh.*

Soon, Ian would have his niece back. And the beginning of the end would finally be upon them…

# 30

*new day, usa!*

## 2 days before the end | Nov 9, 2011

WE GOT HER! The Prophet's sister!" Stacey Morris, lead video correspondent for *New Day, USA!* ran into Rachel Stoltz's office, She was interrupting a phone call the new Director was having with Burke Cummings, now the Producer of the top-rated morning show.

Rachel shushed her with a finger and directed Morris to have a seat. But Stoltz's own eyes were wide with excitement, and she found herself no longer hearing a thing Burke Cummings said.

"Hmmm, yes. Yes. Mmhmm. Okay then, Burke. Sure thing." She hung up and leaned so far forward that another inch or two and she'd be sprawled across the desk. "Stacey, you're shitting me?"

Morris shook her head, brimming.

"It's the real deal this time."

Over the past six years they'd received dozens of leads, most in the late summer of '05, immediately after Diane's story first broke. Every single one had been either incorrect, a desperate attempt at fifteen minutes of fame, or, worst of all, time-wasting pranks.

Not this time, Stacey Morris assured.

"We got a lead from someone inside the Church of the Apocrypha itself. An anonymous email. But I.T. checked its legitimacy and says the IP address, and ISP, and all those other acronyms they like to use, all check out." She lowered her voice which had risen in increments. "We got her, Rachel. We really got her. It took six years, but we have the chance to break the biggest story since The Prophet himself."

Though shaking her head in disbelief, Stoltz unable to keep herself from smiling.

"I can't believe it. God, what did they reveal? Was it how she escaped Barrow Moor, or what she's been up to? C'mon, dish it!"

"How 'bout I do one better than that. In fact, boss, how about I do about a hundred better…"

Rachel Stoltz stood. A slow, incredulous rise from her seat.

"Noooooo, don't tell me…"

Nodding wildly and jumping to her feet, Stacey Morris was a giant smile with a human being attached to it.

"Yes! I do, Rachel. I really do!" It took everything she had to not start jumping up and down. "We know where she is going to be tomorrow!"

Rachel Stoltz mimed like she was having a heart attack. She then came around the desk, wanting to remember this moment without all the papers and glaring computer screen cluttering up the purity of it.

"Well! Go on, God, you're killing me!"

Stacey Morris took a step forward and turned around her notepad so Stoltz could see the four words she'd scribed across the page in great big letters and circled about ten times.

Saint Casimir's Convent Pittsburgh.

"She's at a fucking Roman Catholic convent. Can you believe it? A fucking convent!"

Now she did leap in the air. Just once, and just enough to be noticed, her excitement too tightly wound to stop it.

"Well, I'll be damned," Stoltz marveled. "Talk about sleeping with the enemy. Could this be more perfect? Pack a bag, Stacey. I guess we're heading to the Steel City…"

# MONSTRUM VI

# 31

*karina*

## 2 days before the end | Nov 9, 2011

MARTIN SHADE WAS a normal man. He lived a normal life. With a normal wife. And two normal kids. His house wasn't unlike so many others in that uninspired development: a single-story stuccoed bungalow in a neat little enclave of thirty or forty others. All nestled neatly aside one another like cookies on a tray. He had one dog, two cats (which he abhorred) and drove a meringue-colored Prius for its ecology and economy.

Now, this isn't to say Martin wasn't extraordinary in his own unique way, as are we all. He was quite adept at fixing electronic malfunctions in small and mid-sized appliances. And rather terrific at math, geography, and politics. Also, at taking out the garbage without being asked by wife Marlena.

And Martin was just superb at trivia facts.

The capital of Switzerland? *Not Zurich, as you might think, but Bern.* The 1976 film that dominated that year's Academy Awards and which Robert Redford both starred in and produced? *All The President's Men.* The year Pac-Man took the American marketplace by storm? *1980.*

So you see, he had a talent of sorts.

Now, I know how you're picturing Marty already. Shortish, round-faced, stout, with spectacles and a somewhat nerdish if jolly mannerism about him.

But there you'd be wrong, for Martin Shade was remarkable in another way: He was handsome, beyond reproach. Not those catalog model looks, perhaps, but naturally charismatic enough in a respectably boyish manner to make more than the average woman turn her head, if only for the briefest moment. He often sported a wry and naturally mischievous smile beneath bright blue eyes which glinted in the sun and too easily stole attention away from his fairly well-trained body, above average for a forty-two-year-old. Tall and slim, but with plenty of lean tissue and neatly defined muscles, think Jimmy Stewart meets Mark Wahlberg, and you're getting close.

*And of course, there's one final way in which Marty was extraordinary, but we'll come to that a little later...*

On the day we met, I was already late for work. I'm supposed to be at the club and ready to go on stage at eleven sharp. It was already nearly midnight. One more time, Ambrus Ruud, the club's Hungarian proprietor had told me, and I might as well find somewhere else to dance.

That was two weeks ago, and I'd made sure I wasn't late since.

Until tonight, when I'd experienced—let's just say, something of a difficulty—with a current beau.

It seems ill-tempers and obscene amounts of alcohol don't make for good bedfellows after all.

*Who'd have thunk it.*

Jackson was living proof of this as he came at me insanely fast considering his near incomprehensible stupor, my favorite eight-inch kitchen knife gleaming in star-like twinkles from each serrated edge beneath the stark, fluorescent overhead light.

Jackson thrust it at my face, missed, and struck the wall behind me instead. The fact that I'd kicked him in the nuts may have had something to do with his poor aim. Or then again, maybe it was the eleven beers he'd downed.

*Anyhoo*...it was a brief moment of comic relief as I watched him tug at the knife's handle, doing the best he could to loosen the blade now embedded in the freshly painted drywall. I especially liked when the clumsy attempt caused him to lose his grip and his hand slid down the edge of the blade, opening his palm in a thin but impressively proficient line that bisected the webbing between thumb and index finger.

I backed out of the kitchenette and toward the pantry as Jackson held his hand out in front of him. He stared with an odd mix of curiosity and numb incomprehension as that almost surgical line grew wider, a crimson swell first oozing, then pulsing from it. Moments later, it was a sheet running down his outstretched hand, a trail of great red raindrops staining my new beige carpet.

I think it was this, more than his failed attempt to stab me, that pushed me to do what I did next.

In fact, I know it was.

My landlady Helen is a very pleasant woman, probably in her mid-sixties or early seventies—*I always find it a little difficult to age someone when theirs is so far from my own*—and we're actually becoming something of friends…if a forty-plus year gap between us can allow for such an intimate term. Helen had been promising for some time now that she would redecorate the three apartments above her sprawling home, with mine being first. She'd begun to make good on it too, starting with my new carpet before even looking at the other two units.

*Because you're a sweetheart, and I know you'll appreciate and care for it,* was her reason. *I'll pick you out something nice.*

Now, I'm sorry ladies, but that whole Martha Stewart scene just ain't my cuppa tea. But I wasn't going to argue. At $750 a month the place wasn't bad. Not bad at all. But it sure as shit could use a refresher. So I was happy to let Helen take the reins.

That was barely a month ago. And now the trust she'd so sweetly placed in me was already being obliterated by this mouth-breather of a guy I'd allowed to infiltrate my world, letting him get far too close, way too fast.

Refusing to take my eyes off him, I reached behind me. Rummaging blindly through the partially open pantry doors, I pulled out the first thing my left hand struck upon. I'm still a little intrigued at just how easy it was to swing that three-foot fluorescent tube at Jackson's head. It just sorta came to me, like a matter of instinct. I guess if I were an animal, that's exactly what it would be called. But as I was in fact a twenty-nine-year-old blonde pole dancer, I'll say it was simply having a big pair of cojones, so to speak.

The tube exploded against the side of Jackson's head in a satisfying way I hadn't expected, having never shattered one of these things before. Amid a powdery blast of glass and dust, I was left holding a six-inch piece that had remained intact as Jackson was left holding his temple—*to my disappointment, also still intact*—with the hand that wasn't ruining my carpet. Where I'd expected his head to crack open like a ripe guava, the result instead had been little more than an antagonism.

Ever poke your finger at a wasp you'd caught in a glass jelly jar? It was something like that.

"You bitch! You fucking *bitch*!"

Okay, I guess maybe I deserved that one. This time, at least. But Lord knows, Jackson had accused me of being a female dog every single day this week. Which, by the way, is precisely the total length of time I'd known this latest Prince Charming who I was certain was going to be different this time.

"I'm gonna rip you a new asshole like you never been ripped one before," he warned in a disturbingly calm tone. I was quite sure he had every intent of following through with it as he lurched toward me with that gross, bloodied fist which was starting to look as if it had been dipped in a vat of burgundy wax.

Now, let's take a moment so I can fill you in a little bit.

Jackson may have been pretty, with that long dark hair and perma-stubble that told the world he didn't give a shit what they thought. He was living life his way, your opinion on the matter be damned. But he wasn't exactly the sharpest tool in the shed.

He was strong, though.

And tough.

Also, a good fifteen years my senior.

*Okay, so I admit it. I may have some daddy issues. But what girl doesn't?*

A mechanic for a local custom chopper shop, Jackson builds some pretty sick looking bikes that fetch twenty, thirty, even forty thousand bucks on a fairly regular basis. It keeps him busy from the time he struts into work until the time he shuffles out, tired and worn and ready for a beer...or ten. And the amount of grueling labor those great big grease-embedded mitts of his perform on a daily basis had never been more apparent than in this moment as one of them was coming at me, insanely fast.

It seemed the size of a catcher's glove, and I had no intention of letting it make contact with my face, head, or any other part of my body for that matter. Not if I could help it.

So I ducked to the left.

Jackson's fist slammed into the jamb of the pantry door and the wood crushed a little beneath his knuckles, the paint chipping away to reveal bare, clean wood. Much the same way as the sun-darkened skin over his knuckles simultaneously split to reveal bare, clean bone.

"MotherFUCKER!" he howled as he shook his hand, blowing on it in precisely the same manner as your mother used to do before offering you a spoon of sauce straight from the bubbling pot.

"Hurt much?"

The glimmer of a smile accompanied my question...followed by a sharp and immediate sting of remorse. You might think such regret was out of fear of Jackson's retaliation.

But it wasn't.

It was, in fact, a result of seeing the forlorn, boyish look that swept across his face: bottom lip curling out and down in an adorable pout; eyes filling with that same deeply rooted sadness that had so attracted me to him in the first place.

II

He'd been alone that night he stepped through the doors of the Tangerine Dream. Not with the usual group of drunken cronies so typical of the crowds we get.

*There's safety in numbers, you know.*

And apparently, a little Dutch courage doesn't exactly hurt either when you're trying to muster up enough nerve to ask that sweet little thing over there for a special dance of your own.

You know the girl I mean. That aloof, virginal maiden. Classy. Smart. Unobtainable. The girl you'd love to bring home to Mama but know that she'd never be interested in you in a million years.

In case you can't tell, I'm being facetious as shit. Because the girl we're actually talking about is strutting around half-naked up there, dollar bills bulging from her panty line like stuffing from your favorite old childhood plush. Yeah, that's her. So, I mean, like it's really so difficult? This isn't church, fellas. No one's judging you here. And no one's gonna say no...*ever*.

I mean, it's why we're all here, isn't it?

And trust me when I say, it's nothing personal—just business. Which is why I've never understood how the guys who are filled with such bravado out there in the real world are suddenly so weak and willowy when they come in here.

But Jackson was the exception. Unlike most of them, he didn't stumble to the stage three sheets to the wind, a wad of dollar bills in his sweaty little hand, ready to be shoved down my too-tight G-string. He didn't try to get a cheap thrill by then attempting to brush his fingertips across a certain exclusive nether region as he slid one beer-soaked bill after another between red satin thong and suntanned skin.

It was this restraint—not the product of effete trepidation but a reserved, stoic indifference—that was all it took for me to become attracted to him by illogical measures.

And since he wouldn't come to *me*, I broke all protocol and approached *him* about a private dance.

Not once.

Not twice.

But three separate times.

Far more effort than I've ever invested in another punter. After all, dancing is a numbers game. Pure and simple. You approach a guy once, prefaced of course by that little smile, a cursory glance, a pole-slide or booty-shake. Then you pull away, that fiery interest snuffed as swiftly as it was lit. If the clown chooses not to approach you, that means he falls into one of three categories:

A) he has no money—*not worth your time*;

B) is interested in another dancer—*not worth your time*; or

C) is one of the endless voyeurs who milk a $9 beer while ogling all the girls for an hour, only to leave without so much as a single Washington crossing their palms—*definitely not worth your time!*

Why I then invested so much of my valuable time to attract Jackson remains a mystery to me. There was just something about him, I guess. That boyish innocence behind a hugely powerful frame of a man. A rugged charm that smacked of Bad Boy. But not really bad, more like Hollywood bad.

*Know what I mean?*

Third time was a charm, and we retired around the corner to a deliberately darkened area where Management turns a conveniently blind eye to what—or maybe I should say *who*—goes down there. But make no mistake, this isn't some liberal-minded corporate altruism on their behalf. Despite being optically challenged over what takes place in the private lounge, you better believe they still manage to see the forty-five percent they have coming to them. Believe you me, that part's as clear to them as a fresh turd steaming in the pristine snow.

Behind a curtain reeking of spilt beer and stale cigarettes, we settled into one of the booths where the tables are conspicuously absent. Perching upon the tattered vinyl bench, I collected $50 in tens from Jackson's calloused hand, making sure to slowly run my finger across his palm as I slid out each individual bill. Moments later I was grinding in his lap, teasing his legs, fondling his pecs through that tight cotton T-shirt. All the while whispering sweet everythings in his ear as *Porn Star Dancing* belted out in thumping bass and distorted treble from speakers long ago cracked from ridiculous volumes. Then I did something I've never done before. Well, not for a punter in the Dream, anyway.

Starting at the nape of his neck, I covered him in a hundred butterfly kisses. Making my way steadily down his torso and over his tight stomach, I closed my eyes and thought about nothing but emptiness until the deed was done.

And that's all she wrote. I had become his.

III

Now here we were, in my apartment not even a week later, with Jackson angry and drunk and backing me into a corner for a third time in as many minutes.

My eyes darting but unblinking as he blocked my only way of escape, my fingers again rifled indiscriminately behind me. This time through a junk drawer where a tidy little black number had been buried. From some Dutch company whose name I can't remember and don't really care to, it was the result of an inquiry into self-defense options a while back. I'd been assured by a previous manfriend—one who also happened to be an active-duty Tampa cop—that this company, whose name I can't recall, makes the best handgun for your buck. So, I bought a 9mm semiautomatic with the proceeds of two nights' tips, filled the little cartridge thingy with bullets.

*"Rounds," the cop had corrected me at the time, rather indignantly. To which I simply responded, "Ummmmm, which are bullets...right?"*

And with little further thought, I'd tossed it into the kitchen drawer alongside three old unpaid bills, a dozen colored paperclips, a handful of pens, a wad of plastic grocery bags and about six dollars in loose change.

Feeling the texture of its cool metal grip, I yanked the gun from the drawer. Gripping it way too tight in my left hand, I balanced my unsteady forearm with my right. Just like the cop had shown me. Well, except for the 'way too tight' part.

I was shaking, and it was obvious. But Jackson took no steps closer, freezing pretty much in place like you see in the movies. At the time I thought he respected the show of force. But now I have to wonder if his compliance wasn't merely out of concern that if I didn't calm down, I might just squeeze that trigger by mistake. Five pounds of pressure is all it takes, or so they say. And at this close range, even a child was capable of drilling a hole through a human head and turning it into a spaghetti squash. Sigs were simply that easy to shoot.

*That was it! It was called a Sig ... a Sig–Something.*

"Kandi—" Jackson implored so softly and unlike the ugly thing he had been only moments before. This Jackson was the version of the man I fell in love with a week ago.

By the way, you like my name? Kandi. Kandi Kane. As in, I'd joined the Tangerine Dream at Christmas. And yes, I was at least smart enough to not give Jackson my real name, which is Karina. Not yet anyway. But who knows?

*Give it another day or two, and I might've.*

"Just put it down. And we'll talk," Jackson pleaded quietly and motioned downward with his palms. More blood fell in thick globules onto my new Berber, their red a little darker now.

"Stop doing that, you useless asshole!"

It wasn't a plea but a dictate, and he knew it. Now his hands, like the rest of him, froze where they were. Sort of outstretched and at waist level. He looked as though he were about to get out his prayer mat and face East.

I laughed and waggled the gun at him, telling him to just go. To get the fuck out and leave me alone. And that if he ever came back, I'd kill him.

*And I probably would.*

So, now I was late for work.

And this is precisely where we started, right?

I looked out the bedroom window to make sure Jackson was in fact gone, even though the squeal of his motorcycle's wide rear tire had already confirmed it. Pulling aside the drapes, I watched the chopper angle away from my building, Jackson ignoring the neatly painted lines as he crossed the parking lot. With a deep lean to the left he banked out the exit of the complex and into heavy traffic, somehow avoiding the statistical likelihood of becoming an organ donor in that moment.

The clock radio on my nightstand glowed 11:38.

*Shit shit shit shit SHIT.*

If I said it enough times it acted as a mantra to my getting ready, compelling me forward, pulsing the way the beat of a great song just makes you want to dance.

"Shit!" I declared one more time as I pulled on lacy black stockings and a thong from Frederick's of Hollywood, a plain skirt, cotton blouse half-buttoned, and slipped into my old beaten sneakers. I scurried out my front door with purse and keys in one hand, one of those sturdy designer shopping bags in the other.

You know the kind: the thick waxy paper ones with the wonderfully useful handles. I'd somehow acquired it from some high-end Italian clothing boutique in the Plaza, and it was now unceremoniously stuffed with three different trashy outfits, none of which I'd purchased there.

*Which probably goes without saying?*

It was only then that I realized I still had the 9mm in my hand. How quickly I'd become accustomed to this thing which, while never frightening to me, at least had demanded a fair level of caution when I first held it. Now it seemed as natural a part of me as my watch. Or holding my car keys. Funny. I guess I could see how some folks, some men typically, might become so fanatical about them. There's a certain satisfying sense of power, having the authority of life or death held so effortlessly in your little hand.

But I had no time for such philosophical ponderings right now, so I simply tossed the gun into the big trendy bag with all my other stuff as I raced out to the parking lot. In seconds I was on Madison Avenue and pushing my '02 Mustang convertible (aptly but unimaginatively named 'Sally') for all she was worth as I rocketed onto the connector and up onto the highway.

All the while wondering, what the hell just happened?

IV

The Tangerine Dream isn't much to look at, I'll admit. I cringed the very first time I walked into the place and felt dirty and cheap as soon as I left.

*So, I hear you asking, why the hell would I take a job there?*

And the answer is simple …

… Money. Lots of it. For doing very little.

So, okay. I get it. It's a bit seedy. A little like legalized prostitution, but without having to actually do anything to the guy, if you know what I mean. But for me, when I'm on stage, I just zone out, feeling that beat pulsing through me, the bass pumping loud and mad; guitars screaming and grinding. And just like that, there's no one else there. It's just me and the music.

Now, I'll grant you, it wasn't always like that. The first time, well, that was something to behold, I'm quite sure. Some skinny little girl, all nerves and attitude, trying too hard and even harder to look at. But it's that way for every girl the first time.

*Or two. Or ten.*

Now I just go with it. And in a weird kinda way, I actually enjoy it. A little bit, anyway. If you can look past the pathetic insecurities and creepy sexual compulsions, the punters can actually be pretty nice. And if you treat them right, most'll come back and treat you right, too.

Then it becomes more like visiting with friends.

Except you're at work. Half-naked. And your friends are stuffing dollar bills down your panties.

*But other than that, it's just like hanging out.*

Mustang Sally shot past the gleaming steel and glass of RayJay stadium—*Go Bucs*—and I knew I was just minutes away. Thank God. I'd be late, but probably only miss one dance. And of course, the All-Girl Lineup. But I could work it out. Do some extra special moves, hit the poles one or two times more. You know, basically make good so Ambrus wouldn't up and fire me on the spot. And by tomorrow he'd have cooled down. Probably even forgotten about it and be all aflutter about some other girl, or some vendor giving him shit. Or some betting punter that owes him a fat wad of cash and hasn't coughed up.

*Yeah, Ambrus was running books on the side. But ask me if I've seen anyone in this business that isn't.*

And then Sally veered for no apparent reason.

At least I thought it was for no reason until a sound like a large balloon popping told me that one of my tires had burst and was now transforming itself into a bunch of shredded rubber strips along the blacktop. We—by which I mean Sally and I, of course—narrowly missed a black Malibu coming up on our left as we filled both northbound lanes of Dale Mabry. We then careened sideways as Sally's front end kiltered off-center and the concrete median jumped up from the middle of the road and apparently kicked Sally's front legs right out from under her.

We skidded to a stop with her hood hanging over the center strip, forcing traffic in the southbound lane to swerve in order to keep from spinning us like a bottle at a teenagers' party. With Sally's ass-end obstructing the passing lane of my own side of the highway, northbound traffic was forced to do the same.

So, this just wasn't my night.

I leaned against the steering wheel and held my face in my hands, ignoring the obnoxious *bluuuuuurt* of the horn as my elbows pressed the center of the wheel.

*This was all just too much.*

I'd been cool as a cucumber back at my apartment, unfazed by Jackson's drunken, violent rage. Pulling the gun had seemed so logical and effortless at the time, in the heat of the confrontation. Now, the full realization of what might have gone down was bubbling to the surface and I began to cry, composing a grotesque tune as my sobs intermingled with sporadic pips from Sally's horn when I shifted my weight from one elbow to the other. Then back again.

"Hey," the stranger said softly and with a calculated amount of caution, not wanting to startle me as he leaned down to peer through the door which I now realized had been jarred open by what I thought was only a minor impact.

*Great*, I thought, or perhaps even mumbled aloud as I threw my hands up in surrender. *Not only a crash, but fucking Sally was this close to bucking me clean out of her. Thanks, Sal.*

"Who's Sally?" the man asked as he leaned lower and a little more into the car to get a better look at me.

"Never mind," I said. "Just fuck it."

I pushed open the door with a loud creak and swung my feet out, making sure to give Sally a good swift kick in the dash in the process. All I wanted was to get the hell out of the car and have a look at the damage which I already knew I couldn't pay for. But this dude was blocking my way.

"Uh, excuse me?" I said rather too pointedly but didn't really give a shit at this stage.

He looked embarrassed and moved to one side. Not a lot, mind you. Just enough to allow me to step out while still having to brush up against him. And so now that was just one more thing pissing me off. If you're gonna cop an incidental feel, at least buy a girl a drink first.

"Are you okay?" He seemed genuinely concerned. "I mean, are you hurt or anything?"

Even though I knew I wasn't, I still visually examined myself to make sure. As if this man knew something I didn't. It's the same when someone tells you that you look under the weather. Even though you aren't feeling sick, you'll look in a mirror the first chance you get, just to be sure. Like you can't determine for yourself how you feel.

It's amazing how much of our lives hinge upon others' perceptions of it. I always find that both vexing and a little sad.

In this moment, that mild irritation was heating to all but a boiling rage as I mentally reprimanded myself for allowing this guy to pull me right down into that bullshit societal conformity.

Listen, I know what you're thinking: *Chill girl, he only asked if you were okay. He's going out of his way to do a nice thing.*

And you'd be right. But I wasn't in the mood to be the polite little southern belle at this precise moment in time.

Silent as I looked over the car, I was at least thankful there was no obvious damage from having mounted the median. Only the blown tire which had caused me to swerve in the first place.

"Just a bruised ego," I finally answered the guy with a clinging attitude as I brushed myself down.

*See what I mean—why was I brushing myself down?*

Lord knows. I wasn't dirty. There was no broken glass. It was just another of those stupid built-in automated responses we all have in our behavioral toy box. Goes to show how easily a person can be controlled if you really think about it.

This was now irritating me too, the straw and camel thing I guess, so I kicked Sally's front fender.

It made a small sneaker-shaped dent.

Now there was actual damage. I knew I would regret it later but it sure as fuck felt good right now.

"Piece of shit, Sally," I shrieked. "You metal piece of CRAP!"

"Whoa, okay. Listen—" The man began slowly backing away, his hands open wide and thrust out in front of him. Universal body language that says you have no intention of further poking what is clearly an already irritated bear. "—I just wanted to help, that's all. But now I know you're fine. So, I guess I'll be on my way."

He turned and started for his car, awkwardly dodging late night motorists who all rubbernecked but did little else. Most barely bothered to slow down, let alone stopped to offer help.

Suddenly, I felt like a real piece of garbage.

This guy goes out of his way for a stranger in need—a woman stranded in the middle of a nighttime road—and I basically treat him like he's the source of all my problems. At the very least, that he's a serious nuisance I don't need.

Sighing, I closed my eyes and resigned myself, once again, to the fact that I can be a real bitch.

It was when I called after him, asking him to wait, that I noticed for the first time he was actually kind of cute…in a Good-Boy-Turned-Even-Better-Boy sorta way.

*If you like that kind of thing, that is.*

He smiled, the slightest I think a smile could possibly be and yet still be considered a smile. "Bad day, huh?"

I shook my head.

"You have no idea." Sally was lilting to the front left, her alloy wheel grazed and flattened more than I first realized as it sat on the weed-filled median.

The dude looked at her.

Back to me.

Then Sally, once more.

"Oh, I think I have some idea…"

"Okay," I surrendered. "I guess maybe you do."

I paused to consider what I was about to say next. In hindsight, things would have turned out a lot differently if I'd just let him go. But I have this thing about strays, and for some reason I can't explain, this guy seemed to fall squarely into that category. Something told me he might even be their poster child.

So, I was hooked.

Call it Superwoman syndrome. Needing to be needed. Or maybe, just being way too soft.

*Deep, deep down, that is.*

Whatever you call it, I heard myself speaking the next words before I'd even made the conscious decision to form them.

"Listen, uh—?"

"Martin," he answered and extended his hand to be shook.

"Okay. Listen, Marty. Do you think you could get a girl out of a jam? I need to be someplace, like an hour ago. It really isn't far from here. Would you mind?"

As I spoke, I found myself shaking his hand without even realizing it. It was smooth and gentle. But strong. And if I'm honest, I think I could've stood here like that for hours, just my hand in his.

His smile broadened. "Of course. Wherever you need to go, I'll get you there, Miss, uh …" He tilted his head and those bright cyan eyes found mine in a way that was almost hypnotic.

"Karina." I heard myself completely blurting out. And without so much as a pause, instantly repeating, "Karina Michaels."

*Wait, what? Oh, God. Did I just tell this stranger my real name?*

He seemed utterly indifferent to the inherent vulnerability of such naïve honesty and beckoned me to his car

"Funny name. But okay then, Karina-Karina Michaels. Let's go."

V

As I slid into the passenger seat of his Prius, little did I know just how much shit was on the verge of hitting the fan ...

# 32

*martin*

THE TANGERINE DREAM is an unmistakable landmark, a blight most would say, on the Tampa landscape. But a landmark to all, nonetheless. With its bright orange neon sign that can be seen at least a quarter mile in all directions, it isn't too difficult to establish exactly what kind of establishment the Dream is. NUDE LADIES sizzles in green neon below the name, accompanied by a pair of very suspicious-looking tangerines, the nubby stems of which happen to be positioned conspicuously in the center of both of those round, sumptuous fruits. Anyone would be hard-pressed not to recognize their incredibly sophomoric similarity to a certain pair of body parts found on (rather well-endowed) individuals of the fairer sex.

Surprisingly, the Dream's proprietor, Ambrus Ruud, argued this exact point to the City Council when they tried to block the sign's planning permit based upon public decency laws.

It was merely a matter of coincidence, Ruud insisted as he presented his case to the mostly conservative men and women of the council. Standing in their chamber as full of piss and vinegar as he ever was, Ruud reminded them that he didn't create tangerines. And he sure as shit didn't create tits.

"All of them things is God's work," Ruud reminded the members. "So, you good people can just thank the Lord above for them wonderful additions to our lives. And if the Almighty just so happened to make tangerines and tits look the same, well, that's His doing. And you men—oh, and three council women—just have damn dirty minds. But I'm afraid that's your problem, not mine. So, my lawyer says the sign goes up."

Nobody on the council could find a legal precedent to counter Ruud's overly simplistic, if no less tenable, account of the situation. Which was typically how these meetings between Ambrus and the Council transpired. (And they transpired frequently.)

So, the sign went up.

And from that day onward men have been coming to the Tangerine Dream from all over the region so that they too, or at least a certain part of their anatomy, could also go up.

JUICY FRUIT! was the epic newspaper headline the following morning, the city broadsheet reporting with particular relish upon this latest battle. Even Ruud's most staunch opponents secretly admitted to allowing themselves a snigger or two between sips of coffee as they read the morning news of how Ruud had once again stuck it to the City.

*Who da man!*

## II

Marty and I hadn't driven more than a couple minutes before the neon glow of those tangerines began to create an umbra of the outlying office buildings. As each block drew nearer, that orange light grew brighter. It seemed to burn any thoughts of Sally and my little mishap from my mind, forcing me to focus only on the busy night which lay ahead of me. It was at this point I realized I'd scurried out of the house so fast after my scuffle with Jackson that I hadn't even put on a bra.

And that just wouldn't do.

Not because it was indecent, but because it wouldn't make for much of a striptease if I slowly unbuttoned my blouse, slinking this way and that like a hypnotic snake…only to have my girls just come bouncing out, y'know? Sort of ruins all that delicious anticipation. So, as Martin drove, I sat right there on the passenger seat of his responsible little hybrid and wrestled into an entirely impractical, sheer and lacy plum-colored bra.

Okay, so ol' Marty probably got a bit of a free show.

But who cares?

I mean, it was dark. He was focused on his driving. And I was discreet about it.

*Okay, maybe discreet isn't exactly the word. But I didn't up and shake them in his face either, if that's what you were thinking.*

Besides, the guy was being a good Samaritan. I mean, he just helped a gal out of a real jam.

*Right…?*

We pulled into the Dream's parking lot and Martin sidled up to the back door, the one marked 'Talent.' I thanked him almost as an afterthought as I snuck into the club at precisely three minutes to midnight, hopping on one four-inch stiletto while I pulled and tugged the other over my heel. I made it to the stage just in time for the All-Girl Lineup, slipping into the parade of women in front of Loraine, a.k.a. 'Peaches.'

"Hey!" she protested, smacking her gum too loudly and grabbing my shoulder. I shrugged free of her grip, diamond-tipped crimson talons and all, and we were sauntering in front of a packed house full of drunk, wide-eyed punters before she could do anything else about it.

With any luck, Ruud wouldn't notice that I'd been missing for the past hour. I smiled and winked at him as the line snaked along the front of the stage. Twelve scantily clad women, we ranged in size, shape, race, weight and age. But together, we were a single, lithe, dozen-headed creature whose sole purpose in the Dream universe was to appeal to every man's deepest, darkest, dirtiest, and sometimes downright disturbing desire.

The job description was simple: tease this pathetic pack of strays until they were as close to their fantasy of sex as you could muster. Then withdraw. Quickly, quietly and without apology. Leaving them salivating and, sometimes quite literally, howling for more. The result? Draining them of as much of their money as we could take without actually stealing it. Well, to be more accurate, as much of their money as we and the Dream could take, because like I said earlier, the house of Ruud always enjoys 45 cents of every dollar.

I do feel compelled here to make sure you know the Tangerine Dream isn't a brothel. And Ruud's not a pimp. This is all above board. No actual sex allowed. And in reality, we don't even take their money, the more I think about it.

They quite happily give it to us.

*...Lap dance? Naked, no less? Oh my, no! Honestly Officer, I was only serving that man over there a drink when I tripped and fell into his lap. Thank Heaven he caught me! And I guess he just felt so embarrassed for me that he gave me a nice tip. And by the way, don't you look rather handsome yourself tonight, Officer...*

Ruud smiled his big, curly-lipped smile and winked back at me as though he could read my very thoughts. Maybe he could. Who knows? All I cared was that Ambrus had given me confirmation that I was fine. I still had a job.

So at last, my night had taken a turn for the better.

*If only I'd known...*

III

I don't really remember when Marty came in. I'm guessing it wasn't long after he dropped me off. And then I barely recognized him, if I'm being honest. That's just sort of how I am. I'm okay admitting it, 'cause I've got way too much shit going on in my own life to give much of a rat's about anybody else's. And I guess that spills over into the little details, like really *seeing* somebody when they're right in front of me.

That, and names. I'm just horrendous at names.

You can stand there and tell me clear as day that your name is Susan. I'll smile and nod. But three seconds later it's gone, just another air bubble in the crystal-clear ether of my consciousness.

I don't mean to be that way. It's just how my mind works.

And in my defense when it came to Marty, it's dark as hell inside the Dream. Plus, I'd already had two Jaeger Bombs after the All-Girl Lineup. The combination wasn't exactly conducive to my exhibiting the kind of social graces I should, especially given how decent this guy had been to me. I'd just performed my solo on pole no. 1 to "How Soon Is Now" by The Smiths, my go-to song. Not only is it incredibly sexy to me, but it lasts twice as long as just about every other track the rest of the girls pick.

Oh, yeah. Sorry. I forgot to tell you that part, we get to pick one signature song. And with mine being over 6.5 minutes long, I get way more attention from the guys. And by attention, I think you're getting the picture by now that I mean dollar bills. Okay, so it's a way darker song than something commercial like "Pour Some Sugar On Me" by Def Leppard. But it really suits me to a tee and has kinda become my trademark. If you come see me at the Dream in Tampa, you'll see for yourself.

Anyway, when you've done your solo, you 'sweep up.' That's what we call it when we go thank the guys that came up to stage, hoping they might share a few more bucks, or maybe want a lap dance. And we sweep by the rest of the guys who were too timid to come up, just in case one of them happens to be that diamond in the rough we call a Big Spender. This guy's a lilting wallflower, but sometimes will fork out the most casharoonie. I think it's a lack of self-esteem, and sometimes I feel bad for them. 'Cause once you hook one, they'll be loyal to a fault, giving you all their money and not a cent to any other girl. And occasionally, that even seeps out to the real world and their actual girlfriends, or even wives. But, I guess that's their problem, not mine.

Like I said earlier, we don't really take their money. They give it to us. And who am I to say no…?

Anyhoo, I'd actually walked past Martin at least three times before I recognized him. And to be honest, even then it was only because I'd spotted my bag.

The big waxy paper one with the convenient handles that I'd left in the back seat of his puke beige Toyota.

*The bag I'd tossed my gun into.*

Of course, I wasn't thinking about any of that at the time. I just saw this big, crumpled bag, and was wondering why it was taking up a whole seat next to this guy.

Then the penny dropped.

Martin looked back at me, a little dejected. I could sense it even though he tried to smile.

"Hey…" I pulled out a chair, flipped it around and straddled it like a guy might, spreading each of my legs either side and leaning forward into its open mesh back.

I watched as Martin tried to sneak a peek at my crotch, just like I knew he would. It's why I did it. Let's just call it reparations for me not recognizing him sooner.

Like all the guys, his natural instinct was to try and catch a glimpse of the money shot because maybe, just maybe, my thong wouldn't quite contain me in this pose. But also, like all the other guys, he was hoping I wouldn't catch him doing it.

*Too late, Marty-boy. Gotta get up pretty early if you wanna get one over on this gal.*

The 'chair move' was just one of a hundred tricks I'd picked up during my years here. They're all incredibly easy to master and, frankly, so patently transparent that the first time I tried them I couldn't believe they'd actually work. But they always do.

*I'm tellin' ya, girls. It doesn't take much to rake in a lot of money with this gig.*

"I just wanted to say thanks again. You know, for being my shining knight, and all that."

"WHAT?" he shouted, and I realized just how noisy it was in here if you weren't used to it. Long ago I learned to block out the fact that there was any music playing at all. But now, through Martin's ears, I was made very aware of the heavy rock grinding out of the loudspeakers as a girl calling herself Violet was grinding up against pole no. 2.

"THANKS," I said again as loudly as I could without actually screaming. You know, sort of shout-talking. "YOU'RE MY HERO."

He grinned and shrugged, even blushing a bit.

"So, Marty," this time leaning in close, my mouth all but touching his left ear, "what were your plans tonight, before I went and wrecked them all?"

Beneath the table he touched my leg to see how I would react. I pretended I didn't notice and so he kept his hand there, fingers tentatively stroking my calf.

"No plans at all," he answered. "This works just fine."

As a glaring spotlight swept over the stage and caught us in its path, his eyes shone the brightest blue I think I'd ever seen. Behind them were the echoes of the little boy Martin once had been. Just like I had seen in Jackson.

It was as comforting as it was foreboding.

"A handsome man like you? Nothing to do? I don't believe it."

"It's true, nothing."

"So, where had you been heading when you were so rudely interrupted by this blonde bubblehead careening across the road?"

He looked away and I could tell in that gesture that he had, in fact, been heading somewhere but wasn't about to tell me.

*Fine. Like I cared.*

"Just out. For a drive. You know how it is."

Funnily enough, I did. Many was the night I got into the 'Stang, dropped the top, cranked the tunes, and just kicked it into gear with nowhere to go but anywhere.

"So, you got some time to kill?"

I slid my left hand over and thumbed the side of his thigh, watching the sparkle rise in his eyes. He nodded then swiftly, reflexively looked away.

*Damn, that shy thing always gets me.*

"Marty?" I lifted his face by the chin so that he was looking at me. *Into me.* "Would you like a dance?"

"I dunno. I mean, yeah, sure. But—"

"It's on me," I assured him, stopping him from digging for his wallet. "I owe you that much."

We made our way through the tables, me leading Marty by the hand, and settled into a corner booth under a mirror that allowed me to watch my six. I straddled my new friend's legs and began to glide slowly and firmly, back and forth across his lap in rhythm to the music. I can't even tell you what the song was, only that it had just started, and had a good backbeat full of bass and sex.

Martin leaned back, resting his head against the torn, red vinyl. He closed his eyes. I ground my thighs into his and he pressed farther back into the booth while I pulled myself closer. I could feel his breath, first shallow and then coming faster, little by little. I was kinda enjoying this, and I *know* he was. It seemed like only seconds before the song was already pounding toward its crescendo. Drums, guitar and bass slamming it home. *Bam— bam—BAM.* Then a long, dirty electric guitar note that broke into distortion.

Martin opened his eyes and shook off some image in his mind as I pressed both hands against his shoulders to climb off. I found myself shaking my head as well, feeling like I had to clear my own mind. Which wasn't cool. Because for me, that was a sign that I was beginning to feel emotionally close.

*Again.*

Which was breaking the first rule in this business.

*Again.*

"Okay," I said all chill and detached. "Good?"

"Good," he answered and once more began reaching for his wallet. I declined one last time, taking his hand and lacing my fingers between his as we sidestepped through a maze of tables. Dancers and clients were oblivious as we passed by, as though they were on their own little raft to honeymoon island.

"Hang here. I'll be right back," I instructed as I sat him at the same table where I'd found him, grabbing my bag which was still crumpled on the seat. "Need to powder my nose."

IV

I knew I'd find Amanda—a.k.a. 'Chocolate'—in the dressing room. Chocolate was sometimes milk, and sometimes dark, depending upon her mood on any given night. But whichever version she was to the rest of the world, Chocolate to me was always sweet. And as friends go, she came with a real added bonus: powdered sugar. It had become our shared ritual anytime our shifts crossed, and was the part I most looked forward to on those nights. It got me through the remaining early hours, when the guys grew brasher, the tips grew scarcer, and my patience grew thinnest.

She was already opening the tiny baggie when I came in.

"Want some sugar?" she asked without looking up, somehow certain it was me. I couldn't tell from her monotone delivery if there were a comma in there. 'Want some [comma] sugar?' Made *me* the sugar. 'Want some sugar?' [no comma] made it the *cocaine*.

In the old days, the girl in me would've marveled at how a humble comma could entirely change the meaning of a mere three-word sentence. Nowadays, I couldn't care less. It made no difference to me as both made sense. So, I just leaned in behind her and ran my fingers through Chocolate's platinum weave.

"What do *you* think, babygirl?"

"I think you best sit that scrawny lily-white ass o' yours down and roll up one-a-them Washingtons you got dangling from your pretty lil thong…"

It was good stuff.

My head floated in a rush of blood as shivers ran down my back, fingers teasing down my spine. Nice. If you've never done coke, I can tell you it's not the raging euphoria they so often depict in Hollywood. And you sure as shit don't get trippy. But I felt good, really good. Confident. I was ready for anything again.

"Chocolate, you are just too sweet, girl."

"That's what all them horny lil white boys out there tell me, sugar." She laughed in a sudden, bellowing roar as she threw back her head. If she's anything, Chocolate is addictive. Especially when she's Milk Chocolate, which is how it looked to be tonight. I smiled and laughed with her, bending down to give her a hug and top it off with a kiss on her beautifully sculpted cheek.

"You're an angel," I said as I leaned in, whispering it into her ear. "You know that, girl? An angel."

"Angel…" she repeated and went quiet. "Hmm. I never been called that before. Hell, I been called a lot of things, but angelic sure as hell ain't one o' them."

She lowered her eyes and went quiet.

I kissed her on the cheek one more time as I thanked her for tonight's pick-me-up.

"You got my six one day," she commented without looking up as I was leaving the dressing room. It wasn't a question but a statement, not an ounce of uncertainty in her tone.

And I wanted to think she was right—that I *would* have her back one day if she ever needed me—but so much has happened, I'm no longer sure what I'd do if push came to shove these days. I used to be that person…once…long ago. The one you like. The one you can rely on. But that girl doesn't exist anymore.

Though sometimes, when it's still and quiet and the only sound is the rhythm of my own heart, I can feel hers beating faintly under my own.

Little did I know that Chocolate was actually waiting for an answer, and her eyes bore into mine through the mirror on the makeup table in front of her.

I smiled through the reflected smears and ghost fingerprints, nodding. "Yeah, yeah—of course. You know it."

But the only absolute I knew about any of this was the fact that I didn't have the cash to pay for this regular ritual we enjoyed at least three or four times a week, sometimes more. Chocolate knew this to be true and never asked for anything from me. Not once. Her sugar was my sweet. Simple and clear. So, I just owed her. *Something. Somewhere. Someday.* And that was an unspoken agreement I knew I'd entered into from the very first bump.

V

Martin was waiting for me at his table, a patient little boy who's been told by his mommy that she's just going into that store over there and won't be too long.

*So, you just sit down on this bench here and don't make any fuss. And don't you go talking to any strangers now, you hear?*

"Now, there's a good boy," I said with just enough spice to make him bristle. It could have been sexy. But that wasn't my goal, and my delivery was exactly as intended. Guess I wanted to see how this particular stray doggie would respond. You know, poke him with a stick and see if he snaps at it…or if he shrinks away, back into the corner of his kennel.

Martin responded with a look that conveyed but the barest emotion across his boyishly handsome face. So, the question remained: was this doggie about to bite me…or lick me?

"Why'd you do that?"

"Marty?"

"That. Just now. You think I'm a kid? Some kind of loser, a pushover, because I was a nice enough guy to help you out when you were in a jam?"

He got to his feet, giving the table between us a sharp and deliberate kick. It skirted across the grungy linoleum tile, beer sloshing out of glasses. One toppled over and rolled to the edge, foamy shards spreading in every direction across the floor before I could catch it.

So, I guess I had my answer. This stray was the type to not only snatch the poking stick from my hand, but also chew it up and spit it back out.

Now, let's be honest for a minute. Kicking a table wasn't the worst thing to ever happen at the Dream. But it was enough to attract the attention of Johnnie at the door.

Johnnie was Puerto Rican. Or maybe Hawaiian. I never could figure that one out as his accent seemed to flux on the daily. Whatever his ancestry, I knew he was fit. And handsome in a rough kind of way, despite his pock-marked complexion from severe teen acne that must have made his high school years a living hell. Which also likely explained those bulging muscles, the result of overcompensating at the gym. And overcompensate he did. Because Johnnie was as thick around the chest as he was tall, and not an ounce of fat on him. Which leads me to the other thing about Johnnie…he was tough as nails. But only half as sharp, which didn't much matter, given his job description, y'know?

His tight black tee rippled as he strutted decidedly across the room. SECURITY was emblazoned across it in stark, white letters. Bold, simple and serious. Much like Johnnie's face as he unconsciously swatted customers from his path while making a beeline for us.

*Or more accurately, making a beeline for Marty.*

I shook my head.

"Shit, Marty, what have you done? Johnnie's gonna rip you a new one." Martin started to say something in reply, but I cut him off at the knees. "Listen, you need to just shut the fuck up and let me handle this."

I stepped in front of him so Johnnie would have to go around me. It wasn't going to stop him, but I hoped this slightest of diversions would be enough for the bouncer to cool his flames, just enough to prevent him from going all Three Mile Island on Marty's ass.

*"Heyyyyy, Johnnie!"* I sang-spoke, winking as I tilted my head to one side, all big-eyed and sweet as I beamed my toothiest smile.

"Outta my way, Kandi," he replied with no humor and stretched to see over me. He was about to press me aside when he realized what he was doing. Stopping short, he squared-off in front of me instead.

An oversized rodeo barrel…with a face.

"He's cool, Johnnie," I promised as I broke his focus by softly touching his thick forearm. My fingers were tiny by comparison, my hand barely able to wrap halfway around it. And yet he flinched from my touch as if it were a hydraulic clamp. "I know Marty lost it there for a second, but I don't think he meant to get all full of attitude and shit. In fact, I think it was my fault."

Johnnie started to shake his head in disagreement, but I cradled his chin, preventing him from continuing the motion.

"Yes, Johnnie. I was acting like a bitch. I insulted the guy be—"

"—Because you could." Coming from behind, Martin's voice cut me off. Not the least bit shaky. And that surprised me. 'Cause I gotta tell ya, I've seen some pretty tough and pretty damn big guys in here trying to press their luck with Johnnie. Sometimes it was just to see how hard they could push his buttons. Or maybe to put on a tough guy show for their boys. But they always shat themselves once they'd crossed a line from which there was no turning back. When you've got three hundred pounds of Puerto-waiian Pitbull coming at you, you really have just two options: A) go up against him and face certain annihilation, or B) retreat like a little bitch. And at this point, experience has shown that the latter invariably appears the better option to most.

Sure, they give it a lot of lip service as they back away making out like they're the bigger man for avoiding a physical confrontation. But the tremor in their voice belies the bravado.

Martin's voice, however, was solid as a rock.

"Listen to the lady here, big boy…before this gets ugly."

There was no pleading in Marty's tone. This somewhat athletic but boyish dude, half the bouncer's size, was actually trash talking.

*And he was sober.*

I decided it was probably time to get out of the way, only for the decision to have already been made for me. Ignoring professional etiquette, Johnnie brushed me from his path as easily as he would swat aside a kitten. He reached for Martin with one of those vein-bulging arms and grabbed him by the collar, lifting him from the floor and pulling him close. Martin's feet dangled in the air, a rag doll dancing with an ogre.

"You're outta here, *ese!*"

Johnnie strutted toward the door with Martin seemingly floating in front of him. So, there he was. My previous hero. Working his arms and trying to shake the bouncer's grip to no effect as they continued their surreal and emasculating dance across the Tangerine Dream's main floor.

Then something happened I'd never seen before: Johnnie went down. Like a sack. No warning, just down. Crumpled into a pile, his legs twisted unnaturally beneath him as Marty stepped away, brushing himself off.

I don't know how it happened.

But it did.

*Oh shit,* I remember thinking. *Things just got real.*

Our DJ, Charlie 'C-Dogg' Jones, jumped out from behind his bank of digital mixers and pre-amps. Running toward us, his eyes flicked to me, then Marty, then down to Johnnie. They continued to dart between the three of us as his brain tried to make sense of what his eyes were actually seeing.

Once it did, he stopped dead in his tracks.

It happened so quickly his sneakers actually squeaked. Which made me laugh. Like, *really* laugh. A curt, pitchy cackle as the phrase 'came to a screeching halt' materialized in my mind. Okay, so, seeing as our Puerto-waiian guard dog was lying listless on the floor, it probably wasn't very appropriate of me. In fact, I'm certain it had come off a little disturbing. In hindsight, I'm pretty sure it was me losing it like that which was the catalyst to the hysteria erupting all around us.

In a heartbeat, the Tangerine Dream had transformed itself from a den of (mostly) unrequited sexual longing to a nightmarish scene of chaos. Panicked punters leapt from their seats, unceremoniously pressing half-naked girls from their laps as the dancers screamed and bottles bounced and warm, stale beer splashed everywhere. It was actually kind of funny, if you have the same twisted sense of humor I do.

*And yes, I know. I know. I can't help it.*

Martin rolled his neck as he forced his way back to me through the melee. Clicking it left, then right, the grotesque *craaacks* were actually audible above the thumping music.

"Let's go," he demanded as he grabbed me by the wrist.

I found myself acquiescing as he tugged me toward the door.

*Still laughing ...*

# 33

*road trip*

## 31 hours before the end | Nov 10, 2011

CRESTS OF WATER glimmered under the moonlight as we drove in silence across one of the three bridges that traverse Tampa's Bay. I think it was the Gandy. In the distance, a lone boat bobbed lazily on the water, its red and green lights dipping up and down with the mild chop.

Marty stared a mile down the road as the sound of the tires droned, a rumbling cadence from the expansion gaps between the spans of the seven-mile bridge. Every few moments the glow of an oncoming car would dimly illuminate his face. And though I studied it hard, I could find only a blank, emotionless canvas there. His bright blue eyes had darkened to colorless pits, the bottoms of which I couldn't see.

I think it was that, more than anything, that made me feel the anxious weight of reality pressing down upon my chest. Since that confrontation with Jackson earlier tonight, a steady stream of adrenaline had been coursing through my body. All at once, that adrenal high had conceded to cold, stark reality. A cinder block now compressed my rib cage. I could feel it as surely as if it were there.

*Fuck. Oh fuck! I didn't have a job.*

"Oh FUCK," I blurted out. In the silence it sounded ridiculous and out of place.

Martin didn't flinch.

I was in the car with a zombie. A shell. The façade of a man wrapped around a lifeless automaton filled with circuits and pulleys and gears. For a second, I thought I could even hear them whirring. Then, with no deviation from that emotionless stare, he reached for the center dash and pressed the tiniest button I think I've ever seen. How he managed without taking his eyes off the road, and without his fingers fumbling across the panel, is beyond me. Muscle memory or something. The radio burst to life, washing the Toyota's cockpit in a soft blue glow as Debbie Harry yowled, "Call Me."

I've always hated that song. Gives me the creeps. And now I'll forever correlate it with this moment: this surreal, unsettling, singular moment in time.

It felt like someone had taken an ice cream scoop and hollowed out my insides.

Despite this, or maybe because of it, I smirked.

*Why? Who knows.*

Perhaps I was becoming a zombie, too. A wraith. Just like Marty. Or maybe I was finally coming to terms with the fact that today was just one more shit show on the endlessly bizarre network of my life.

You've heard that Oprah's about to launch a cable network called OWN? Apparently, the idea is that it will air only positive, enlightening shows to help improve your outlook on life, love, family and friends. Well, welcome to *my* network. We'll call it DISOWN. The antithesis to anything cultured, noble, or worthy of the slightest joy.

Love?

*I've chased it. Thought I'd even caught it. Only for it to break me. Every. Damn. Time.*

Friendship?

*Not sure I can say I've had one strong enough or long enough to know what that really means. Not since I was a kid, anyway.*

And family?

*Well, yes. I used to have one of those. Long, long ago ...*

"Hey, would you mind telling me where the fuck we're going?" I found myself just blurting out of the blue. I had no idea why I was in this stupid Prius in the first place, let alone cruising with some stranger to the other side of the bay. In the middle of the night, no less. Yet somehow, I felt as if being here was exactly what was supposed to happen, my own free will be damned. "Hey. Uh, helloooo? Did you hear me? *I said,* where are you taking me!"

Marty said nothing. He didn't look at me. He just drove. And Lord knows why, but I didn't resist. Like I said, it felt like it was supposed to happen.

I used to get those feelings. At least I think I did.

*Whatever.*

There was nothing I could do about any of this right now. I was surely fired from the Dream after these shenanigans. And, if by some miracle I wasn't and Ruud actually allowed me back in there, tonight was not the night.

So, with nerves frayed to about their very last thread, I simply closed my eyes and allowed the droning of the tires to lull me to deep, welcome sleep...

# OMEGA

# VII

# 34

*waking up*

# 17 hours before the end | Nov 10, 2011

HEN I OPENED my eyes, I was no longer in the car. I didn't know where I was, exactly. I mean, Tampa Bay is a pretty big place. Okay, so it's not like New York or anything. Not that I'd exactly know what the Big Apple is like, other than movies and TV shows. But lots of towns make up this sprawling metropolis I call home. I used to like Clearwater the best. But it's getting so busy, I think St. Pete is where it's at now. Unless you're a tourist. In which case, yes, please stick to Clearwater Beach. Thank you.

*And thus concludes my Public Service Announcement,* I giggled to myself, making the voice in my head the kind that you'd expect from some stuffy white guy in his fifties. Doing this kind of stupid stuff is how I keep myself from freaking out, y'know? Gotta make it light, 'cause God knows life is short enough…and shit enough.

Anyhoo, like I said, I had no idea where the fuck I was. But I knew it sure as shit wasn't the passenger seat of a Prius.

And my head was ringing. Bad. My mouth felt like I'd just had a visit to the friendly neighborhood taxidermist. Yeah, to say it was dry was an understatement. If I spat, I expected wood wool to come spewing out instead of, well, instead of spit.

*Did that motherfucker roofie me?*

"Mar—" it was hard to speak, and the dude's name wouldn't

come all the way out. I cleared my throat and tried again. It was still wispy, but at least it was a name this time. Well, it sorta was. "*Mar-r-tinnn.*"

I sat up and held my breath to listen for the guy who I had thought was my KISA (Knight In Shining Armor) as the girls at the club call them. Only to find I was in a bedroom.

And now my skin began to crawl.

*No, no, no, no no no no nononono.*

I sat bolt upright in the bed, still in the same bra and panties I'd been wearing at the Dream when the whole kerfuffle between Martin and Johnnie broke out.

*Again, my stupid mouth getting me in trouble. When was I going to learn? Now look at me.*

Trembling, I slid my hand under my panties but felt nothing. No nasty moisture. No swelling and absolutely zero hint of pain. Everything felt normal. Still, I pulled them off and examined them for—well, you know what for.

Nothing.

Cringing, my chest tightening over my ribs, I smelled them.

*Just the scent of me, thank God.*

I looked at my fingertips. No blood. No wetness. Dry. And, again, just my scent. I began to cry. Mostly from relief, but also from the smallest uncertainty still lingering in the background.

After several minutes of feeling sorry for myself, even though there was no indication that I should, I pulled it together and the tears were replaced with anger that I was even here. In a bedroom I didn't know, in a house I didn't know, in a part of Tampa Bay I didn't know.

*Goddammit!*

For years I've worked at the Dream and kept this sort of thing from happening. At least six times…that I'm aware of. In my line of work there were usually signs, you know? Things like the guy holding onto me a little too tight; not letting me get up from his lap the first time I try; telling me he would love to take me out on a real date and asking if I'd like to go to his place for that lap dance.

"Think about this," he'd add to justify the proposition, really selling me the idea. "Then you'd get all the cash. I mean, I'd pay you, say, twenty percent less. But it would save you the thirty percent the house takes. So, we both win."

Now *that's* how you sweep a girl off her feet.

*For a start, buddy,* I'd want so badly to say, *the house take is forty-five percent. And you think I'd really go to your rundown crack trailer of a place just to save a few bucks? In your dreams.*

Instead, I'd say, "How clever. Let me think about it!" Then I'd get up, blow him a kiss…then blow him off—

*but not in the way he was hoping*

—for the rest of my shift. Of course, I'd make sure all the other girls knew it and blew him off, too, avoiding the piece of shit like the plague he was.

When you never saw him again, that's when you knew your instincts were right.

## II

*So, how had I been so oblivious this time…?*

## III

There were jeans and a hoodie folded nicely on the chair next to the bed. Exactly my size. Which creeped me out even more.

I threw them on and opened the door to the hallway as quietly as I could. It creaked a little, but nothing too harsh, so I think I was safe at this point.

I was in an upstairs corridor with a bunch of doors. Probably other bedrooms. But, why so many? Was this some kind of B&B, or a creepy-assed boarding house like you see in horror movies?

One was ajar and I peeked in. Modest. Light grey walls. A simple silver crucifix hanging above a double bed with one of those old wrought iron decorative headboards.

*The kind that are just fantastic for handcuffs,* I found myself thinking without being able to help it. Because it was true. Many was a time I found myself at some hot new beau's place and would've killed to have a headboard like that.

But today, not so much. Today, it felt like bedroom décor for the serial killer in your life.

*'And now, from Bundy-Dahmer Furniture, we're excited to bring you the new Serial Killer Collection of autumn bedroom furnishings and accessories…'*

Again, the voice in my head was that fifty-year-old coiffured spokesman dude, taking bit parts for regional cable commercials.

I pulled the door as near to the closed position as I thought I remembered finding it, and made my way to the stairs. Slowly, and as quietly as I could, I took each step, one at a time, stopping to keep my breaths from coming too fast or loud so I could listen as I descended to the first floor. The stairwell itself was gorgeous. Oak treads and ornate banisters, with those old, really tall baseboards everywhere. The stair treads were kinda odd, partially covered with some kind of sage green linoleum type of material mottled with streaks of white. Protectors of a sort, I guessed, but thought how much nicer they would look if just the wood itself were allowed to be the star of the show.

After a few deliberate minutes going as carefully as possible, I was finally downstairs and in the entry of the ground floor.

And still undetected.

There were voices coming from one of the rooms down the hall. By the looks of it, probably the kitchen. The entry was much more grand than my little apartment on the third floor of Helen's place across the bay, over in Tampa. But then again, Like I said, I only paid $750.

*You want fancy banisters? Pay the rent for them. As for me? I was fine with Helen's plain ol' stairs. I'd rather keep my cash.*

Still, I tried to take in as much as I could about the place, because you never knew when this was gonna be the kind of stuff a detective would ask you. After you make your big escape, I mean, and end up flagging down a postal van with some genuinely nice guy who takes you to the nearest cop shop.

*For those who have never been arrested, that's the police station.*

Now *that* would be the kind of story TruTV fans would love.

There were two very unique features I'll never forget about the foyer. First were the walls. They were tiled, all the way up to about somewhere between my tummy and boobs. That, to me, was unusual enough. But the pattern was especially odd: like a brown cross set inside an ivory background. The second, and the most downright impressive feature, was the stained glass. Just stunning, it was in both the door itself and the transom window above it. The colors were so opaque you couldn't really see out, but I could tell by the way the glass didn't shine that it was the middle of the night. In the daytime, I'll bet it was incredible. Probably projected those geometric designs in reds and purples all over the entry hall walls.

Oh, and there was one other thing.

A face.

The stained glass had a portrait of a guy in it. A face and torso, with his hands folded in front. I'll never forget it... or the fact that it was comprised of exactly thirteen individual pieces of colored glass. Beneath it, the pieces had been fashioned to read:

*St. Casimir.*

Lost in thought examining it, I completely forgot where I was (or wasn't) when a voice from behind called out my name and I clutched at my chest to keep my heart from bursting through—

# 35

## 15 hours before the end

**D**ON'T OPEN THAT door," they said in a voice that was all the more commanding for it not being raised. I spun around, my heart trying to break through my ribcage. The voice wasn't Martin's.

It was a light-skinned Haitian woman with the kind of eyes that can melt you on the spot.

"Jesus...*Christ*...you scared me." I was patting my chest as if I needed to resynchronize my heart or something, and gulping for air like a carnival prize guppy. "Where the fuck *am* I...and who the hell are you?"

"You don't know me," she answered in a lilting southern accent. "And where you are? Well, where you are is somewhere safe."

*What the fuck kind of answer was that?*

"So, I'm with a strange woman in a strange house, in a strange neighborhood, brought here by a strange man. But I'm safe."

I was acting the tough girl, sure enough. Straightening myself, shoulders back. A scowl souring my face. The body language equivalent of 'KEEP OUT – NO TRESPASSING.' But inside I was a little girl and about three seconds from crying out for my mommy.

"Yes," she confirmed without even a hint of the sarcasm or vexation I had anticipated in my mind. She had looked past the tough-girl act to see only the scared little girl squirming deep inside. "Again, you don't know me. But my name is Della."

She extended her hand. It might as well have been a dead fish. I stared at it with incredulity until I felt silly, for she hadn't retracted it. Eventually, I stepped forward and shook it at last as I started to tell her my name. She stopped me, letting me know that she was already aware of not only my name, but where I lived, worked, and why I was here.

"You must be hungry, Karina."

## II

There was another woman at the round kitchen table sipping a latte: a cop if ever I saw one. At the stove with his back to the three of us stood Marty. He dropped something in a pan and it sizzled with vigor.

"What's with SVU here," I asked Marty with not a small amount of sourness as I thumbed toward the cop, acting all hard. Though I think we both know I was more relieved than I can tell you to spot that shoulder harness. The cop just sorta looked at me without answering, so I clarified the reference. "C'mon, you know. Mariska Hargitay? Plays tough girl cop Olivia Benson?"

*Crickets.*

"Jesus. Law & Order? Still nothing…?"

"I know who you're referring to. And I'll take the compliment. I'm sorry, I'm just a little shocked, I guess."

I tilted my head. *She* was shocked?

"You just aren't what she was expecting, sugar." Della was trying to soften the uncomfortable intro.

"No, no, stop." The cop waved her off. She looked me square in the eye. "I just thought you'd be. I dunno. *Nicer*, somehow."

I was about to sit down but popped right back up. Squared off a little. Pulled my chair from in front of me so there was nothing but a few feet of table between me and Angie Dickinson here.

*And don't be so shocked that I know who Angie Dickinson was. My mom and I used to watch reruns, too. Jesus, I wasn't always a stripper.*

The chair made a metallic scraping sound against the tile floor and for a moment I felt something pulse through me. Like a memory of something that never happened to me. You ever get one of those? My mom used to call it *déjà vu* and I think she's right.

"But you sure are a pretty girl," the cop lady said. And she meant it. Not in a creepy way. It was the way your aunt from across the country looks at you after not seeing you for a while. Know what I mean? She's genuinely taken aback, in the most complimentary manner, at how much you've matured.

This completely disarmed me and I had nothing else to say. I guess I shoulda at least said thanks or something. Instead, I just sat down.

Marty was almost done with the curry. I didn't even have to ask, as its scent preceded it. Lamb. A light korma sauce. Cashews. I've always had a sensitive nose and since I'd been in Tampa Bay, had become something of an Indian food connoisseur.

"Where were you before Tampa, Karina?" the cop asked, and in my periphery, I saw Della shoot her—*I think she said her name was Margaret, or Marge, or something*—a look. Margie acted as if she hadn't seen it and was kinda staring me down. Just a little. I didn't care. I was never one to mind eating while people watched. It's why I can go out to eat on my own. I can do that all day long. I just couldn't give a shit if people are looking at me. But I know a lot of people aren't like me in that way. I guess it may have something to do with my childhood. *Which I was having a weirdly hard time remembering all of a sudden.* Maybe it had nothing to do with that at all, but in reality was due to the fact that I can strip naked before a room full of strangers without so much as blinking an eye. Or maybe that childhood thing I couldn't remember and the stripper thing were both the same thing.

*Who knows…*

With a mouthful of korma and naan bread I didn't think it was polite to answer Marge. Which was a good thing, 'cause for some reason I couldn't think where I had lived before Tampa Bay, either. That was a bit odd, don't you think? Not able to remember my childhood, or where I'd lived just a few years ago?

But I never had to reply, because the subject of conversation had already changed by the time I'd finished chewing.

"Her name's Magdalena," Della reminded me, gesturing kindly toward the cop. "Or Maggie."

Weird. I hadn't said any of that out loud, of course. So, how she knew I couldn't remember the cop's name was freaking me out a little. Even more than the fact that I was sat here having a lamb korma with a group of strangers in the middle of the night. I had no idea where I was. Yet strangely, it was Della's ability to read me that was the most disconcerting. Other than that, for some reason—just like when Marty plucked me outta the Dream and started driving—I felt at ease, like this is where I was supposed to be. *Go figure.*

"So," I piped up as I slid my plate into the sink. "Does anyone wanna tell me what in the capital H-E-double-hockey-sticks is going on, why this curry-cookin'-psycho here kidnapped me, and what I'm doing in your house?

III

We moved to one of the drawing rooms and when they told me the place had once been a convent, I was like, *aaaaah, yes.* Now that I was able to view it through this lens, it was plain as day: the many bedrooms, the austere décor, the old beautiful woodwork and that stained glass above the door.

It still didn't tell me why the fuck I was here with a cop, a guy who'd all but abducted me, and a gorgeous voodoo-lookin' chick who, even though she was a bit older, would slay it at the Dream. I bet she could really rock that goth look, y'know? Maybe I'd introduce her to Ambrus. I know I could get my job back if I brought someone of her caliber along for the ride.

Maybe I'd talk to her about it. If they gave a satisfactory answer as to why I'd lost my job in the first place, that is.

"I didn't know we had any old convents like this around Tampa Bay. I mean, is this town even old enough?" I was looking at Martin, though I don't know what made me think that he, in particular, would know any more about it than the other two. Something just told me it was his kinda thing. Like one of those history buffs.

He was seated on what looked like an Eastern European pouffe, and leaned forward with a deep breath as if what he was about to tell me was going to be more shocking than I wanted to hear. I didn't like it, and I got up from my chair, suddenly filled with anxiety. Up till now, it was sort of like hanging with some new friends. Given the job I did, it wouldn't be the first time I ended up at a party somewhere with a bunch of strangers, the booze and blow flowing. Neither were flowing here, though. And the silence was making my skin crawl.

"Marty? What the fuck is going on here?"

I began backing toward the corridor, but Maggie slid behind me and closed the door, blocking it as she stood there with her arms crossed and that gun in her shoulder holster glimmering.

Feeling caged, I moved to a part of the room where I could see the three of them at once. While Maggie was stalwart, Della's emotions were coming off her in waves. It wasn't weakness, it was kindness. It felt like love.

Marty was academic.

"We're not in Tampa, Karina."

I looked at him, dumbfounded. "I know we're not in Tampa, dude. I was awake when we drove across the bay on the Gandy bridge at like two in the morning. What I want to know is, where in Tampa Bay is this convent, and why have you brought me here."

"Karina, we're nowhere near Tampa Bay anymore."

"Okay, so…?"

He shook his head.

"We're in Pittsburgh, Karina. Well, sort of. What I mean is, we're—" he gestured at the three of them, but Della shook her head, curtailing his explanation. She stepped toward me, hands out and speaking softly as I felt nausea swamp my stomach, my head going light.

I didn't hear a word she was saying. I burst past the cop, pressing her aside so brusquely she probably landed on her ass in the middle of the drawing room. I don't know, because I was already sprinting down the corridor and yanking open the front door. I tugged on the handle and it wouldn't budge.

One. Two. Three deadbolts.

I undid them all, and as I was turning to the side to open the door, I could see Della holding back Maggie, who looked as if she were about to pull that weapon of hers.

She didn't, and I swung the door open.

The sky was filled with white, every streetlamp and city light reflecting off the snow as it drifted to the ground in an infinite number of prisms. In the distance, the distinctive tower of the Cathedral of Learning stood proud above the University of Pittsburgh campus. I recognized it immediately, because my dad—

*I suddenly was able to remember my Daddy*

—had told me about it and described the incredible library it housed. He did this often when I used to share my stories and would tell him how badly I wanted to go to college there, just like he did, so I could become a famous writer and make him proud.

*Oh, God. I wanted to be a writer. I remembered that now, too.*

It was all coming back. And I was caught in some kind of

accelerated spiritual withdrawal, as if I'd just given up meth cold turkey. My muscles tightened and cramped, hands and feet pulling into claws. Doubled over, rivers of sweat poured into my eyes like I was baking in hundred-and-thirty degree weather, not thirty. My pulse was a machine gun. Rapid bursts of pain stung my neck, the veins bulging as it stiffened.

Then I saw it—*really saw it*—for the first time.

In a shallow indentation of the sidewalk, a small puddle had frozen over. Smooth as glass, the ice perfectly reflected the shimmering snowflakes as they danced in the amber streetlight.

Its mirrored surface also perfectly reflected me. Bent over, grasping my knees…staring into a face that was not mine.

I screamed and clawed at the air, smashing the ice mirror with the heel of my foot.

The last thing I heard before the seizure shorted my nervous system was Della's voice, over and over she was promising me it was *all going to be okay, Diane…*

# 36

*purgatorium*

# 7 hours before the end

I DON'T REMEMBER coming out of it. I just remember the nothingness of my unconscious cocoon becoming a different kind of nothingness.

An *external* nothingness.

It lasted forever. Or maybe just moments.

Wherever I was now, time no longer existed in this tomb of blinding darkness. I have no idea how long I sat there on that mattress, either hyperventilating or feeling like I wasn't capable of breathing at all.

However long it was, my eyes had finally adapted to a lack of light so deep that I could only see my hands when I brought them within a foot of my face. When they were outstretched before me, all I saw was half of each forearm blending into the void.

I swung my legs from the mattress. Instead of dropping some twenty inches below me, my shins immediately banged against the floor. A sharp yelp escaped my throat, only to be so fully absorbed in the blanket of darkness, I might as well have barked it into a pillow.

Behind me, I felt no headboard.

Just empty air.

The mattress had been laid directly on the floor I could not see despite it being so near. Which meant I was no longer in the room where I'd awakened earlier.

Barely capable of pushing myself up from the floor with arms that had turned to rubber, my thoughts careened out of control as I stumbled to my feet and inched through the darkness. With every hesitant step my legs became heavier, anxiety tightening my chest the farther from my mattress island I moved. Repeating this three more times, I was able to find no edge to my dark universe. In any direction. I now mentally marked the mattress as the center of a room that was impossibly large for a modest convent nestled on a South Side city street among other homes, shops, and of course, the church to which it was attached.

*What the fuck, what the fuck, what the FUCK WHAT THE FUCK.*

I bit my lip so hard that the metallic taste of my own blood temporarily overpowered the weight of the overwhelming dread roiling in my abdomen. My arms twitched, legs quivering. Violent paroxysms you'd expect from a reflex test…or mild electric shock. Yet I was aware of each fitful jolt only because it was felt, not seen.

"Martin!"

The sound of my kidnapper's name sucked back into my throat the moment it left my mouth, unwilling to forge its way through the black void. I cupped my palms to either side of my face, a cone to amplify the sound. "Della!"

Again, it was muted before the air flowed fully across my lips.

*Breathe, Diane. You've got to breathe.*

I had no idea how long it had been since my subconscious self had acknowledged my real name.

Hours? Days? Years?

One moment I'm climbing the stairs of Uncle Eddie's cabin alongside Slaughter Creek, the next I'm staring at a stranger's reflection in a frozen Pittsburgh puddle.

It had to be a dream. A dream I was still having.

Because my mother's voice was calling me—

*my dead mother's voice*

—just as she'd done when I was a teenager.

It was faint, but I knew it was her.

Tearless, hiccupping sobs bubbled from my diaphragm as I spun to face the direction of her voice, but everywhere I turned it was somewhere else.

"Mama?" I cried out, now weeping.

"I need you to wake up now, baby."

"Where are you? I'm trying—"

"—Follow my voice, Diane."

"Mama? I can't find you, Mama!"

"I'm with you, baby." Then a silence like death. "I'm always with you."

"Pl-pl-please, Mama! I'm lost. Help me...!"

I rotated 'round and 'round, dizzying myself though I saw nothing to gauge the motion. I was blindfolded, spinning through the darkness of nights on a sadistic theme park ride.

"Listen," is all she said, so gently it was a whisper in my ear. The hairs on my neck stood proud, the tingle of emotion traveling down my spine the way her fingernails would gently do while she sat behind me, brushing my hair as a young girl.

I stopped turning to find her, choosing not to stumble blindly through the dark. Instead, I focused only on the sensation of my mother's fingers trailing down my back. Centering myself, I did as she asked.

*I sat in the dark and listened...*

II

My mother's fingernails were still playing down my spine when the sound of them over the fabric of my hoodie became the sound of paper brushing slowly across more paper. Now her nails were teasing my lower back as I sat upright on the mattress, shrouded in a darkness to which my eyes refused to adapt; my visible world still a two-foot bubble fading into a darkness as black as tar.

But the fear it had conjured had waned as my mother's gentle touch transformed the suffocating black into a swaddling blanket. I relaxed into the feeling, accompanied by the soothing sound of her nails across my back, and leaned forward, lifting myself to a kneeling position. With my arms at my sides, my own fingers grazed the mattress. Though blind to it, I felt the cool folds of the linens between my fingertips as Mama's now trailed down my left arm. With my hoodie sleeves pulled up to my elbows, her fingers were cool as they ran over the bare skin of my forearm, causing pinpricks to rise between my shoulder blades.

But the paper-on-paper static had grown louder, even though Mama's fingernails were no longer scratching across the hoodie's fabric. It also wasn't isolated to where she was stroking me, having somehow expanded to fill every part of the room.

A room I was still able to discern only by sound, not sight. And that sound was now more defined; more rhythmic. More disagreeably familiar.

I bristled as Mama's cool fingers coiled around my wrist, the static rustling paper sound burgeoning to become a hundred plastic baby rattles that shook all around me—behind, in front, to the side—*beneath me.*

Something brushed my other wrist, another weight slithering across my hand and I flinched away, repulsed.

Now a heavier girth moved across both calves as I knelt upon the mattress, while the folds of the linens I'd gathered in my left hand coming to life.

Something writhed between my fingers.

Jerking backwards and screaming, I became tangled in the sheets and found myself sprawling across a squirming mass. My mouth widened in terror, a broad, arrow-shaped head appeared inches from my face, mimicking my reaction as it unhinged its fat jaws, tongue darting to taste my fear as its body expanded and contracted in a wave down its long, scaly length.

I struck at its head, closing my eyes and knowing I was bitten before I even felt the fangs embed in my arm; the hot injection of venom flowing through blood it would soon thicken.

But the bite never came.

Instead, the room had gone quiet. And bright. A blinding light even through eyelids that were clenched so tightly shut. There was an audible sigh of relief from several points around me. As they faded to silence, one descended into a low, soft keen.

"He's coming," Della cautioned as I squinted through the intense glare to see the shadow of her figure glided from view...

# 37

*detox*

## 3 hours before the end

GULPING DOWN ELECTROLYTE and glucose drinks, the cramps and dizziness slowly subsided along with my confusion and fear.

I won't say I just accepted the fact that yesterday I was Karina Michaels, oblivious little pole dancer, and today I was Diane Cockerton, fugitive sister of The Prophet, but I wasn't fighting it anymore, either.

Because I knew it was true.

All of it.

I remembered now: about my dad, about Andrew, Barrow Moor...Uncle Eddie. *My mother.* If I seemed unfazed, it wasn't because I was such a tough gal, but because I was numb. To all of it. The equivalent of four hundred milligrams of Novocain injected straight into my brain. But, just like at the dentist, I knew I would feel it later. And when it hit, and I mean *really* hit, I only prayed I could handle it.

Remember, I had been in that place of denial before when I was young. *Just not for six fucking years.* Back then, my conscious mind took a break from reality for a little over a year. That was when I was twelve, after my father was killed. After they found me in the Little Woods, dangling like a puppet from the grips of 'something unimaginable,' as my mother had always told me. Well, they were right. Except now, I didn't have to imagine it anymore.

I was living it.

"How did I get from that bedroom to this dining room?" It didn't come out that cool and collected the first time I tried. At first my words were stuttering, my mouth a desert wasteland that wouldn't allow me to shape them properly. It took several attempts before I could string the whole sentence together.

"What bedroom?" Maggie asked and I spotted Martin and Della swapping knowing glances.

"Was it dark?" Marty asked as I slugged more of my drink. "By which I mean, Diane, was it a darkness so black it was almost thick, like a blanket?"

I nodded. He responded by doing the same.

"And did you move around? Was it big?"

I cleared my throat. The words were raspy. "Massive. I couldn't find the walls, no matter how many steps I took."

"You weren't in a bedroom, darlin'." Della's voice was soothing, and I allowed it to wash over me. "You had a kind of, well, let's call it a psychic seizure, for wont of a better word, at the front of the convent. Martin carried you straight in here and laid you on your side. There was really nothing more we could do until your psychic balance returned."

"Then where was I? Because I sure as shit wasn't here."

"Purgatorium," Martin said candidly, not elaborating, and Della's eyes on him hardened. "There's an intermediate spiritual place for expiatory purification. Neither this realm nor the next, it is a place of atonement."

My stomach began to grow heavy again. "Are you saying I was in purgatory?"

"I'm saying you were in a spiritual place that is the final purification of the elect. For many, this is the next step after death. It is neither Heaven nor Hell, but both have access to it."

I sat in silence, my right hand index finger tracing the scar on my left wrist. "I heard my mother. I *felt* her."

Appearing as though she were about to tear up, Della nodded. "Yes, baby. I know you did. You have a lot of people to greet you on the other side. Too many for such a young woman. But I know when the time comes, your mother will always be the first one waiting for you."

Now a tear slowly glided down my cheek and Della held me.

"Her voice changed though. Everything changed. What was warm and filled with love became cold. Dangerous." I paused before adding, "Vile."

"The Purgatorium is the realm of ultimate balance," Martin stepped in. "Both Light and Dark have access to it. Your balance is yet to be found. The Darkness attacking you is still too powerful."

"Those snakes," here I shivered, "were they something to do with my brother?"

"Please don't think of him that way, sugar." Della was solemn but intense. "He's no part of you. Or your mother. That thing masquerading as a child is the most powerful and merciless harbinger of hate and pain, and all things borne of the Darkness, this world has ever witnessed. And the time has come to stop it…"

She paused, considering the weight of that statement before finishing her sentence. If the hesitation was for dramatic effect, she nailed it.

"…Or not."

I tossed my plastic sports drink bottle across the room, a slam dunk into the garbage can. Clearly, I was finding my footing again. At least physically. Deep down, I was a cheap, shredded facsimile of a person. Literally. I had no idea who I'd been for—according to Magdalena and Della—the last six years. But again, as that Novocain wore off, I was sure it was all gonna come back to me. How I then reconciled those two lives was a different story.

*If I even had a life to reconcile when this was over, that is.*

From what I was learning, shit had really gone down while I had cocooned myself away in Tampa. Thankfully, the one thing I still had no recollection of was my crucifixion. I did remember Simon's followers, freaks in cowled robes dragging me to the cathedral's altar. I still felt that fear as they pinned me down to that huge cross. And the sound—

*its broad head peals in metallic, ear-splitting chimes as the mallet slams against a rusty nail as thick as a railway spike, ripping me from the salve of unconsciousness*

—of Ian bringing down the hammer, again and again.

I examined the scars in my wrists, able to recall nothing more past that point. Until the bus ride. I remembered the bus ride, all the way up to the moment I was walking in the dark up Edie's stairs as the lighting flashed and the thunder rumbled.

And Lizzie.

I remembered Lizzie.

We had made a real connection that day. The one pleasant memory I have of that whole period of my life—the fact that she genuinely made me laugh for the first time since the morning of Thanksgiving 1997, the morning before everything changed.

Now I found myself wondering if Liz had even died that night or if she were just one more person who was using me, manipulating me, and generally fucking me over for their benefit.

Della saw me tracing the scars on my wrists with my fingertips, and I know it made her feel like shit. She was, after all, the one who had led me to the place where she knew Simon Peter and his cuntbag cronies would find me. I still didn't understand why she did it, but had a feeling I was about to find out.

"You're not like us," she said as she sat across from me, gesturing at Maggie then back to herself.

*So, I was right. Here it comes.*

"There's something you need to know…"

## II

Frankly, I wish I had more time," Della qualified. "But that's one thing we just don't have. And there's something I need to tell you. Once I do, it's going to all start to make sense." She looked at the pendulum clock on the wall and I followed her eyes.

*7:58 a.m....*

## III

"Simon Peter had that baby torn from your mother's womb for a good reason. Or, I should say, for a very bad one."

"Uh, yeah. 'Cause he's a sadistic fuck."

Next to me, arms folded, Maggie sniggered in agreement. This cop chick was growing on me.

"Because that unborn baby boy was a serious threat, Diane."

"It can't have even been close to term. How was it possibly a threat? In even the tiniest way?"

"It was the biggest threat he'd face in over two thousand years. After you, that is."

The pendulum clock struck eight times and we all counted every one of them. At least I know I did. We then sat in silence as if expecting something intense to go down that very moment.

It didn't.

But damn, you had to hand it to her. Della was good at this building drama thing.

"Trust me, DeLaCroix. I have no intention of poking that hornet's nest. So you can assure the little freak I'm no threat to him, or his little empire, at all. Just drop me back in Tampa and we'll call it all even."

"It's far more than a little empire, sugar. At just sixteen years old, Simon Peter is on the brink of becoming bigger than Christ Himself. Little by little, he's blown out the candles of hope. And he's done so in a way that no one has even noticed. In fact, they've willingly participated. They *want* him to. Do you understand?"

I shrugged. "So, let them. See if I care. I have my own prob—"

"DIANE!" Della was on her feet. I don't know if I was imagining it, but I'm pretty sure the whole dining table had shaken. Taken aback I reflexively jerked my hands from its surface as if it were about to bite me. "IT'S TIME TO GROW THE FUCK UP!"

Shaking her head and clutching her temples, she turned away, pacing back and forth but not looking at me.

*Unable to look at me.*

I lurched from the seat, a pang of remorse mixing with the anger that had been simmering just beneath the surface of my restraint. Then I screamed. *Really screamed.* A sound like every tantrum I'd ever wanted to have culminating in this one moment.

And the dining table, a good eight feet long if it were an inch, heaved of its own accord halfway across the room. Maggie jumped out of the way just before it plowed into her chair and all the others down that side. Slamming them across the room, the whole mass careened toward Della who did not turn to look, nor flinch from its path. She just stood there as it ground to a deafening stop, inches away.

One chair pivoting on a single leg performed a little pirouette. It then toppled to the floor the way anthropomorphic characters do when they die in children's cartoons.

Maggie was slack-jawed. And to be honest, so was I.

Did I just make that happen? If so, just how long has that little parlor trick been hiding away inside me? I sure could've used that when Jackson had come at me in my kitchen.

*Jackson. My apartment in Helen's place! Things were starting to come back to me already.*

Martin lifted an eyebrow, appearing a little impressed if I'm honest. While Della failed to acknowledge the feat at all.

Sighing without attempting to hide her chagrin, she simply

turned and asked, "If you're done, may we continue?"

## IV

"I'm sorry," Della said as we all worked together to move the massive table back to where it belonged. "I did *not* mean to yell like that, sugar. Really. You're mother…she…she wou—"

Her grief was as palpable as it was sudden, and I put her out of her misery. I had a feeling my own was going to be that, and so much more, as this mental Novocain wore off.

"My mother would have been ashamed of me for acting like such a brat," I assured her. Because it was true.

"Oh, Deedee…"

I felt the tears welling and quashed that shit straight away. I'd had more than enough of those to last a lifetime now. Maybe two lifetimes. And besides, now wasn't the time. At least, that's what Della had begun to share before I tossed a three hundred pound table halfway across the room without even touching it.

"So, you were saying something about me being a threat?" I shrugged my shoulders comically, an *'I have no idea where you get that from'* kind of stance. In the corner of the room, Martin laughed. Then Maggie realized it was okay to, and let out a sharp hoot. Finally, Della came over and hugged me.

And we all needed that release, let me tell ya. Because what I was about to learn was going turn my entire life upside-down.

*For the third time…*

## V

"You've always had the ability to do so much more than most people, Diane. But have you stopped to question why?"

I thought about my Interruptions that allowed me to know things other people didn't; about the way I could hear people's thoughts, and, with the right ones, hold a whole conversation without speaking a word. I thought about the way I had once, so long ago, spun a handgun from under a bush and then made my uncle's finger squeeze that trigger, a memory so faint now it hardly felt real.

"Yes, Diane," Della replied, hearing my inner monologue as clearly as if shared it aloud. "That, and so much more. I once told you just a few of the things you were capable of. That within you something powerful exists beyond a psychic's gifts alone."

*...Alone with her in the vast emptiness of the dark cathedral, Della is staring at me with clouded eyes you would expect to be blank. Instead, they are filled with insight and emotion. I find myself melting into them. Becoming one with her. A million strands of information passing between us.*

*Astral projection. Bilocation. Clairvoyance. Dream telepathy. Precognition. Remote viewing. Retrocognition. Telekinesis...*

*"You claim to have these abilities?" I ask her. Again a questment, and not a very nice one. It's dripping with sarcasm and disbelief. My years at Barrow Moor have turned me into a mini-me of Dr. M.*

*"I possess some of those blessings, child. Yes. But far from all," hesitating before adding, "unlike you, Diane..."*

I remembered. And felt a distant pulse throbbing in the back of my skull. A sensation not yet painful but one of those you can tell has the makings of a real shitstorm of a migraine.

Nodding, I remained silent. This humility was something new to me. And I knew it was warranted.

An inexplicable warmth exuded from Della, a depth to her eyes again so beautiful and light they were almost grey. It was hypnotic. "I once shared with you about the Watchers, Diane. How the fallen had become the Shadows, while those that stayed in God's Universal Light were tasked to keep them in check. Banished to earth with their dark counterparts, these became the Shadow Watchers. Do you remember this?"

I nodded.

"The offspring of those angels were called Nephilim. A soul neither human nor angelic, a Nephala exists in a realm all his own. The reason Ian's child was a threat to Simon Peter, so much so that the demon prophet had it torn from your mother's womb, was because that baby was a Nephala, Diane. The offspring of a Watcher's comingling with a human."

I didn't know what to say. The idea that Ian was some kind of angel—fallen or not—brought bile to my throat.

"I asked you that, Della. Goddammit, I asked you that in the cathedral! You told me no. I remember it as clear as if it were yesterday. You said to me, 'Ian Cockerton is very much human, child. As am I.' Do *you* remember?"

"Yes, Deedee. I remember."

"So, which one is he, Della? Is Ian one of the Shadows or is he a Shadow *Watcher?*"

"I've never lied to you, Diane. I may have failed you, and others, in the past. But lie to you, I never have. And I don't plan on starting now, today of all days."

"If that baby was a Nephala, then Ian has to be one or the other. A Shadow, or a Shadow Watcher. Goddammit, tell me!" On the verge of making something bad happen again, something I knew I couldn't necessarily control, I took a deep breath. Long. Slow. Lowered my voice, making a concerted effort to sand down that harsh, splintery edge it has these days. "I'm sorry, Della. Please, which one is he?"

"Neither." Della's eyes softened. "But your mother was."

# 38

*an angel in our midst*

## 2 hours before the end

I'D GOTTEN SO caught up with the idea that an angel would always be in the image of a male, I hadn't seen what was right in front of my eyes.

"Rebecca—your mother—was a Shadow *Watcher*, Diane. Yes. A luminous soul unlike any I've ever met."

"You go around meeting angels a lot?"

I couldn't help myself. A smartass, even now. I wonder what Doc M would say about that. Probably something about it being a defense coping mechanism.

"More than you realize," Della answered, also adding that yes, she thought that was exactly what Doc M would say. "And by the way, so do you. Meet angels all the time, that is."

I was perplexed and didn't hide it. Okay, so I know I said I wasn't going to fight everything. And I wasn't. Promise. But I had to feel like I had *some* control in my life, and a little healthy skepticism was perhaps that last bastion.

"Everyone does, sugar. They just don't realize it. Or they feel it, but refuse to believe it. For some people, being a skeptic is all they have left to feel like they're still in control of this world that spins faster and faster from their grip every day. Sad, really."

She smiled, teasing me.

Okay. I guess I wasn't getting anything past Della. Not anymore at least. Not even a personal thought. She was always good, but those skills had come a long way in the six years since I'd seen her last.

*'That's correct, babygirl,'* she broadcast by way of reply and Martin also grinned. *'So, what say we just stop trying? Hmmm?'*

Unintentionally isolated from the mental dialog, Magdalena seemed lost as we three made facial expressions you'd expect during a conversation, though no words came from our silent mouths. She realized with a decree of: "Oh, the telepathy thing…"

Must suck to not be able to do this. So, yeah. I guess I was as close to being along for the ride as I was ever going to get.

*Whatever* happened next.

Then Martin Shade took off his shirt.

He stood there, all toned Mark Wahlberg abs in Jimmy Stewart's lanky body, and a boyish face whose cheeks you just wanted to pinch.

*Whoaaa.* I jokingly tapped my chin upward as if it were necessary to shut my mouth that was agape. I'm sure if it were summer, I'd have caught a housefly or two. If only I'd known, back in the Tangerine Dream, that's what Marty was hiding beneath that sensible polo shirt, I might have been a little nicer to the guy.

*Well, maybe I would've.*

Maggie's eyes were just as alight as mine. Whereas Della's were honed in only on me. That girl's got some self-control.

"Ooh, I love this part!" Maggie exclaimed, her eyebrows high, eyes wide as saucers.

Marty bowed his head, focused, and began lightly flexing his trapezius muscles, or traps for short. For those not into the whole biology or gym rat lingo, those are the sexy-assed muscles either side of the neck that run down the center of your back in a 'V' shape. And when those bad boys are swollen, they look incredible. Real gladiator stuff.

Now Martin flexed one more time, the veins in his neck bulging as if he'd just finished a forty minute workout, and they pumped full of blood, rising either side of his neck.

And so did the great wings that unfolded from his back with a tearing sound before extending a good six feet either side of him as he beat at the air and a wave of circulation buffeted me where I stood all the way across the room.

Holy SHIT.

"Holy?" he rebutted. "I hope so. But shit? Let's hope they're somewhat a grade or two better than that."

"I m-me-meant—"

He put me out of my misery, laughing as he let me know he was joking. So, angels can be cute *and* smartasses. Who'da thunk it?

*This angelic Adonis of mine.*

Um, I meant, of Marlena's.

Yes. His wife, Marlena.

*Eh-hemm.*

"Lucky Marlena Shade is all I can say."

Cringeworthy. I know. But, hey, it was an honest response. And, oh, I was wrong a moment ago. With the whole telepathy thing? When I said that, in that moment, I was as close to being along for the ride as I was ever going to get?

That was horse hockey.

*Now* I was all in...

II

"You just happened to be cruising up Tampa's Dale Mabry highway when my Mustang got a flat tire, hey Martin?"

"In your uncle Eddie's Mustang, you mean? Yes. And...no."

Oh shit. Now that part I'd forgotten. When Liz had driven up Blood Mountain in her badass blacked-out Jeep, we parked next to Eddie's car in front of his cabin.

*Next to Eddie's Mustang, the car I stole when my uncle told me he was the one who set off this whole shitshow. When he, or should I say some demons fucking with him, admitted that he, or maybe they, had manipulated Reicher Winslow. That they made the poor sap think he had been one of the boys that killed Matt Chauncey in the woods that day, so many years ago.*

"There are no coincidences, sugar." Della was sage smudging the convent and praying. "I taught you that long ago."

Which led me to my next question: Why were we here? And I meant this in both senses. What, exactly, was about to go down that was making Della so nervous about our time running out? And why was this convent the place for it to happen?

"I'll answer the latter," she offered, dipping two fingers in holy water and making the sign of the cross over my forehead. I didn't ask her to, but I also didn't decline it. To be honest, with my stomach feeling heavier by the minute, and the scratchy feeling in my chest feeling more and more like my ribs were slowly being wrapped in steel wool, it was the most comforting thing I could imagine experiencing in this moment. "This was your uncle Eddie's parish when he first graduated the Seminary."

"You knew Uncle Eddie?"

"Oh, babygirl. Who do you think sent your mama's letter to his cabin for you six years ago?"

*I hadn't thought about that. But why Eddie? And how did she know I'd be there?*

"Your mama, darlin'. She knew he was your last hope. Even if Rebecca didn't know just how deeply the Shadows had gotten their claws into him by that point."

By now, that mental Novocain I'd mentioned had completely worn off and I couldn't help but see that last image of Uncle Eddie in my mind. My chest tightened and I felt my skin go clammy as I remembered the look on his face as the things inside him spoke to me as if we were old pals. That thin, inane grin while his eyes blazed from the pain as he snapped his own fingers, one-by-one.

Then the hundreds of crucifix spears that pierced and skewered.

I still can't remember how that happened, exactly, or how I got out of that room. All I remember was running. Then driving. As far away and as fast as I could.

Della felt, perhaps even saw, every bit of what I remembered, and she lowered her gaze.

"He was a good man, Eddie. He protected you. For *years*, Diane. Starting with the safety of Barrow Moor. Then refusing to give you up even when you appeared at his cabin and were right under their noses. They attacked him. Incessantly. For over a decade. Until he couldn't take the suffering any longer."

I suddenly felt sick to my stomach, wanting to retch.

But tired of being the hunted, something like a light switch flicked inside of me, and instead I started to get angry. Not at Della, but at Simon Peter.

*And, if I'm honest, at God, too.*

"It's why I've been in hiding, Deedee, for most of the past sixteen years. And why they've now turned their attention to Maggie. They've been hunting the one loose thread with the power to unravel a cloak of Darkness they've been weaving for thousands of years. Because it only takes one."

"And I am that loose thread..."

### III

Della didn't respond to that. She didn't have to. I'm pretty quick, but there was a lot of information—and intense emotions—for me to process here. So, while others may have done so sooner, I'd finally figured out that since Mama had been a Shadow Watcher, that little baby boy Simon Peter killed wasn't the only Nephala. I was one, too. And I was okay with that. It actually explained a lot and was already helping me with some of the missing pieces.

So, when Simon ripped Gabriel from my mother's womb—

*I've decided that baby boy deserves not only a name, but a beautiful one. And with no one left but me to do it, I've chosen Gabriel. I feel it's fitting.*

—and then had me crucified, he thought the path was clear. Full steam ahead to Hell town. He didn't expect me to get up and walk away from that morgue on the third day any more than I did. So you see, I became a major stumbling block for that little shithead. And he's been after me, and everyone associated with me, ever since.

I guess I've known it for years. Deep down. Even when I blocked it all out by becoming Karina Michaels, I still felt it. Gravitated toward it. Even though I didn't know what *it* was.

Now I did, and to say I'd gravitated toward it would be an understatement, right?

Because not only was I here, but so was everyone else who was still left in my life. Even if I hadn't known them before now. We clearly all had a purpose. And I understood now why the clock was ticking.

Bringing this to an end was now or never. We'd either overcome what was headed our way, or die fighting.

To that end, and doing a little mental tally of our resources, this is what I figured we had in our corner: A theological Voodoo Priestess and Tavern Owner; a retired cop who'd pretty much been asked to remove herself from the force; a drop-dead gorgeous nerd who was actually one of the glorious Shadow Watchers; and of course, yours truly—a zombie pole-dancing Nephala, or whatever the fuck I was.

A ragtag crew if ever there was one.

But they were my crew.

*So I say, bring it on...*

# 39

*revelations*

## the end | Nov 11, 2011 | 11:11am

**M**ARTIN WAS IN the sanctuary, meditating. Maggie was loading and unloading her gun incessantly, more of a nervous tick than a legitimate set of checks. Della was continuing to smudge the entire convent, walking all three floors and alternating between the Lord's prayer, a Haitian Voodoo chant of protection, and a recital of the Hail Mary with such emotion that I got goosebumps between my shoulder blades that crawled down my back, arms and legs.

It was quiet, tranquil even. The calm before the storm. I don't do well with silence, and with too much time to think, I came to the realization that I wasn't ready for what was about to happen after all. So, I'd had a moment of bravado earlier. But let's face it, some stories are just better without the happy Hollywood ending. And something told me my life was gonna be one of those stories.

I was about to approach Della to talk about it, really in need of one of her pep talks, when the thunderous sound of the gunshot made me jump back. I slammed into the wall and an old black and white photo of a group of nuns, as well as a painting of the crucifixion at Golgotha, both jumped from their hooks and dropped to the floor, picture glass shattering.

Della was already running down the stairs; Martin bounding across the corridor. My fingers were digging into the plaster surface behind me, the pounding of my heart surely audible as my feet were encased in concrete at the bottom of legs which had turned to jelly.

It was Maggie's icy shriek of terror that cut through my hesitation like a razor, and I found myself running down the hallway. Her scream was so high pitched it was all but the howl of an injured animal.

*And it still hadn't stopped.*

I skidded into the room behind Martin.

But Maggie was nowhere to be found.

The room was empty as the scream continued to echo from the walls. The only movement was the gun spinning to a stop after skating across the hardwood. I squeezed past Martin, who suddenly seemed the size of a small tree, and called out Magdalena's name.

I was answered by silence, my own voice curtailing the scream.

Della appeared in the doorway panting, eyes alight.

"What hap—" Scanning the empty room. "Where…?"

The striated wail came from the second floor this time, somewhere above us, and we were up the stairs and checking each of the rooms before I realized it.

Martin was the one who found Maggie beyond the door I first opened last night, the one with the wrought iron headboard from the serial killer's collection of furniture.

Sitting on the bed cross-legged, Magdalena was staring into one of those antique oval mirrors she was holding in her hands.

"I like puzzles." Her voice was monotone but the pitch of a child's. Enthralled by the mirror, she gazed deeply into its reflection as if it were endless. "I like puzzles," she repeated, but this time in the whisper of a secret shared between friends.

Her head slowly cocked to one side, then the other, enraptured by the thing in the mirror that followed her every move. With her free hand she waved at it, the way a child tentatively responds to a stranger because she's been taught to be polite, but also taught the rhyme, 'Stranger Danger.'

"Maggie, can you show me what's in the mirror?" Della approached the bed with care, slowly extending her hand. The retired detective seemed to not notice her, smiling bashfully at her own reflection.

Until Della touched the mirror's handle.

With the unexpected speed of a striking snake, Maggie bit Della's hand. Her teeth clamped down hard and fast. Then she jerked her head violently back, lifting a small flap of DeLaCroix's skin. Della yelped and reflexively yanked her hand away, and the skin peeled back and tore away.

She stumbled in shocked silence as a sinewy, crimson flap about the size of a quarter hung from Maggie's mouth.

The retired detective jeered, then sniggered, her laughter rising to an uncontrolled, hysterical warble. She then stared directly at Della as she sucked the flap into her mouth, never breaking eye contact while chewing it with the zeal of a starving dog. She swallowed with a gasp of satisfaction.

Between giggles she asked again, "Do *you* like puzzles?"

Horrified, and with red hot pain at last finding its way to her brain, Della was mute.

"Do you like puzzles!" Blood-filled spittle flung from Maggie's mouth. "DO YOU LIKE PUZZLES!"

"*I* like puzzles!" I shouted in reply, stepping in front of Della so that Maggie's eyes were forced to fall upon me instead. Then more gently I repeated, "I like puzzles, Magdalena."

Maggie tilted her head, her grin widening. "Oh, good! It's been too many years since we last played. Uncle Eddie won the last round. Can you redeem yourself...or will Maggie take round two and reap all the rewards?"

My blood ran cold as Maggie's face rippled, the skin moving of its own accord to take the shape of Simon Peter's, then Maggie's once more, then a very young girl who resembled me long ago.

"Answer me this, *Deedeeeee*," she posed, snickering with childlike delight, her teeth stained red with Della's blood. "In shadows deep, where souls are bound, her husband awaits, finally found. A punishment grim without cessation, what does she fear?"

Repeating the riddle in my mind, my hands had begun to visibly shake as the fear took hold and the temperature of the room plummeted. Tufts of steam began rising from my mouth.

"WHAT DOES SHE FEAR, DIANE!"

"She—" I replied, buying time as I ran the lines through my mind. "She—"

"YOU'RE STALLING, DIANE! OR SHOULD I CALL YOU KARINA MICHAELS?"

Maggie exploded into laughter.

Then she smashed the mirror into her face.

Some pieces of the glass remained intact while others fell to Magdalena's lap. Thin red lines began to swell in a helter-skelter patchwork across her face.

"ANSWER ME!"

*...punishment grim without cessation...*

"—Eternal damnation!" I blurted out as the answer came. "A punishment grim without cessation, what she fears is eternal damnation!"

The corners of Maggie's mouth drooped in mock disappointment, the melodramatic expression of a clown.

"Oh my. Well, I'll get you on this next one. Best out of three, or the forlorn wife will meet the end she most fears!"

Magdalena plucked a triangular sliver of glass from the frame and held its shimmering point to her face. Staring into the shattered mirror, the woman recited in the voice of the little girl she once had been: "Mirror, mirror, in my hand, who's the fairest in the land?"

I knew what Simon wanted me to say, the sick little psychofuck. He wanted me to stroke his frail, twisted ego. Just like the pathetic losers at the Dream who wanted you to stroke their pathetic little cocks because they couldn't get it anywhere else. But just like them, I knew he would beg for it if I made him.

And begging was a willing transfer of power.

"Oh, I know the answer to that one, Simon," I crooned in my most seductive, throaty voice. Approaching the bed, I leaned in toward Maggie, my breath in her ear.

Excited, she started fidgeting.

Then quaking.

Moaning.

Her hand that gripped the mirror shard lowered to the bed.

"Mmmm, that's right, Simon. You like it when Karina talks to you this way. Because you *know* that I know the answer. We *both* know, don't we? We both know what you want..."

Now Maggie's hand was quivering beneath the sheets.

"That's right, Simon," I whispered. "Tell Karina what you want."

I could tell he was already on the verge of breaking. When he did, I also knew he'd have to release Magdalena, whose hand now convulsed violently in her lap, the bedsheets shredding from the shard she gripped.

She was moaning louder and louder, until it was no longer Magdalena Romano on the bed at all, but a sixteen-year-old Simon Peter. He was still staring at the handheld mirror, but instead of the glass shard, in his other hand Simon was gripping himself. Stroking faster and faster, he brought himself to climax, moans rising until he released onto the mirror. As the semen seeped down, the broken glass sizzled as if it had been spritzed with acid.

In an instant, he was Magdalena once more. And in her hand, the glass shard.

A circle of darkest red began spreading across the sheets as that same hand at her groin slowed to a stop and Maggie groaned in ecstasy, her eyes rolling back.

She cackled as she then licked the length of the blood-soaked shard, oblivious as her tongue sliced in two and the ends flickered like a snake's.

"Mmmmm. Thank you, you little slut," Maggie slurred. "But you still owe me an answer."

She played the shard of glass over her face, running it seductively over her nose, mouth, around her eyes.

"Mirror, mirror, in my hand, who's the fairest in the land?" Now she was the young Magdalena, the little girl smiling and tilting her head to and fro as she watched the glass shard in her hand trace fine pink lines between the bleeding gashes already dripping. She giggled with innocent glee as she connected the dots of broken, shining fragments of mirror which had embedded into her face.

"Stop it!" My breath was visible in the freezing air as I lunged for the mirror.

"WRONG ANSWER!" Simon bellowed and an invisible wave blew through the room, knocking us all to our feet—

—as Magdalena plunged the shard into her eye.

She extracted it, the optical fluid spraying from the socket, then plunged it again.

And again.

All the while cackling, "I am I am Iam Iam IamIamIam!"

The sound of the gunshot was as intense as an explosion in the small bedroom, and a crisp circle appeared in Magdalena's forehead. There was the briefest of delays before she slumped against the headboard now spackled in the substance that had once been the powerhouse of her nervous system. The mirror still clutched in her hand, a gnarled grin was frozen across Maggie's face.

In the doorway, Ian held the sidearm that had been hers.

A wisp of smoke plumed from the barrel in the frigid air then disappeared just as quickly. While a similar plume of steam rose from the back of Maggie's head and hung there.

"Well, we were done with her anyway," Simon Peter admitted as he stepped into the room next to my uncle. "She served her purpose by leading us to you."

He sniffed his hands, then brushed them on his pants.

"But that was a bit of good clean fun, no?"

He was looking directly at me.

I wanted to retch, to scream, to cry.

Instead, I pulled the gun from Ian's hand. I did this without moving a muscle, the thought becoming reality and so much more powerful than my physical grip would ever be against his.

It flew into my hand, already pointed at Simon Peter.

I pulled the trigger.

But it spun from my grip before the action could be completed and was now in the hands of the sixteen-year-old…

…And aiming directly at me.

"I find these so uncouth, don't you?" he asked, the question a real one. I said nothing and he shrugged as a result. "Well, I do. So violent. And so…*unnecessary*."

The semiautomatic's carbon steel barrel began bending, until the metal blistered and cracked down to the trigger guard.

Simon tossed it to the floor.

"Speaking of uncultured—" He now addressed Della who was gripping her right hand wrapped in a piece of torn shirt around the bitemark. "Those clues you sent to the detective were all rather…transparent…don't you think?"

*Your Shadows didn't think so.* It was a reply in thought, but we all heard it as plainly as if spoken. *They never suspected a thing.*

"Well, that's true enough," Simon Peter admitted as he stepped closer to her. "But then again, just because you're angelic doesn't mean you're necessarily the brightest spark. Some of my Shadows are little more than mindless heavies. Grunts, eager to hurt and maim. Even in the netherworld, it takes all sorts. Isn't that true, my dear?"

He leaned in, so close that his sewer breath wafted Della's hair. He peered into her eyes with a dark intensity, gesturing at them.

"By the way. I trust they're serving you well, the eyes?"

Della spat in his face.

It dripped down his chin and Simon thrust out his tongue, reptilian thin and impossibly long for a human's, and slurped up her spittle with a gasp of delight.

"My, DeLaCroix. You taste as succulent as you ever did."

Della cringed.

But she also did something else: she looked at me in a way that made me think she was hiding something. If she were, she was doing much too good of a job for me to catch it telepathically. But there was something she didn't want me to know.

*I could feel it.*

As could Simon, who was all too pleased to share it.

"Oh my! How delicious. You never told her!" He began laughing. Bent over belly-laughing. The way you only do with your closest friends. "Now, that truly is evil. How did I not know this?"

"Know what?" I yelled. "What don't I know, Della?"

She began backing out of the room and I followed, Martin slamming Ian and Simon both aside to allow me to safely pass.

Simon laughed at this. "Easy there, big boy." He licked Martin's bulging bicep. "*Yummm.* You know, when this is all over—which it will be any moment now—I could use a strapping lad like you on the team. Come see me after."

Martin ignored him, his shirt ripping as two great wings burst through and unfurled. I heard them beat against the air as he pinned my uncle and half-brother to the wall.

On the landing, I confronted Della who continued to retreat. "What don't I know, Della? Tell me!"

My anger was a vibration of energy that flowed from me in ripples, a rock skipping across a pond's glassy surface.

She backed away more. Timorous.

Nothing like the Della I knew.

"Tell me, Della! What am I not seeing?"

It happened so fast I couldn't stop it. Pulling out a serrated kitchen knife, Della sliced her own throat. Her skin gaped open below her left ear, unfolding behind the knife as it traveled across to her right.

"I'm so sorry, hun! Follow the voice. And I pray you'll forg—" her mouth continued to form the words *'forgive me,'* but the air that should have passed over her vocal cords hissed out of her sliced larynx instead.

Dropping the knife and clamping both hands over her gushing neck, Della stumbled backward across the second floor landing, her eyes wild with terror. When her left foot slid over the top step, she lost her balance. Thrusting out both arms, it was temporarily regained. But then she reflexively clamped them again over the geyser that pulsed in a jet from her throat.

And her balance was irretrievably lost.

Pinwheeling, Della spun forward just in time to see her unstoppable descent down the stairs. She hit the third step from the bottom and her neck bent with a perverse cracking sound.

With the flow of blood from her throat temporarily clamped by her neck rotated fully around, she gulped. Opened her eyes. Gulped again.

My disbelief was the last thing she'd ever see.

For it was not DeLaCroix Laveau twisted and broken at the bottom of the stairs...but Elizabeth Winslow.

Palms cradling my head I began screaming, a tumult of emotion threatening to shred my last tenuous grip upon sanity. Simultaneously, Simon Peter shoved Martin aside as easily as I'd seen Martin take out Johnnie at the Dream.

"Della's dead." Simon Peter sidled up to me. "And I don't mean that stupid bitch down there. I mean, the real witch."

Invigorated by my fear and longing, he ensured I was looking into his eyes before he would share the next piece of information.

"Just like Judas Iscariot, she did herself in. The same night Rebecca, that whore masquerading as our mother, went to serve my father in the depths. Now they're both sucking Satan's cock. Day and night. Eyes forever stinging with tears as he gags them so they may offer penance for their allegiance to the false one."

He slapped his thigh as if the thought just tickled the shit out of him, and again was bent over, guffawing. Too busy enjoying the imagery, he failed to receive the message Uncle Ian floated weakly into my mind. It was so much information, and so quietly broadcast, I barely caught it myself; fragmented bits and pieces, disjointed and out of order.

'—tect you—forsaken you—judgm—Della is gone—o stop the unstoppable—show the worl—low the voice—'

I was so lost in my focus upon it that I didn't notice Simon nose-to-nose with me. Head tilted.

Listening to my mind interpreting the words.

"It's sad, really. Don't ya think, sis?" The way he emphasized every 'S' ensured that each became the long, slow *hissssssss* of the snake from my Purgatorium. "You see, without Judas, the blood-soaked crucifixion would never have taken place. There had been plenty of chances, don't you know, but it took that catalyst to really make it all come to fruition."

He was pacing circles around me.

*Slinking around me.*

"Soooooo, if God is, in fact, all knowing. And Christ really was his Son. And if dying such a humiliating death on that cross alongside a couple of common criminals—as Barabbas walked free by the way, a deranged rapist and murderer—if that was the one act required to unify a movement to last through the millennia, then wouldn't Judas be a hero? Are you following me, *sissssssssss*?"

He grinned, and for a moment I was certain his face had morphed into those fat, unhinging jaws; that arrow-shaped head.

"No Judas, no crucifixion. No crucifixion, no Christianity. And Jesus becomes just another delusional dude."

I felt sick to my stomach. I wanted to run. But the bowling ball in my gut had turned to lead, and that molten poison had melted and filled a pair of hollow legs I could no longer move.

"So, poor Della. She believed so much in 'the cause' that she was willing to give you up for it. To create a new movement. One that might actually have the power to oppose me and thereby retain the Universal Balance I'm about to destroy. And destroy it I will. Finally and indelibly. But alas, just like my old pal, Judas, she couldn't bear the guilt. The imagery of watching you hammered to the timbers and tortured, in front of our own mother no less, was just too much to bear once mommy left her all alone in this world. So..."

Preferring to play a sick game of charades rather than tell me, he pantomimed the act of hanging himself. Jerking his head up and to the side by a pretend rope, his tongue shot from his mouth.

I was helpless as he licked my face while squealing with arousal. Violating my soul in low, basal vibrations, the light all around me was being absorbed like water into a sponge by the demonic thing Simon Peter was becoming before my very eyes.

No longer a teenage boy, his physical form was shedding, daring at last to wrest from the skin and tissue that no longer served it. Emitting a stench of sulfur, it slithered and extricated itself from what had appeared a person, but was in reality a shell to house the hideous aberration my mind was barely able to comprehend.

II

Cresting the stairs at the end of the hallway, Stacey Morris of *New*

*Day, USA!* fired up the broadcast camera, too astonished to yet be afraid. Petrified but resolute beside her, Rachel Stoltz desperately prayed that someone, somewhere, was picking up the live feed.

She prayed even more desperately that help was on its way…

# 40

*an audience*

FIVE MINUTES BEFORE they appeared in the second floor hallway, Stacey Morris and her Director, Rachel Stoltz, were on the street outside the convent. They stomped their feet and blew into their cupped hands to keep warm as they set up the final broadcast installation.

It had been strangely quiet for over an hour, but at precisely eleven minutes past eleven came the unmistakable report of a gun being fired.

"That was a gunshot. Oh my God, Rachel, that was an actual gunshot!" As giddy as she was apprehensive, Stacey Morris's eyes lit up as she hoisted the camera to her shoulder. "Do we call the police, or do we go in?"

Rachel Stoltz, Director of *New Day, USA!* stared at the three-story convent without responding. Then came the nerve-shredding yowl from inside the building. A sound like the cry of an injured animal, it trilled for nearly a minute before it was cut short as sharply as a speaker plug being pulled.

Then the street was again a hush of snow-filled silence.

To go in risked becoming part of the story rather than merely reporting it. But then again, if she had followed the rules six years ago, she never would have broken the story of The Prophet. Or secured an exclusive interview. Or the prime time special which followed. All of which made *ND-USA!* the number one show, by a mile. This, in turn, earned Rachel her rise from Floor Manager, pushing Burke Cummings even further up the broadcast ladder. His new position was now the next target in her sights. And the decision she was about to render would make or break that opportunity with an absoluteness not to be trifled with.

*'Stop it!'* A woman's voice. Coming from one of the street-facing second floor rooms.

*'WRONG ANSWER!'* A man's voice. Deeply brutal. A chilling, demented intonation that made Rachel's chest tighten.

Then a mad cackling followed by a young girl's voice that squawked, *'I am I am Iam Iam IamIamIam!'*

A second gunshot thundered inside the convent, a flash of light illuminating what appeared to be the same second floor window.

"Both," Rachel finally answered Morris as the blistering crack echoed down the street. She dialed 9-1-1 as she jumped into the rear of the satellite truck. As she raised the twenty-foot telescopic broadcast antenna her voice shook despite her best efforts to keep it from doing so. "T-th-that was a young girl, Stacey—my God, didn't that sound like a young girl to you?"

Morris nodded, a mix of nervous energy and the bitter cold, wet morning making her shift from side-to-side.

"It did, yeah... I don't like the sound of that, Rachel. Like, at all. We need to do something!"

Stoltz nodded without making eye contact, her breaths rising in steam as she spoke to the emergency operator while flicking switches and turning knobs to link the truck with the studio.

"We have less than seven minutes before the cops bar us from that place. But Stacey? Once we go through that door, we're as much a part of the story as whatever the fuck's going on in th—"

Broadcast camera in hand, Stacey Morris was already running toward the front door as the second floor window began to glow like the summer sun...

# 41

## the end

THE RADIANCE FROM the room had grown so gradually, it was the last thing my mind had registered. When I heard my uncle Ian's voice—*truly heard it, as I had as a child*—the glow became all but blinding to my eyes.

For the first time in sixteen years, a vibration like a rich harmonic chord was being cast from him to flow into my core in bold, strengthening waves. Now the garbled, incoherent message he'd broadcast only moments ago was clear and loud, surfacing as his light shone bright to dispel the darkness he had submitted to in my stead. And I heard—*I felt*—the soul of the man he was born to be, the beautiful innocence of a child before an ancient prophecy stole it away:

*'I tried to protect you, Diane, but in doing so I know I have forsaken you, and for that, my judgment is upon me. If Della truly is gone, you know that she too will have died to protect you. And you know in your heart that your mother loved her babygirl to her very last breath and tried so hard to stop the unstoppable. But now the whole world will see. Follow the voice, Diane! Follow the voi—'*

Simon Peter was upon him, tearing the skin from Ian's body. He bludgeoned the traitor of the new church with fists like boulders, and a river of blood poured from my uncle Ian's temple, his pain releasing in a haunting wail. It reverberated in piercing echoes through the woods in which he now saw himself. In his mind, Ian was again the twelve-year-old boy in a wooded glade filled with the promise of summertime fun. But the darkness has fallen hours before dusk, and he has become disoriented, horrified as the Beast Bear from his recurring nightmares closes in. Then Ranger Rob, the amiable cartoon ranger appears. A little man, short and plump, with little round glasses, Ranger Rob is here to protect him. He promises that he will not leave the boy as Martin Shade embraced Ian and absorbed blow after thunderous, buffeting blow.

Now the abomination that had been Simon Peter loosed a cry of its own. Every minor chord in jarring unison, it was the shrill whistling of a thousand discordant flutes that set fire to my nerve endings.

*This can't be real*, Ian Cockerton, the boy, lied to himself as Martin Shade wrapped around him, shielding the child inside. Fully free of the Shadows' grasp for the first time since they had doused his light, Ian Cockerton, the bewildered and anguished man, cried out: "This isn't real!"

Folding into my uncle's shape, Martin unfurled his great wings and hammered the space above them. But savoring the rising acid taste of Ian's terror, the beast that had been Simon Peter shrieked with rapture—a warbling, ear-splitting squall—as it pounded and beat and tore at its victims beneath.

The last thing Ian Cockerton would ever see was the dimming light in Martin's eyes. Refusing to yield, the cartoon ranger only held Ian tighter as their bodies were pummeled in the mud and stinging rain of another time and another place, beneath a canopy of nonexistent trees.

Again.

And again.

And again.

As Ian's last breath left his body, the Little Woods dissolved to become the convent bedroom once again. And with each merciless blow, the demon's squeal grew in equal proportion to Martin Shade's failing light.

When that golden rod was extinguished altogether, the beast roared as all became nothingness…

…And I was again in the Purgatorium.

## II

The darkness is complete. Where before I was at least able to make out what was immediately in front of me, now I am effectively blind. I hold my hand to my face and know it is there only by the soft flutter of air as I wave it back and forth.

Where all sound had previously absorbed into the consuming void, it is now filled with harrowing screams drowning beneath spine-chilling yips—the curt, choppy laughter of hyenas—and moans that can just as easily be of pain and torment as those of sexual release.

But one sound rises above the rest: it is the singsong voice that once belonged to the toddler Simon Peter.

"I *seeeeee* you, *Deeeeee*deee."

My mind sizzling with a veil of static, white-hot pokers of adrenaline again suck away my breath.

"Look, Deee*deeeeeee!*" he insists and lifts my blindness to show me my adopted brother. Andrew is laughing, but the sound is perverse; he is smiling, but it is a macabre imitation of joy. Before my eyes, his body twists and implodes, his head twisting as his skull caves. He cackles, throwing his head back to loll grotesquely from his neck as he takes on Simon Peter's infant voice: "Simon says flwy, Andweww, flwwwwyyy!"

The bowling ball in my gut pushes the bile up my esophagus. My pulse is a jackhammer. I know my heart is way too burdened; the rests between becoming dangerously short.

*...thum thum ......... thum-THUM ... thum-THUM...*

My blood feels so cold and thick that my hands tingle with frostbite. I can't breathe; my throat suddenly too small.

"Simon says come play with me, Deeeee*deeeee*!"

I feel I am being scraped from my body.

I feel that I am dying.

—*Deedee*—

Behind the tumult of screams and jeers and a caterwaul of suffering, my name comes to me, an impossible whisper. But this is not Simon Peter's mocking voice. It is warmth. And Light.

I have fallen to my knees, unable to catch my breath...

—*Deedee*—

...panting as wisps of bright tendrils of light coil from my mouth. Every hue I've ever seen swirls around me, but mostly deep blues, indigo and violet. And then the white. So much bright, crystal white! Toddler Simon Peter sucks them into what I used to call his infant duck lips. His soft, innocent little hands touch my cheeks, and he smells like toddler. He's holding my face so close I can taste his breath, that sweet and sour scent of milk, and my laboring heart hastens even more.

*... thum-THUM-thum-THUM...*

The swirling colors are less defined now, and I feel so weak I can barely hold myself as I crouch on hands and knees. If not for my sweet little brother holding my face, I know my neck would no longer support my head and it would crack against the floor.

—*Deedee*—

That voice again. Louder. But I am so tired, I lean into my half-brother and he giggles with delight. He does not hear the voice which is so clear to me now that it has become part of me.

—*Deedee*—

But my breath is now little more than a puckering gasp.

*... thumTHUMthumTHUM...*

The searing pain in my chest and the thrumming which has

begun to cycle at the back of my skull, none of it seems to matter anymore as Simon Peter's squeals of joy eclipse the hellscape of sounds. The vapors of color he inhales are no longer distinct trails, having become a weak haze that mixes and comingles until the colors are diluted, muted; an unpalatable smog. It feels wrong, and the sweet scent of the toddler's breath has gone with them, only the sour milk stench remaining.

His squeals of joy have intensified and shortened, mutating into the jagged, sawing yelps of a hyena over its kill. And I know I am but a handful of fragile heartbeats from death. I close my eyes as the incubus demon I cannot beat takes the last of what I am.

All, that is, but an image of my mother.

In a flowing silk tunic—a mauve so dusky it could have been soaked in French Mourvèdre—she's exquisite beyond reproach. Her trademark complexion of natural porcelain is flawless to the point of glowing. Draped over her shoulders, a long charcoal scapular flows in undulating waves. Peeking from what I can only describe as a Benedictine veil, her resplendent strawberry blonde hair has been pulled back to reveal the steely gaze of blue eyes amplified to crisp, aquamarine ice.

She is alluring. Powerful. And as gorgeous as she is fierce.

*In short, my mother is one savage, badass bitch of the Light.*

An indomitable energy pulsates from her in oscillating, thumping, currents. It regulates my heart's tempo and pumps breath back into my beleaguered lungs.

As her spirit appears, the Purgatorium explodes into brilliance.

The thing that was Simon Peter snarls...but then cringes with a yelp, backing away in cowardly retreat as it shields its empty eyes from her glorious light.

'*Deedee,*' she calls out to me, and her tone is neither gentle nor patient. '*Come help me put Simon Peter to bed?*'

She says it like a question, like she's giving me options. But we all know there's really only one right answer...

# 42

*the beginning*

## 1 year after the end | Nov 12, 2012

THAT'S HOW IT happened. Of course, that's not what the *New Day, USA!* camera broadcast. What the world saw on live TV was its beloved sixteen-year-old savior attacking his church's Archcardinal and beating to death with his bare hands the man who had thrown himself between them. They did not see Martin Shade's wings like solidified light, or the angelic aura as the Shadow Watcher's spirit departed the shell it had occupied for a few short decades.

No, all the world saw was a mortal man, a hero, punched and thrashed and battered by Simon Peter until Martin slumped lifeless over Ian Cockerton, giving his life that the other might live.

As police in tactical gear restrained The Prophet, the world watched with bated breath as paramedics worked tirelessly on his shunned and forsaken half-sister. Little did she know that the transference of loyalty of the majority watching was already taking place in that moment, the woman becoming an instant icon for the lost and lonely and disenfranchised.

II

*And of course, that woman was me.*

Uncle Ian coded in the convent and officially died. But they managed to resuscitate him, and after spending nearly a month in the hospital, he's doing much better. He's been working hard at physical therapy and even regained his ability to walk without assistance now. He does still have to use a cane, but I think it's actually a rather debonair vibe. I had it made specially for him, with an exquisite raven's head hand piece carved out of ebony.

Between you and me, Uncle Ian and I have also been working privately on what I've come to now call our special 'clairs.' Meaning, the abilities we once shared though we didn't even know it—like the power to speak to one another through clairaudience. But that part of us seems to be either gone, or in very deep hibernation. And isn't that just like life? When we had it, we didn't know it. Now that we know we had it, we don't anymore.

*C'est la vie.*

At least we both live together as a family again, just like we did when we were on the Upper West Side. Though I have to say, this location is rather different than our apartment on West 93rd Street, across from Central Park.

For a start, this place could fill a fairly respectable portion of the park. And it's all ours. You see, the funny thing is, as I'm legally Simon Peter's nearest surviving biological relative (apparently half-sister trumps half-uncle), all control of property owned by the Church of the New Apocrypha reverts to me.

*Oh, wait! I forgot to tell you what happened to that little shit.*

Well, there really was no trial, as such. Simon Peter's attorneys—court appointed Public Defenders—pled 'No Contest' after the entire western world had seen the footage of his brutal and unprovoked attack.

Over and over and over.

*Good luck getting an impartial jury of your peers after that reel went viral!*

And if you're asking why his attorneys were court appointed as opposed to the finest in the land, or why he didn't just buy himself a 'Get Out Of Jail Free' card, the Federal Government froze all accounts pending the outcome of the trial. Now he's been hauled off to serve a life sentence with no chance of payroll.

And guess where…!

Did you guess? That's right. The most secure facility in the country for the truly criminally insane: Barrow Moor.

*Just how deliciously ironic is that!*

Which takes me to where I started.

As the law doesn't allow felons to be anywhere near a non-profit organization, let alone operate one, all control of property owned by the Church has now reverted to me. That includes the campus comprised of Simon's sprawling mansion, the church itself, the homes that once comprised the old neighborhood…

…And the $2.2 billion in the bank account.

Yes, that's billion with a big fat capital 'B.' And since a non-profit legally only has to account for about ten-percent of its funds being allocated directly to its mission, Simon squirreled most of that cash away in special little funds. Including a fucking vault stuffed with actual currency.

The best part? The church is a non-profit, so there are no taxes.

I've been thinking what to do with all that asset, and realized I've got time to figure it out, y'know? No hurry. It'll come to me when it's supposed to.

But it sure as shit ain't gonna be a church.

In the meantime, there are a couple things I've already started in motion. For one, do you remember Amanda, a.k.a. 'Chocolate' who never asked me for a single dollar, but still let me bump with her anytime I needed a little extra something to get me through the night? Well, as of a month ago, she's the new Managing

Partner of the Tangerine Dream in Tampa. Yep, Ambrus was more than happy to sell when I offered him twice the Dream's value. In cash. After all, what do I care? We're talking something like four million total. Such a small amount, the meter hardly budged.

You wanna really *feel* how much money Simon Peter, that little freak, pulled in from donors all around the world? Just start counting with me, one (million dollars) per second of the clock.

Okay, let's start:

*One million dollars...*

*Two million dollars...*

*Three million dollars...*

...and just keep on counting. When you get to two thousand, one hundred and ninety six, let me know. If you're curious how long that'll take, at one count per second, it'll be over thirty-six minutes from now. And every one of those seconds you count represents a cool million in the bank. That's how much is still left, even after taking care of Chocolate.

Oh, and Helen, my landlady? I paid off her mortgage. Anonymously, of course. She's such a sweet lady, she'd never take a penny if she knew it was coming from me. 'Save your cash,' I can hear her saying now. 'You never know when you might need some for a rainy day.' So adorable, that Helen. Oh, and yes, I also bought her a new carpet to replace the one that my assclown ex-boyfriend, Jackson, ruined by letting his stupid big bloody mitt of a hand drip all over the place. And still, doing all of that for Helen was barely a half-second off our thirty-six minute clock.

*So yeah. I think I'll survive.*

As for the mega campus in Pee Aay, I have some ideas!

Now...hear me out. I was thinking, just because I'm Diane Cockerton again doesn't mean I have to forget all about Karina Michaels, or pretend she never existed now, do I? That girl got me through more than even you may ever know.

So, how about this? Wouldn't that elaborate new church in the woods make one seriously badass adult recreational center? I mean, just think about that for a moment. Clubs for him, for her, for them, you name it. Fantastic restaurants. A casino. Anything your heart desired. It would be an entire resort campus in the woods where you could rent a room—a whole house—hell, a whole damn neighborhood, if you wanted—and do nothing but spend your days, nights and everything in between satisfying your every whim.

*Now, that sounds like a lot more fun than the apocalyptic hellscape Simon Peter had planned for it. Don't ya think?*

And besides, I still got the moves. Seems a shame to let them go to waste. It's only been a year, but I'm already itching to hit that pole and get lost in the music, gyrating to something with a sexy, dirty dubstep beat.

So yeah, I think that's what I'm gonna do.

A pleasure resort in the old Little Woods. Everyone's own personal happy place. Kinda like that old TV show, *Fantasy Island*.

But real.

I'm not gonna lie, I know people are going to despise me for it. And if I'm really honest, I can't say that I blame them. I mean, I took away their clear and easy hope. But this is the real world. And out here, things aren't always black and white. Morality can be a slippery bitch. And hope—I mean *real hope*—is the most beautiful thing you can find in this messed up world of ours. But it's not always easy to secure. And it's never found in some quick fix of an empty promise.

So, you can judge me. Or you can join me. The latter will be a whole lot more fun.

*Just think about it.*

And maybe I'll see you in the woods...

∞

# DID YOU ENJOY THE STORY?

I'd be grateful if you'd take a moment to post a rating with a brief comment on Amazon, Goodreads, or your favorite book site. Your positive feedback makes a big difference for independent authors like me by helping the books you love reach more people. Thank you for being a reader!

# JOIN MY 'INNER SANCTUM'

Receive personal updates before anyone else, pre-release offers, free book swag and more! Sign up for free at
AGMOCK.COM *OR* EPOCHTHRILLERS.COM

# STRIKE UP A CONVERSATION

Instagram • Facebook • Twitter • YouTube
@AGMOCKAUTHOR

# COMING SOON!

Two standalone supernatural thrillers in 2024!
Follow the author on any of the channels above, or by following his author's profile on Amazon.com